# PARADISE PRIDE

## BOOK 3 THE RESORT SERIES

### LISE GOLD

Edited by Debbie McGowan

Cover design by Neil Irvine Design

One's destination is never a place, but a new way of seeing things.

— HENRY MILLER

# 1

## MEGHAN

"*R*emind me never to take a shuttle bus again." Meghan felt clammy and tired from sitting in the stuffy vehicle for over two hours. The hotel wasn't even that far from the airport, but it had stopped off at fifteen other hotels before they finally arrived at their destination: Paradise Hotel. Waiting for their luggage to be unloaded, she glanced at the entrance of the tall, rather unappealing building and frowned. "What's with all the rainbows?"

"What?" Her friend Kim was panting as she joined Meghan with their suitcases.

"The rainbows." Meghan pointed to the rainbow flags in the pineapple palms by the door and over the entrance.

"I don't know." Kim sighed. "And I don't care. I just want to shower, get changed and have a drink by the pool before I meet Andres." She looked over her shoulder as the shuttle drove off. "Seems like we're the only ones who got off here."

"Hmm…" Meghan grabbed her case and followed her friend into the reception area. From previous experience with packaged holidays, she'd expected chaos at check-in, but there was no one. "Hello?" she yelled, only to be answered by the echo of her own voice. "Hello, is anyone there?"

"Hi, can I help you?" A man came out from the office behind the reception desk and stared at their suitcases. "I'm afraid we're not open. We're preparing for an event, so if you have tickets, you can come back tomorrow."

"No, that can't be right," Kim said in an irritated tone. "We've booked an all-inclusive holiday with you. I have the confirmation right here."

"Maybe you got the date wrong?" The man took the confirmation Kim had printed and furrowed his brow as he looked it over. "Did you not get a follow-up email from us, offering you an upgrade in one of our other hotels?"

"No, we never got anything," Kim said, sounding like she was close to panicking. She was here to see her Spanish boyfriend, Andres, whom she'd met on holiday last year, and she'd asked Meghan to tag along so she wouldn't be alone during the day, when Andres was working. She'd been unbearable for weeks, talking non-stop about him and spec-ulating whether he would introduce her to his family. Because Kim was only here with one goal in mind: she wanted a ring.

"Okay, my apologies." The man backed away. "Please give me a moment. I need to start the system so I can check the facts. Take a seat. I'll be right back."

Meghan dragged her case along to the reception seating area and slumped in a chair. "I didn't get anything," she mumbled as she scrolled through her emails. "I'm sure of it."

"Me neither. If anyone's been double and triple checking

the facts, it's me." Kim groaned and covered her face with her hands. "Oh God, this is a disaster. He's not lying. It looks closed, and even if they offer us an alternative, we won't be as near to Andres' bar as we are now. I only booked this place because it was walking distance."

"Don't worry. They'll come up with a solution. They have to." Meghan couldn't have cared less where they were staying as long as there was a pool and the drinks were included. Being thirty-four and single, it was hard enough to find people who wanted to go on holiday with her. Most of her friends were married with kids, and the few single friends she had were too wild for her to spend more than a night with. When Kim had suggested going to Spain together, she'd immediately said yes because it seemed like the perfect solution. During the day, they would sunbathe, gossip and have cocktails by the poolside, and at night, Kim would see her boyfriend, which would give Meghan space to go out, explore and maybe meet new people. After all, what was the point of being single if she didn't chase opportunities?

"Now I'm going to be late, and I'll look like shit," Kim said. "And my ankles are still swollen from the flight. I need to put my feet up ASAP. I was hoping I could do that by the pool."

"I'm sure Andres will understand if you're a little late." Meghan turned to her friend, who was about to lose her temper. "He loves you, and he'll be happy to see you. He won't care if your ankles are swollen."

"He *says* he loves me," Kim corrected her. "I'm here to find out if he really does, or if he's just some lothario who still sleeps with tourists on a regular basis. But if he does love me... If he *really does* love me, then I want to look my best for him, so he'll realise we should be together forever and—"

"Ever and ever," Meghan interrupted her. She'd heard this so many times before, and although she was happy for Kim, it was getting old, especially after a ten-hour journey during which Kim had talked about Andres non-stop. "There he is," she said, relieved to see the man come out of his office. He was clearly not on official duty, as he was wearing jeans and a T-shirt, but at least he seemed helpful.

"Apologies for the wait, ladies. There was a glitch in our system. We sent an email to everyone who had booked for this week, but for some reason, yours wasn't sent, and it's still pending."

"Great." Kim tilted her head as she looked him over. "So, how are you planning on solving this? I have somewhere to be in two hours, and I'd really like to get ready."

"Of course. My name is Robert, by the way, and I normally work behind reception—when the hotel is open," he added with an apologetic smile. "I've just called my manager. The good news is I'll be able to give you an upgrade and check you in, and we'll give you a refund for tonight. The bad news is that we can't provide food for tonight, but there will be a member of staff behind the pool bar to serve you." He hesitated. "Unless you'd rather go to one of our sister hotels? I can find out which ones have availability."

"No, that works for me," Kim said, getting up. "A room is all I need. Are you okay with that, Megs?"

"Fine with me." Meghan was surprised at how quickly the problem had been solved, and she, too, was dying to get changed.

"Oh, one more thing." Robert slipped back behind the reception desk and picked up a flyer. "As I said, there will be an event here this weekend. It's a Pride event. Women only," he added, holding it up for them to see. "I just need to check you don't have a problem with that."

"No problem at all." Meghan smiled. "As long as the bar is open."

## 2

## FLORENCE

"You want me to work the bar tonight?" Florence stared from the pool bar to Robert and frowned.

"Only until midnight—if you don't mind," he said. "I'll stay on reception. I can sleep in the back." He sighed. "We screwed up with their reservation, so it's the least we can do, but I understand if you can't at such short notice. I can ask someone else."

"No, it's fine. I could actually do with the overtime, and with only two guests it's easy money." Florence picked up a rainbow garland that had fallen off one of the palm trees and reattached it.

The preparations for the women's Pride festival were finally done, and most of her colleagues, including Stella, her manager, had left. A few were still hanging around, smoking a cigarette before heading into town for a drink.

"Hey, guys. Just go without me," she yelled at them. "There was a fuck-up with a reservation, and a couple of people just arrived, so I'm staying here tonight." Her announcement was met with some protests, but the boys would be secretly relieved she wasn't coming. They loved hitting on the ladies, and even though she did too, people always assumed she was dating one of them.

She waved them off and turned back to Robert. "So, how does this work? Do I turn the music on? The lights?"

Robert shrugged. "Honestly, this is a first. I have no idea, but I don't want to bug Stella again. I just called her, and she was already in bed. I'd say do what you would normally do, apart from the announcements over the speakers."

"Yeah, that would be weird." Florence chuckled as she imagined her voice blasting through the silence, aimed at only herself if these guests didn't come down to the poolside tonight. "Well, I'll get the bar ready. Do you want a beer?"

"No, I'm good," Robert said. "I'm technically on duty, so I'd better not." He gave her a pat on her shoulder before he headed back into the building. "And no drinking for you either. Thanks, Flo. This should be an easy one."

"Sure. Easy-peasy," Florence muttered to herself as she turned on the pool lights and the string lights that adorned the tiki bars and the plants around the pool. Paradise Hotel wasn't the best or the prettiest hotel in Benidorm, but with the rainbow decorations and the lights, it looked pretty charming tonight. She connected her phone to the speakers and put on her own playlist instead of the standard corporate one. If she was going to be here all night, she might as well enjoy herself, but first, she needed something to wake herself up. The hotel's new coffee machines that had replaced the old, noisy ones were a blessing.

As she made herself a cappuccino, she heard one of the balcony doors above her open and looked up to see two women staring down at her. Unable to resist, she turned on the microphone. "Hey, there! The bar is open, ladies. Special one-on-one service, tonight only." She smiled when she heard them laugh.

"Thank you!" one of them yelled back at her. "I'll be down in a bit!"

Florence leaned on the bar and scrolled through her dating app, grimacing at most of the men and women who had 'liked' her. With the local dating scene being limited, she usually looked out for tourists, but there wasn't much choice this week. She was excited for tomorrow, though: working at a women's only weekend was right up her street. Personal relationships with guests were off-limits, but a little flirting was innocent and just what she needed.

"Hi."

Florence jumped and almost dropped her phone in the sink. "Oh, hey! Welcome to Paradise."

"Welcome to Paradise? Is that what they make you say?" The woman laughed. "It looks pretty cute out here, but I can assure you, our room is far from paradise, even though your boss gave us an upgrade."

"Robert?" Florence chuckled. "He's not my boss. He just happened to be here when you guys showed up, so they put him in charge." She winked. "I don't think it's gone to his head yet, but let's see what the night brings. And as far as the rooms are concerned, I agree with you. They're not great."

"It's fine. I'll be outside most of the time anyway." The woman took a seat at the bar. "Are you here just for me?"

"For you and your girlfriend," Florence said. "My name is Florence."

"Nice to meet you, I'm Meghan. It's just me tonight, and Kim is not my girlfriend."

"Oh, I'm sorry. I shouldn't have assumed. I just thought you were here for the Pride event and—"

"No, no, no," Meghan interrupted, waving a hand. "My friend is here to see her boyfriend, who's a local, and I'm tagging along. Neither of us is gay, nor are we here for the event." She leaned closer and lowered her voice, even though there was no one else around. "Are we going to be the only straight women here over the weekend?"

"I'm afraid so." Florence shot her an amused smile. There was something adorably innocent about this woman. "But it'll be fun. There's live music and a DJ, and everyone will dress up."

"I don't have anything to wear," Meghan said.

"No problem. Just grab one of those garlands. They're everywhere." Florence pointed to the cocktail menu. "By the way, what can I get you?"

Meghan shook her head. "I can go somewhere else. I'm sure you'd like to go home."

"Now that we officially have occupancy, even if it's just one room, someone has to be here, so you might as well stay." Florence shrugged. "The drinks are free, and I can be good company. I'd love to have someone to talk to while I sit out my shift, and besides the drinks on that menu, I can make you anything you like."

Meghan ran a hand through her long, dark hair and smiled. "Okay. But only if you have a drink with me."

"I'm not supposed to drink on duty." Florence glanced at the building. Robert always took naps on his nightshifts, and with hardly any guests in the hotel, he was sure to be fast asleep by now.

"There's no one here." Meghan pointed to the empty poolside. "It's just you and me. If there was ever a time to have a cheeky drink at work, it's now."

"You're right," Florence said after a moment's hesitation. "As long as you don't tell anyone."

"My lips are sealed." Meghan's smile widened, and she tapped the bar. "So, what are we having?"

## 3

---

# MEGHAN

"It's good," Meghan said as she sipped her margarita. She studied the attractive bartender, who was a little younger than her.

"Thanks." Florence was petite, but she seemed to have a big personality. Her wild, dark, curly hair was loosely pinned up, framing her heart-shaped face. She had a deep tan from working in the sun and big, hazel eyes that sparkled in the dim light of the bar. Wearing nothing but a slinky, grey vest top, a pair of tiny jersey shorts and flip-flops, she looked like she'd jumped straight out of bed onto the job, and as the hotel was closed, Meghan suspected that might have been the case.

"It could be a lot better. Our tequila is not of the best quality, but it does the job." Florence smiled widely and clinked her glass against Meghan's. "So, you're third-wheeling? Is that what's happening this week?"

Meghan laughed. "Yeah, something like that. I don't mind, though. I can entertain myself, and Kim will be here during the day while Andres, her boyfriend, is working."

"Well, you have me tonight." Florence pulled a chair

behind the bar, propped her feet on the edge of the sink and sat back. "And tomorrow, you'll have two hundred women fighting over you, so you won't be short of company then either."

"I don't mind making new friends, but as I said I'm not—"

"I know, you're not into women. I was only joking. Do you have a boyfriend?"

"No, I'm single. What about you?"

"Me too. Single and ready to mingle. I'm excited for the festival."

"Oh, you like women?" Meghan blushed and felt silly for it. She often ended up in gay clubs on Saturday nights, and she'd even kissed a girl on a drunken occasion when she was younger, so her reaction made no sense.

"I've dated men too, but I prefer women." Florence locked her eyes with Meghan's as she sipped her cocktail. "Physically, I mean."

Meghan nodded, a little uncomfortable under her intense stare. "Are you allowed to personally engage with guests?"

"No. I'm not allowed to drink on the job either." Florence suppressed a smirk as she held up her glass. "What can I say? I'm easily tempted."

"Then you must get in trouble a lot," Meghan joked. Florence had a permanently mischievous look on her face, and that amused her.

"Not really. I keep myself entertained, but I know my limits, so I tend to get away with a lot. Where are you from?"

"London. It's good to get out of the city for a bit, and we haven't had much of a summer. It's rained non-stop for weeks." Meghan looked at her arms, which, like the rest of her, were terribly pale compared to Florence. "What about you? Do you live in Benidorm?"

"For now. I'm a seasonal employee. I'm here in the summer. In the winter, I work for a hospitality employment agency in London. It's restaurant bar work, mainly, but they occasionally put me on events and weddings too."

"That sounds fun."

"It can be. What do you do, Meghan?"

"I manage a casino. A small one in Southwest London."

"Cool." Florence looked her over and frowned. "I find it hard to imagine you as a casino boss. You look so innocent."

Meghan threw her head back and laughed. "You've been watching too many movies. I'm not a gangster. I just manage the day-to-day and the staff."

"But you wear a black suit?" Florence asked with a chuckle.

"At work, yes."

"Do you smoke cigars and drink whisky in your office?"

Meghan laughed even harder now. "No, I don't smoke, and like you, I'm not allowed to drink on the job." She shrugged. "But unlike you, *I* play by the rules."

"Hey, that's not fair! You were the one who insisted I have a drink with you." Florence's eyes widened in amusement. "So, you never get up to anything naughty at work?"

"Never. I'm not involved with money laundering or blackmail, I'm afraid, and I don't go around breaking people's legs. Sorry to disappoint you."

"Bummer." Florence slapped her thigh with a comical grin. "What about office affairs? A bit of fun on your desk after hours?"

"Nope. I share an office with the head of payroll and the head of HR, and they're both old enough to be my parents."

Meghan held up her hands in defeat. "I'm basically super boring."

"We'll see about that." Florence pointed to her glass. "How about another margarita?"

Finishing her cocktail, Meghan already felt it going to her head. She hadn't eaten anything yet, but she was enjoying having a drink with Florence and didn't feel like venturing out in search of food. "I'd love another, but I need to eat. Do you know a good place that delivers?" She opened one of the international delivery apps on her phone and handed it to Florence. "Are you hungry? Please order whatever you like."

"I do know of a place, but I don't want you to buy me dinner. Let's split it."

"Please. It's the least I can do when you're keeping me company," Meghan insisted. "And I'm a big casino boss, remember? You're just going to have to do as I say."

Florence arched a brow and chuckled. "Okay, big shot. How about tapas?"

# 4

## FLORENCE

*A*s they unpacked the food together, Florence felt pleasantly surprised with how her evening had turned out. Meghan was fun to talk to, although she was a little different than their regular guests, and Florence couldn't quite figure out why.

"I feel like we need candles," Meghan joked, carrying the food over to the poolside table Florence had laid out with plates and cutlery from the hotel kitchen.

"Good point. I can arrange that." Florence grabbed three candle holders from behind the bar, put in fresh candles and lit them. "Here you go," she said, placing them in the middle of the table. "It doesn't get any more romantic than this."

Meghan laughed. "I know. The sea breeze, the candle-light, the food..." She looked skyward. "And the full moon. Let's not forget about that."

"Yes, and you look dazzling in the moonlight, darling." Florence made a show of pulling out a chair for Meghan and then sat opposite her. "Honestly, this is so weird. I've never dined in my own workplace, and I've never been here while the hotel was deserted. I was planning on a few drinks with colleagues, but this is so much better."

"I'm glad you're not bored with me."

"Not at all. Have you heard from your friend?"

"Oh...Kim! I'd totally forgotten about her." Meghan checked her messages and nodded. "She's fine. She's telling me not to wait up for her."

"That's good. For her, I mean," Florence said. "For me too. I'm having a really great time."

"Same here." Meghan plated her food. "It smells amazing. Is this one of your local takeaway places?"

"Yes. It's a small restaurant where we often meet up after work. It belongs to one of my colleague's cousins. He appreciates our business, and we get a discount on drinks." Florence tore off a piece of bread and dipped it in the albondigas tomato sauce. "So, how does a big casino boss end up in Paradise? Isn't it a bit..." She thought long and hard about how to phrase the question, as she didn't want Meghan to feel judged. "I mean, there are a lot nicer hotels along this strip."

"As I said, I'm not a big boss." Meghan looked up with a humorous twinkle in her eyes. "And as far as the accommodation is concerned, Kim picked it. Not that I care where I stay. As long as there's a bed, I'm happy, and besides, there's something comforting about cheap package holidays.

"Really? How so?"

"My parents used to take me to a hotel nearby. They had me very young, and we lived on a council estate. They were always struggling with money, but they still managed to save up enough for a ten-day holiday every year. I looked forward to those trips for months."

"How sweet. How old were they when they had you?"

"Seventeen." Meghan chuckled when Florence gasped

and almost choked on her food. "I know, it's crazy. But guess what? They're still together and very happy."

"Now that's a unique story. I take it you didn't follow in their footsteps, as you didn't mention having kids?"

"No, no kids. You?"

"God, no. I'm barely an adult myself." Florence laughed. "I'm twenty-five. But because I'm petite and look younger than my age, I still get ID'd. One of my friends is thirty-five, and people often mistake him for my dad. I hate it when that happens."

"Ouch." Meghan grimaced. "Well, all I can say is, it might be annoying at times, but enjoy it while it lasts. I'm turning thirty-five soon, and I feel like everything has started drooping."

"How can you say that? You're so not drooping." Florence didn't mean to stare, but she did. Meghan's cleavage was enticing in the low-cut white top she was wearing, and she had a great figure. "You're hot, girl. You're—" She bit her lip, stopping herself. Although she was enjoying Meghan's startled expression and flushed cheeks, she was worried she'd gone too far. Meghan was a hotel guest, after all, and she didn't want to make her uncomfortable. Luckily, Meghan's face broke into a smile as she sat back, creating some distance between them.

"Are you hitting on me?" she asked. "Because that's not going to work."

"No." Now it was Florence's turn to blush. "No, I wasn't." She shook her head with a grin. "All I'm saying is, I think you're beautiful."

"Oh." Meghan stared at her. "Thank you."

"You're welcome." Florence didn't know what to do with herself in the uncomfortable silence that followed, and she was thankful Meghan changed the topic.

"So, Florence, tell me about the festival. What can I expect tomorrow? Just so I can prepare Kim when she comes back tonight." At that moment, Meghan's phone lit up, and she raised a brow as she read the message. "Never mind. Kim's staying with Andres."

"Are you surprised? You seem disappointed."

"It's not that." Meghan stared up at the building. There was only one light on in the enormous block, which was in her room on one of the top floors. "It was creepy when we went up there earlier, but at least we were together so we could laugh about it."

"Wait. Are you scared?" Florence shot her a teasing smile. "You are!"

"Just a little uncomfortable." Meghan hesitated. "Would you mind walking me up to my room later?"

"Of course not. But just to get things straight. If anyone's watched too many movies, it's you."

Meghan rolled her eyes. "I know it's silly. There's no one in the building apart from the reception guy, so there's nothing to be worried about, but I get..." She swallowed her words and fiddled with her napkin.

"You get what?" Florence saw a hint of genuine distress in Meghan's features. Although she didn't know her, it was clear this wasn't a cry for attention, and she felt a stab of guilt for making fun of her.

Meghan was silent for a long moment as if there was something she wanted to tell her. "It's nothing," she finally said. "I'll be fine once I've locked the door behind me."

# 5

## MEGHAN

"*I*'m sorry about this. I'm not usually such a coward." Meghan felt her legs shaking as the lift went up. Not because she was afraid right now, but because she knew she would be once Florence had left. She'd be sitting up with the lights on, her body tensing at every noise. It was going to be a long night.

The evening had been so much fun, but eventually Florence had to close up as they weren't allowed to be there after midnight, and as she'd helped her clear up, her growing anxiety reminded her she'd be alone soon.

"Don't apologise. I'm with you. You're totally right. It's spooky here when it's so quiet, but I can assure you, this hotel isn't haunted." Florence's attempt to make her feel better didn't help one bit because it wasn't a fear of ghosts that had her on edge.

The ping of the lift echoed eerily through the empty hall as they stepped out and headed for her room. Meghan scanned the ceiling for security cameras, but she didn't see any. Surely, they would have some form of surveillance here, or at least a security guard on duty. Knowing the receptionist was asleep didn't fuel her confidence either, and as she stopped in front of her door, her heart was pounding hard.

"Are you okay?" Florence asked.

"Yeah. I'm just going to check the room. Do you mind waiting?"

Sensing her distress, Florence stopped her. "I'll do it. You stay here."

Meghan watched her from the doorway while Florence checked the closet, the bathroom and even went on her knees to look under the bed.

"All clear," she said with a sweet smile.

"Thank you, again." Embarrassed and worried Florence might think she was a paranoid wreck, which admittedly, she was, Meghan returned her smile and straightened her back as she headed inside. *There's no one here*, she told herself. *You're safe.*

"Are you sure you're going to be okay?" Florence leaned against the doorpost and studied her intently. "I can stay if it would make you more comfortable." She held up her hands. "I'm not hitting on you. I want you to feel safe, that's all."

"That's very kind of you, but it's not your job to make me feel safe." Meghan took her hand and squeezed it. "I've had a great evening. You go home and get some sleep. You'll be super busy tomorrow."

Florence nodded and turned to walk away, but before Meghan had a chance to close the door, she came back. "Wait." She reached out for Meghan's hands. "You're trembling. I felt it earlier, but it didn't register."

"I'm just cold." In truth, she was shaking all over and the tightness in her chest that had started as soon as she'd gone inside was growing.

"It's not cold here, and you look terrified." Florence

glanced at the two beds. "Look. I have to be here tomorrow morning anyway, so if you want, I'll stay with you. That way, we'll both get more sleep. My housemate works here too, so I can ask him to bring me some clothes, and housekeeping will change the sheets so your friend will be in a clean bed when she comes back." She paused. "And I doubt I'd get into trouble for sleeping in a guest's bedroom because the whole creepy-empty-hotel scenario is a great argument."

"It's still crazy and not your job," Meghan said again, but she stepped back to let Florence in. She'd hoped the alcohol would relax her once she got upstairs; instead, she was on high alert and had sobered up within minutes.

"No, it's not my job, but I want to." Sitting on the bed, Florence bounced to assess the mattress and laughed. "Besides, this is so much better than my own bed."

"You're full of shit. Those beds are terrible." Meghan joined her and chuckled when the bed creaked, threatening to break. "You'll regret this."

Florence laughed and turned to face her. "You haven't seen where I live. It's basic at best. In fact, it might be worse than here, but I'm hardly ever home, so I don't care."

"That's not possible." Meghan shot her a grin.

"Oh, yes, it is. Like I said, I'm only here through the summers, and I'm outside all the time, so I get any cheap room nearby that's available. This year, I'm sharing a house with my colleague and bestie Manuel and another woman. It's crammed, but we get along." Florence gestured to the room. "And I wasn't lying when I said it looked a bit like this. Dated, ugly and mildly uncomfortable, but this is still better."

"That makes me feel less guilty." Meghan let out a deep breath and cradled her knees. Her anxiety was slowly subsiding now that she knew she wouldn't be alone. "Why are you doing this for me?"

"Because I'm having a good time, I'm not bothered about my own bed, and I like you and want to help you," Florence said, and Meghan believed her. "Are you tired?"

Meghan looked at the other bed and shrugged. "I'm wide awake, but you must be tired."

"Far from." Florence got up. "How about I get a bottle of wine from downstairs? It's not the best wine, but if you're not fussy..."

"Never fussy," Meghan said. She pointed to the balcony. "We could sit out there for a while? This room is stuffy, even with the balcony doors open."

"Sounds good. Are you okay to wait here? I won't be long."

"Yeah, I'll be fine." Meghan forced a smile. Surely, she'd be okay for ten minutes. Her logic told her this was a perfectly safe place, yet her heart started pounding in her throat as soon as Florence left. Taking a couple of deep breaths, she fought the flashbacks that started attacking her.

# 6

## FLORENCE

"One for you." Florence poured Meghan a glass of white wine and handed it to her. "And one for me." She sat next to her and leaned back against the balcony door. "Do you want to tell me why you're so scared of being alone?"

Meghan silently sipped her wine as she stared down at the poolside. "I'm not afraid to be alone per se. I'm fine at home. It's just hotels that make me uncomfortable when I'm by myself." She paused. "I knew there was a chance Kim wouldn't be here at night, and I honestly thought I'd be okay but..."

"But you couldn't have foreseen staying in an empty hotel." Florence placed a hand on her shoulder. "It will all be better tomorrow when it's busy and noisy."

"I know," Meghan said. "What are you afraid of?"

"Hmm..." Florence could not think of a single thing that scared her. She was fearless, according to her friends, perhaps even a bit reckless, and she never said no to a challenge, no matter how ridiculous. She'd bungee jumped, ziplined, paraglided, and she'd jumped out of a plane on several occasions, loving the rush of those first few seconds before she opened her parachute. She was comfortable in water too; she'd swum in wild shores and was a confident cliff diver.

"Nothing?" Meghan asked when she still hadn't answered.

"I don't think so. Well, maybe apart from missing out," Florence joked. "But that's not serious enough to call it a fear. I worry about others, of course. I want my family to be safe and healthy, but when it comes to myself, I always trust that everything will work out. Maybe that's naïve."

"Maybe. But still, it's nice. I used to be like you."

"What changed?"

"Something happened." Meghan shrugged and didn't elaborate, so Florence didn't enquire. If Meghan was uncomfortable talking about it, she wasn't going to push her. "Tell me more about you," Meghan said, diverting the topic away from herself. "Do you date a lot?"

"I have fun." Now that she was off duty, Florence was really enjoying the wine, as she didn't have to worry about being caught. "I was in a long-term relationship with my first boyfriend until I was twenty-one. He was a DJ, and I thought he was the coolest person in the world." She chuckled. "And then I developed a mad crush on a woman, so I broke up with him. I wanted to explore my sexuality, and he was my best friend, so it was difficult. The woman in question was a colleague in a hotel where I worked, and we hooked up a couple of times. It never got serious, but it did open my eyes, and after her, I was in a couple of short-ish relationships with women. On an emotional level, I like both men and women. As long as there's attraction, it works for me. But on a physical level, I prefer sex with women."

"Oh." Meghan turned to look at her curiously. "Why is that?"

"I don't know. There's something more intuitive about women, I suppose, and I just love their softness and their curves..." Florence watched Meghan's eyes darken, and she wondered what she was thinking. "Have you ever tried it?"

"I've kissed a woman, but I've never gone any further than that." Meghan pursed her lips, and her eyes darted to Florence's mouth for a split second. "It was a long time ago, though, in uni."

"Was there alcohol involved?"

"Yes," Meghan admitted. "The girl stayed on my mind for a while. Not in the moment, but after we'd kissed."

"So you felt attracted to her?" Florence asked.

"I'm not sure, but as I said, she was on my mind in the weeks following. It happened at a party. She took me by surprise, said she wanted to kiss me. I was a bit tipsy, and she was cute, so I let her. The next day, I couldn't remember her name and I never saw her again, so that was that." Meghan finished her wine and held out her glass for a refill. "But I'm not bisexual. I've never been in love with a woman."

"But you've been in love with men?" Florence realised the conversation had turned very personal, but she liked how Meghan was opening up to her.

"Yes. I was in two long-term relationships. It wasn't perfect, but we had the same interests, and we were happy. The only reason I ended it on both occasions was that I didn't feel it was going to last forever. Not from my side, anyway."

"How did you know it wasn't forever?"

"I guess I've always wanted what my parents have, and it wasn't that." Meghan smiled. "They can't bear being apart, not even for a day, and they always have each other's back. They're like two peas in a pod." She paused. "And your parents? Are they still together?"

"No, they divorced when I was young, but I have a good relationship with both of them. My father is British and my mother Spanish. I grew up here, but I have dual nationality. That's why I work in the UK over winter."

"Nice. You've got the best of both worlds."

"I guess. I can't complain."

Meghan leaned back and looked at Florence's curls. "And your hair? Is that from your mother's side?"

"Yes." Florence laughed. "My father is a tall, bald, pale Englishman, so I certainly don't take after him. My mother is a bit of a hippie, and they couldn't be more different. No wonder their marriage didn't last."

"A hippie?"

"Not in the literal sense of the word," Florence said. "She doesn't live in a commune, and she doesn't wear headbands or tie-dye, but she's into auras and the universe and that kind of stuff. She has a small practice in Altea where she does crystal healing."

"Fascinating. Then you must know a lot about it."

"I have basic knowledge of crystals, but I've never been very interested. I may have got my looks from my mother, but in essence, I take more after my father. He's a dentist, and with his medical background, he doesn't believe in alternative medicine. Growing up, I never saw any evidence of actual healing, so I decided my father was right."

Meghan nodded. "I've always been curious about alternative healing."

"Then maybe you should visit her practice," Florence said. "I'll give you her details so you can make up your own mind."

# 7

## MEGHAN

*I*t was two o'clock in the morning by the time they'd finished the bottle, and Meghan could hardly believe how quickly the time had flown by. "I'm so sorry," she said. "I didn't realise how late it was. You've been working all day. You must be exhausted."

"Honestly, I could happily sit here and talk to you all night, but I should probably get some sleep." Florence checked her watch, stood up and stretched. "In that wonderful Paradise bed."

"I'm sure it will be a treat." Meghan laughed and stood up too. Her legs were stiff from sitting in the same position on the small balcony, and the wine had made her light-headed. They'd talked non-stop since she'd sat down at the bar, and Florence was right; they could have stayed here until the sun came up. "I don't have any spare toothbrushes, I'm afraid." She pointed to the bathroom. "But please help yourself to a towel and any toiletries you need. I'll get you a T-shirt and underwear."

"Thanks." Florence locked the door behind her, and Meghan heard the shower running. She imagined her stripping off and stepping in, running her hands through her wild curls as water trickled down her face and shower gel slid down her body.

*Why is my mind even going there?* Suspecting their conversations about sexuality and the wine had something to do with it, she shook her head and sighed as she rummaged through her suitcase and pulled out two white T-shirts and two pairs of white panties. She was sharing a room with a woman she'd only met seven hours ago, and now she was having intimate thoughts about her, which was ridiculous. Her breath hitched when the bathroom door opened again, and Florence appeared with nothing but a towel wrapped around her. Her hair was wet and her skin shimmered from the lotion she'd applied; she let out a dramatic sigh as she fell back on Kim's bed.

"That was so nice. I was seriously clammy from setting up all day."

"Good." Meghan caught herself staring and threw one of the T-shirts and pairs of panties at her. "Here. You can wear these." She rushed into the bathroom and consoled herself with the thought that when she came out, Florence would have put on the clothes so Meghan couldn't gawk at her anymore. Florence was pretty without even trying. In fact, Meghan didn't think she knew how beautiful she was. She giggled as she looked at the top of the mirror, where a smiley face was drawn on the condensed glass.

As she'd already had a shower when she arrived, she settled for a quick one and left the water running while she took her time to check herself in the mirror. Uncertain why she felt the need to look good, she combed her hair thoroughly and applied moisturiser and a little bit of mascara before getting dressed for the night.

Florence's eyes fell upon her breasts as she came out, and Meghan instinctively crossed her arms.

"Glad to see you're wearing one of those see-through T-shirts yourself, or I might think you gave it to me on purpose."

Meghan hid her face in her hands and laughed. "Sorry, it's what I sleep in. I don't have anything else."

"I'm just messing with you. It's fine. Nice and airy for a warm night." When Florence sat up in bed, the outline of her breasts was clearly visible through the thin top, and Meghan swiftly looked away. "Well, I think I'll try to get some sleep." Florence yawned through her words. "Thank you, Meghan. I had a lovely time with you." She hesitated. "Maybe we can meet up again sometime while you're here?"

Meghan's face broke into a huge smile. She had no problem going out by herself; she easily made friends, but she loved Florence's company and was eager to spend more time with her. "I'd like that." She got into bed and turned on her side, facing Florence as she slipped under the covers. It wasn't awkward but certainly unusual, having someone other than Kim there. She didn't feel like she was taking up Florence's time or asking for too much, though. This was a two-way understanding, and she was pretty sure Florence wasn't here because she took pity on her. "Goodnight."

"Goodnight, Meghan."

Meghan turned off her bedside lamp, leaving the room in the dim light from the poolside and the full moon. Sea breeze was flowing through the balcony doors, and in the distance, she heard music coming from the clubs and bars along the promenade. She was mindfully aware of her own body and the fact that Florence was lying in the bed next to hers. The image of Florence's breasts hit her, and she shook off the thought.

This made no sense. She'd come here with the intention of flirting a little, perhaps even have a holiday fling. It had been a year since she'd ended her relationship with Tom, and she was ready to have fun again, but with a man, not with a woman.

Her mind went back to the girl she'd kissed at the university party. Meghan hadn't thought of her in many years, but talking about it tonight brought it all back, and she could vividly remember her face now. A sharp jawline, big, blue eyes and short, ash-blonde hair that fell over one side of her forehead. She'd been confidently charming and assertive, something Meghan wasn't used to back then, not even with boys. And her lips had been so soft...

Meghan closed her eyes, attempting to relive the moment. She'd kissed her soft and tenderly at first, then more persistent and hungrily as their hands explored each other's waist and hips—until one of Meghan's friends had pulled her away from the girl because they were leaving. During the cab drive back to their campus, they'd teased her relentlessly, and Meghan had laughed along, blaming her out-of-character behaviour on too many cocktails, but she'd never forgotten, not really. The memory turned vague, and then darkness took over as she slipped into a deep and dream-filled sleep.

# 8

## FLORENCE

"Yes, I'm coming!" The knocking was hard and persistent, and Florence rushed to the door and opened it.

"The stuff you wanted," Manuel said, sticking his head into the room. As soon as he saw Meghan in her bed, he quickly retreated and mouthed, "What have you been up to?"

"Nothing," Florence whispered. "I swear. The hotel was empty, she was scared, I was here, and it saved me going home and coming back." She took the bag from him. "Thank you. Did you get my toothbrush too?"

"Yes, it's all in there." Manuel looked her up and down and decided she was telling the truth. "Aren't you going to get into trouble for this?"

"Of course not. If anything, they should thank me for helping out a terrified guest who was here all alone."

"Right. That makes sense." He stepped back and pointed to her messy hair. "You'd better get ready, though. You're looking a bit rough, and we open in half an hour."

"What?" Florence grabbed his wrist to check his watch.

"Oh God. I forgot to set the alarm." Behind her, she heard the bed creak as Meghan stirred awake and sat up. "Okay, I'll see you down there. Thanks, Manuel." She closed the door and turned to find Meghan smiling at her.

"Good morning. Did you sleep well?" Meghan yawned and rubbed her face, looking adorably sleepy.

"Yes, like a baby." Florence returned her smile. "Must have been the wine. You?"

"Yeah. I had weird dreams." Meghan frowned as if she was trying to remember, then subtly shook her head. "Really weird dreams."

"Care to share?"

"Best not." Meghan chuckled. "Anyway, it's all fading now." She got out of bed, stepped onto the balcony and leaned over the railing, taking in the final preparations that were going on around the poolside. "Wow, it's a beautiful day."

"It's going to be a great day." Florence couldn't help but stare at Meghan's perky behind, only sparsely covered by her white lace panties. Her T-shirt didn't help either, as her shapely waist was clearly visible through the thin fabric. A tightness grew in Florence's core, and she tried to think of something else. Anything else. Last night, she'd put her subtle flirtations down to the alcohol and the full moon, but now that the sun was up, not much had changed. She still felt the need to let Meghan know she appreciated her looks, and as she joined her on the balcony, she attempted to bite back the flirtatious comment that was dying to slip from her lips. *Don't say it.* "I hope you're going to cover up that cute ass today, or you're going to have women flocking around you like there's no tomorrow." *Damn it.*

"What?" Meghan's cheeks flushed as she looked at her, wide-eyed. "Me?"

Florence could've kicked herself for her impulsiveness. "Do you see anyone else here? Yes, you." She laughed it off as a joke and sincerely hoped she hadn't offended her.

"I guess I'll take that as a compliment." Meghan turned and arched a brow as she eyed Florence's T-shirt. "And I hope you'll cover up those puppies for the sake of all the single women who are dying to get it on with the bartender."

"Hey, if it catches your eye, it may work with others." Florence grinned as she met her eyes. "Unfortunately, I have to wear the Pride top the organisation provided me with, so there will be no flashing action behind the bar today." She held Meghan's gaze, and Meghan didn't shy away.

"Shame. I guess all the attention will go to me and my cute ass, then."

*Am I mistaken, or is she flirting back?* "I guess so. Are you ready for that?"

Meghan shrugged. "As long as you look after me, I think I'll be fine." It wasn't so much what she said as the way she said it that caused a stir in Florence's core. Meghan's voice was sultry, and her eyes were twinkling with mischief.

"I can do that." Florence hesitated, contemplating what to say next. She wanted to ask Meghan when she was free to meet up, but she was worried it would come across as if she was asking her out on a date. "I'll look after you if you let me take you out on Monday."

"Deal." Meghan's face pulled into an amused expression. "But I'll still be straight on Monday, so if you get a better offer over the weekend—"

"Then I'll tell them I already have a lovely, purely platonic date planned. And if you decide to venture out into town and you get a better offer from a handsome young man, then—"

"Then I'll tell them the same," Meghan said. "Monday is on, no matter what."

"Good. I'm already looking forward to it." Florence inched back when she saw her manager, Stella, crossing the poolside. "They're expecting me downstairs soon. Do you mind if I use the bathroom first?"

"No. Please, go ahead."

"Thank you." Florence slipped past Meghan, and again she felt a flutter as her leg brushed Meghan's thigh. When she turned on the shower and condensation settled over the mirror, she chuckled. There was another smiley face next to the one she'd drawn last night, and this one had a winking eye.

## 9

## MEGHAN

"Which one?" Kim scanned the poolside from the balcony. "Her?"

"Yes, the one with the curly hair behind the first bar." Meghan studied Florence as she moved effortlessly, whipping up cocktails and delivering them to patrons, always with a dazzling smile. "She's so nice." She'd filled Kim in on last night's happenings after Kim had finished her hour-long monologue about Andres.

"How lovely of her to stay here with you." Kim rubbed Meghan's shoulder. "I'm so sorry about that. I didn't think of how scary it must have been for you on your own in an empty hotel."

"Don't worry about it," Meghan said. She'd never told Kim about her hotel anxiety, and Kim didn't need to know why she panicked. Dealing with it the best she could, she hoped her trauma would heal eventually, and that one day, she'd be fine on her own again. Apart from her parents, the police and her therapist, she hadn't told anyone what had happened two years ago. The past was in the past and there was no point reliving that awful night just for the sake of telling someone. "Neither of us saw it coming," she continued. "Not the empty hotel, and not this..."

"No, certainly not this." Kim chuckled as she spread her arms and gestured to the women below. They were wearing rainbow bikinis, T-shirts, outrageous shades, hairpieces and wigs. The poolside was quickly filling up, with half of the sunbeds already taken, and the DJ was just setting up for her first set. "It'll be fun. Something different for a change, right? Or would you rather go to the beach?"

"No, no. I'm happy to stay," Meghan quickly said with more enthusiasm than she'd meant to. "Shall we go grab some breakfast before we find a spot?"

"God, yes, I'm starving." Kim grinned. "I've been up all night playing with Andres' glorious—"

"Spare me the details, please. I'm happy for you— delighted, in fact—but just fade to grey, will you?" Meghan tied a sarong around her waist, grabbed her straw beach bag and put on her shades. "I don't want to picture my best friend in action."

"Boring," Kim shot back at her. "Who else am I going to tell about my new experiences with tantric sex? The ladies downstairs won't be interested."

"You never know. Why don't you try them?" Meghan turned to her as they headed out of their room and called the lift. "So, when am I going to meet your man?"

"Whenever you want." Kim sighed dreamily. "He's so passionate, Megs. I just can't believe this is happening for me. He's perfect in every way, and he loves me."

"Aww, Kim..." Meghan pulled her friend into a hug.

"He said it to my face this time, and it felt different." The nervous and neurotic Kim from the past weeks was gone and here was a brand-spanking-new Kim, who was still talking Meghan's ears off about Andres but in a happy and excited way, and that was adorable. "And I said it back, of course. And now we're, like, super official."

"I think it's safe to say I won't be sharing this room with you, then."

Kim winced. "Probably not. But you'll be okay, right? Now that there are guests here?"

"Of course." Meghan painted on a smile. Even with a hotel full of women, she wasn't sure how she'd feel, as she hadn't tested the theory yet.

"How about Monday night? We could have a drink somewhere in town, the three of us? I just know you'll love him. He's super funny and sweet."

"I can't do Monday, but any other night works for me."

"You have plans?" Kim frowned. "With whom? You don't know anyone here."

"With Florence, the woman who stayed over last night. She's taking me out," Meghan said, then corrected herself. "I mean, we're going for a drink."

"Oh, that's nice.

"Uh-huh." Meghan took Kim's hand and pulled her out of the lift towards the breakfast buffet. "We get along, and I figured since you were busy with Andres, why not?"

"Sure. Then we'll do Tuesday," Kim said, taking a seat at one of the tables in the outdoor area. "I love travelling with you. You're so independent and I never feel like I have to worry about you."

"I have to be, babe. I'm single." Meghan sat back, enjoying the mild morning temperatures. Since most guests were yet to arrive, it was quiet in the dining area, but she suspected it would be chaos tomorrow. Scanning the other tables, she saw couples, mainly, or at least she assumed they were couples as they seemed so comfortable with each other. Some were younger than her, some older, all of them smiling, visibly excited for the weekend ahead. "Do you think they think we're a couple?" she asked, lowering her voice to a whisper.

"Gross. I hope not. I wouldn't do you in a million years." Kim grimaced and got up when the staff showed no intention of serving them. "Come on, I need coffee."

"Thanks for the confidence boost, arsehole. Same here," Meghan joked. She left her bag on her chair and followed Kim to get breakfast.

"I feel like everyone's checking me out," Kim said with a nervous giggle as she piled scrambled eggs onto a slice of toast.

"They probably are. Take it as a compliment." Meghan slapped Kim's behind playfully. "You're looking lovely, by the way. Is that a new sarong?"

"Yes. Andres might pop by on his break. I said I'd meet him in front of the hotel." Kim picked up a fork and pointed it at Meghan. "But you look nice too, darling. Who did you dress up for?"

## 10

## FLORENCE

"What can I get you?" Florence put on her most charming smile as she leaned over the bar. "Three beers? Sure, coming up." She kept half an eye on Meghan, who had just chosen a sunbed on the other side of the pool, facing her. The other woman, whom she assumed was her friend, had applied sunscreen to her back, and Meghan was returning the favour. She'd put one of the hotel's garlands around her neck to make up for the lack of colour in her black bikini and matching sarong, and her long, dark hair fell over her shoulders with bouncy, curled ends. Florence was hoping Meghan would order a drink from her, and her smile widened when she finally walked over with her friend. Typical that of all the women here, she only had eyes for one of the two straight ones.

"Three beers for you," she said, placing them on the bar. Wanting to impress Meghan, she rushed to get a margarita ready as she arrived.

"Hey, there. I hope you're not too tired?" Meghan asked, twirling a lock of hair around her finger as she propped her elbow on the bar.

"Not at all. I'm feeling great today, and you look fantastic."

"Oh, thanks." Meghan looked her up and down. "So do you. You're rocking the rainbow top."

"Thank you." Florence felt her cheeks turn pink as she put the margarita in front of Meghan. "Here, your usual," she said with a wink. "Or would you prefer something else?"

"Ehm, it's a bit early for alcohol, but I'll have one." Meghan chuckled. "You're quick."

"I told you I'd look after you." Florence turned to Meghan's companion, whose curious eyes looked her over. "You must be Kim. I'm Florence. It's nice to meet you."

"Very nice to meet you too." Kim smiled. "And thank you for staying with Meghan last night. It's so sweet of you."

"Trust me, the pleasure was all mine. What can I get you?"

"I think I'll have the same. But don't make it too strong. I'm seeing my boyfriend later," Kim announced loudly enough for everyone around her to hear it. She was clearly a bit uncomfortable being straight amidst queer women, but she seemed nice nevertheless, Florence decided.

"Don't listen to her, she'll have a double." Meghan took a sip of her drink and nodded slowly as she shot Florence an approving look. "It's good, babe. Just have the same as me, you'll be fine," she said to Kim.

"Will you be here later?" Florence asked. She just couldn't help herself. "There's a dance competition on at eight."

Meghan laughed. I'm a crap dancer, so I won't sign up for that, but I might come and watch."

"You should." Florence had specifically mentioned the last event of the day, hoping she'd be able to catch Meghan before she went to bed. "I'm a crap dancer too, but I might give it a go anyway."

"Oh, are you feeling it?" Meghan asked.

"Yeah, I'm kind of bouncy today." Florence chuckled when a couple of women cheered at her comment. She hadn't realised people were listening in and had totally forgotten about her job, which was to serve people. Not just Meghan, but everyone. "I'll see you around," she said with a cheeky smile. "I'll be here."

"So will I." Meghan turned and walked off, and Florence wished she wasn't at work, so she could talk to her some more. "Who's next?" she asked and laughed when at least ten women raised their hands. Manuel came back from his break, and she let out a sigh of relief. "You take the left side, and I'll take the right," she said, giving him a fist bump.

Manuel arched a brow at her when most women shifted over to the right. "Check you out, little Miss Popular," he muttered. "How do you do that?"

"Just be nice," she mouthed back. "That's all there's to it."

"Like you were nice to that hot brunette over there last night?" Manuel glanced in Meghan's direction.

"Hey, I told you, nothing happened." Florence had to up her pace, as more and more women were gathering in front of her. She lined up as many cups as she could fit on the bar and started making cocktails in batches so everyone could help themselves. "We slept in separate beds."

"I believe you." Manuel smirked. "But that doesn't mean it will stay that way. Are you seeing her again?"

Florence decided it was better not to answer that. "She's straight," she said instead.

"Really?" Manuel's smile widened. "I knew it. I got a

straight vibe from her when she was checking me out earlier. I think she likes me."

"Don't you get any ideas. She probably just recognised you because you brought my stuff over." *She's mine*, Florence wanted to say, but that was ridiculous. Maybe Meghan *was* attracted to Manuel. A lot of women were, and just because she was flirting with Florence, it didn't mean she wanted anything more. Besides, there would be no such thing as fighting over guests when it could get them fired. Mixing Unicorn cocktails as fast as she could and throwing in decorative straws, she raised her voice and looked at the crowd. "Help yourself, ladies. Unless you want beer, then Manuel here is your man."

# 11

## MEGHAN

"So, Florence, the bartender..." Kim took a sip of her drink before she continued. "She seems to have a way with you."

"What do you mean?" Meghan pulled her shades over her eyes so Kim couldn't see she was watching Florence. She knew exactly what Kim meant, though; there had definitely been playful interaction between them.

"She was flirting with you. Didn't you notice?"

"No," Meghan lied. Her stomach did a flip when Florence looked up and glanced in her direction. *She's watching me too.* "It's just her extraverted personality. She's like that with everyone."

"Not with me." Kim paused as she followed Meghan's gaze. Florence was saying something to a group of women, which made them laugh loudly. They stood gathered around the bar, scrambling for her attention, and one of them had been there for a while now. "Is she gay?"

"She's fluid." Meghan attempted to sound indifferent, but the truth was, she constantly found herself staring at Florence. She'd watched her from the balcony before Kim came back, and now she was doing it again. Something about Florence attracted her, and that brought along a whole arsenal of questions she had no answers to.

"She's definitely fluid for you, that's for sure," Kim said in a teasing tone. "Maybe by the end of this week, you'll be fluid for her too."

"Ha-ha, very funny." Meghan slapped Kim's thigh. "You can give up on the shipping. I barely know her and I'm not into women."

"Hmm..." Kim rolled on her side to face Meghan and lowered her voice to a whisper. "But let's say if you *were* into women, who would you go for?" She subtly pointed to the group of women at the bar. "Someone like them? The feminine type? Or someone like that woman in the pool? The butch one with the baseball cap."

Meghan sipped her drink and shrugged. "I don't know. What about you?"

"I think I'd go for the butch one," Kim said. "There's something cool about her, and I imagine her being gallant and protective. I love her tattoos, and I think she'd be great in bed too."

Meghan turned to Kim and lowered her shades. "Really? You've thought about this?"

"Uh-huh. Well, just for the past hour," Kim clarified. "It's hard not to think about it, with all these women flirting and kissing." She poked Meghan's shoulder. "Okay, I've said it. If I were into women, I'd gladly spend a night with her. Your turn."

"How can you ask me what my female type is when I don't even know what my male type is?" Meghan hoped her argument would get her out of answering the question because it felt awkward. If she hadn't met Florence, she'd probably have fun with it, but now she was paranoid Kim would see her gaze darting towards Florence. Not that she fancied her; she didn't. *Okay, maybe a little.*

"At least you're consistent," she said, steering the attention away from herself. "You tend to go for the tough, dark types, and that woman you pointed out falls into the tough and dark category, but me? I've dated just about every type of man under the sun."

"Fair point. They were all very different, but attraction is still attraction. So, if you had to...if you had to pick one of these women to sleep with or you would die..."

"I would die?" Meghan chuckled.

"Yes, you would die a horrible death if you didn't pick one right now. Who would it be? Dark, curly hair, perhaps? The cute smile, big eyes, outgoing type?"

Meghan laughed when Kim pointed to the bar with a mischievous grin. "Fuck off, Kimbo. I know what you're trying to do, and I'm not falling for it."

"Bugger. I give up. Well, if you're not going to misbehave in lesbian paradise, I'll just have to set you up with one of Andres' friends. One of his colleagues is super handsome. Tall, dark, rugged... I met him last year, and he had a girl-friend back then, but now he's single. I'll ask Andres to invite him on Tuesday."

"Please don't set me up. It's awkward." Meghan pleaded.

"It won't be. We'll just tell him we're meeting up for casual drinks, nothing official. If you like him, take it from there." Kim persevered when Meghan kept silent. "Come on. You need this more than you know. When was the last time you had sex?"

"That's irrelevant, I'm not desperate for sex," Meghan said. She really wasn't. It had never been that great, and she was sure she was one of those people who could easily live without. What she liked was someone to fall asleep and wake up with; someone warm to hold her at night. "I'm just not interested when there's pressure." She sighed. "Look, I'm open to meeting someone, but I'm not in a rush. You just want me to date your boyfriend's friend so we can move here and live happily ever after together. Isn't that it?"

"You know me so well." Kim laughed. "Of course I hope you'll like him, but no pressure. It's just an innocent drink, nothing official."

Knowing Kim would never give up unless she agreed, Meghan groaned in frustration. There was only one way to shut her friend up. "Okay, okay. But to be clear, I'm coming to meet your boyfriend. I'm not going on a date."

"I swear, it won't be a date." Kim crossed her fingers and shot her an innocent look. "Tuesday. You, me, Andres and Tiger."

"*Tiger*? What the actual fuck?" Meghan's eyes widened. "Is that his real name?"

"Yes, but you can't judge him on that. It's not his fault."

"I don't care if it's his fault or not. I'll take any of these women over someone called Tiger," Meghan joked. She randomly pointed to the first woman who walked by. "Her," she said. "I'd rather date her."

# 12

## FLORENCE

"Hello, bartender." A woman leaned over the bar and made eyes at Florence. "You're cute."

"Thank you," Florence said, amused by her directness. She was tall, blonde, and tanned, dressed in a bright-yellow bikini and denim shorts, and she made sure Florence saw the rainbow bracelet she was wearing. "You're very cute yourself."

"Thank you back..." The woman reached over the bar and pulled Florence closer by her nametag. "Florence. Nice name. I'm Amber."

"Nice to meet you, Amber. What can I get you?"

"I think I'll have a beer." Amber shot her a flirty look. "And I wouldn't mind a kiss too."

Florence laughed. She wasn't one to shy away from kissing a beautiful woman, but this was a whole new level of overconfidence. Amber was pretty and she knew it, and Florence suspected she usually got what she wanted. "I'm flattered, but I'm working. I'm not supposed to fraternise with guests."

"Shame." Amber jutted out her bottom lip. "What about after work?"

"Still the same. You're a guest." Florence hadn't played by the rules when she'd asked Meghan out for a drink, but Meghan was an exception, she'd told herself. Besides, it wasn't a date, so she wouldn't be crossing any serious boundaries.

"But I'm not staying here all week, I'm only here for the Pride event," Amber said. "I'll be at the Seabreeze further down the strip as of Monday." She batted her lashes and flashed her pearly white teeth. "So lucky for you, you can kiss me then."

"Lucky for me, huh?" Florence handed her the beer and chuckled. Amber seemed fun and she was certainly attractive, so why would she even have to think about it? "I'm actually busy on Monday, but we can go for a drink on Tuesday if you're free?"

"Tuesday... That's a long wait, woman." Amber borrowed a pen from the bar and scribbled her number on a napkin. "But I'm a patient girl."

"You don't strike me as the patient type," Florence joked, tucking the napkin into the back pocket of her shorts.

"You're wrong. All good things are worth waiting for." Amber flicked a lock of hair over her shoulder and winked. "Message me. I can't wait for that kiss."

"Holy shit, Flo." Manuel, who had been listening in on the conversation, nudged her. "Did you cover yourself in lesbian nectar this morning? She was all over you, and from what I've seen so far, she's not the only one wanting a 'kiss'." He made quote marks in the air.

"I can't help it that women like me," Florence shot back at him with a grin. She was never cocky, apart from with Manuel, who considered himself the hunk of Paradise. "It must be tough for you, not getting any female attention for once."

"Trust me, it's painfully frustrating. They don't even look at me. It's like I don't exist," he said with a huff. "And you?" He looked her over. "I don't get it. You're not all that."

"Thanks, Manuel," Florence said in a sarcastic tone. "Always the gentleman." She gestured to their customers and grinned. "Well, we're already out of beer again, so they're all yours. I'll go and get a new keg."

"I can do it," Manuel said, staring at Meghan, whose sun lounger was on the route to the outdoor drinks' storage.

"It's fine. I promised to bring the DJ a drink anyway." Florence patted his shoulder and slipped out from behind the bar with a large margarita. The party was in full swing now, with women dancing in and along the pool and in front of the DJ booth. She could feel eyes on her as she handed the drink to the DJ and wondered what it would be like to be here as a guest. If she were, she'd probably be in someone's hotel room by now.

"Thanks, babe," the DJ said, then turned on her microphone. "Everyone, give it up for Florence, our lovely bartender!"

The overenthusiastic cheering made Florence grin sheepishly as she crossed the poolside. Meghan's oiled-up skin was shimmering in the sun. She and Kim were talking to two other women on the beds next to them, and she seemed entirely at ease. Meghan spotted Florence on her way over.

"Hey!"

"Hey. Are you having a good time?"

"We are." Meghan smiled. "And you, Miss Popular?"

Florence laughed. "Don't be fooled. I'm only popular because I hand out free drinks."

"I doubt that's the reason." Meghan, who was on her fourth cocktail, sounded flirtatious, and Florence caught Kim shooting a curious glance at her. "I mean, you're very nice," she quickly corrected herself. "That's why everyone likes you."

"We were just discussing with these lovely ladies here what our type would be if we were gay," Kim chipped in. "And although she denies it, I have a feeling you might be Meg's type."

"Kim!" Meghan nudged her friend and let out a nervous chuckle. "You're embarrassing me." She turned to Florence and waved a hand. "Don't listen to her, she's had too much to drink already."

"I'll say it, you're definitely my type, Florence," one of the other women yelled over the music, saving Meghan and Florence from the awkward exchange. Florence wasn't easily taken aback, but hearing those words from Kim did something to her, whether they were true or not.

"Thanks. I'm feeling good about myself today," she joked and gave them a quick wave before she walked off. "Enjoy the party, ladies."

## 13

# MEGHAN

"Are you sure you're going to be okay, babe?" Kim was dressed ready to go out, and a trail of strong perfume wafted around her as she got up and hung her handbag over her shoulder.

"Yes, stop asking me that and go!" Meghan waved her off. "Have fun with your man and don't worry about me."

"We'll take care of her," Sammy, one of the women next to her said. She was from the UK and holidaying with her partner Laura. They were fun and chatty, and Meghan and Kim had been talking to them for hours.

"And we'll let you know what her type is tomorrow," Laura yelled when Kim blew them a kiss. "Sorry, no offence. I couldn't resist," she said with a grin, clinking her glass against Meghan's.

"No offence taken." Meghan sat up and took a sip. Feeling light-headed, she searched for her water bottle in her purse. Downing the bottle in one go, she looked from Laura to Sammy and back. They were sweet and constantly fussing over each other. "So how did you two meet?"

"We met at a festival similar to this one, in Greece," Laura said. "Sammy bravely saved my life. I stupidly went into the sea against all warnings as the current was strong that day, and I got pulled under." She put an arm around her girlfriend and kissed her cheek. "And then Sammy dove in and rescued me."

"How romantic. That's quite a story to tell if you ever get married."

"Yeah, right?" Laura beamed. "As soon as I caught my breath and came to my senses, I looked at her and I just knew she was the one."

"So did I," Sammy said. "Call it luck, call it fate, I couldn't keep my eyes off her."

"Even though I looked like a stranded whale once she'd pulled me onto the shore." Laura laughed. "My bikini was all over the place, there was sand everywhere, my skin was raw from being dragged over the sea floor, and I think I was drooling."

"You looked beautiful," Sammy said. "But her thighs and one ankle were quite badly hurt, so I took her to A and E. When we came out of hospital, we passed this super-cute restaurant. I asked if she wanted to have dinner with me and the rest is history." She cupped Laura's face and looked at her so lovingly it brought a lump to Meghan's throat. "I love you so much."

"I love you too." Laura shot her a cute smile before she turned back to Meghan. "Anyway, that's our story."

"It' so, so sweet." Meghan noticed they were running low on drinks, and although she'd had enough herself, she was happy to stand in line at the bar and maybe talk to Florence for a few minutes. "Can I get you a drink?" she asked, getting up. "Same?"

"Yes, please! Are you going to order from that bartender you spent the night with?"

Meghan rolled her eyes and chuckled. "How many time do I have to tell you?"

"Sure. You're not gay and you don't fancy her." Sammy arched a brow at her. "Come on, Meghan. I may not know you very well, but I've seen you checking her out, and she's been doing the same. There's nothing wrong with being gay for a day."

Meghan shrugged, hoping they couldn't see how flustered she felt. "I know there's nothing wrong with it," she said. "But I'm not gay, not even for a day. Not yesterday, not today, and not tomorrow." Heading over to the bar, she noticed the queues had died down, and she could see Florence behind the handful of women who were clearly not there to get a drink. *Just like me.*

"Hey, there." Florence waved at her before she'd even reached the bar, and to Meghan's delight, she ignored everyone else. "Would you like another margarita?"

"No thanks. Just two Unicorns for those women next to me." She pointed to Laura and Sammy. "And a water for me, please."

"Okay. A water for you..." Florence made a show of making her the most beautiful pint cup of water with lots of ice, lime and so many sparkly cocktail sticks and decorated straws that it made Meghan snicker. "And the Unicorns," she added, handing Meghan two cocktails she'd made earlier. The DJ announced the dance competition over the speakers, and she arched a brow at Meghan. "Are you sure you don't want to join?"

"No chance. I'm a terrible dancer," Meghan said, even though she secretly loved dancing and the alcohol had put her in the right mood for it. "Are you dancing?"

"I will if you do." Florence started shimmying her shoulders when 'Lambada' blasted through the speakers. "I'm not a bad dancer." To Meghan's surprise, she came out from behind the bar and yelled at her colleague. "Hey, Manuel. Watch that for me for five minutes, okay?"

Meghan blushed profusely when Florence ran up to her and pulled her along the poolside. "Leave the drinks, we're going to dance." Heading for the podium in front of the DJ booth, she shouted, "We're first!"

"Okay, we've got two contestants here already. That's a great start. What's your name?" the DJ asked Meghan, whose heart was racing now. So many women were staring at her, and suddenly she couldn't feel her feet anymore.

"Meghan," she said, shuffling on the spot. She was tipsy, and she hardly dared look in the direction of Laura and Sammy. She was pretty sure they already had their phones out, ready to snap pictures for Kim to see tomorrow.

"Okay. Our cute bartender Florence and the beautiful Meghan will have the first dance. Please give it up for Meghan and Florence!"

"I'm sorry," Florence whispered as cheering broke out again. "I was always going to start the first dance. Someone had to, and I tend to volunteer for events. And then you were standing there, and I couldn't resist."

"You're evil," Meghan said with a chuckle. "I told you I can't dance."

"But, you lied," Florence said matter-of-factly. "I've seen you today, and you danced several times when you thought no one was watching."

*So you've been watching me.* Meghan couldn't help but smirk as Florence took her hand. Her hips started leading a life of their own when the DJ turned the volume up, blasting salsa beats over the premises. She was barefoot, which limited the risk of tripping, and with a sarong wrapped around her waist, she didn't feel too self-conscious, so she figured she could handle it.

"See? I was right." Florence pulled Meghan closer and wrapped an arm around her waist. "You can dance."

"Only because you're leading." Meghan met Florence's intense stare and gave her a small smile. "And you're still evil for dragging me into this." Florence's grip was firm; she was much stronger than she looked. Her thumb on Meghan's back moved slow enough for people not to notice, but Meghan could feel the caress against her skin, and it made her shiver.

"Don't fool yourself. You look like you're enjoying this." Florence spun her around and laced her fingers with Meghan's. Their feet moved fast, and their hips shook and rolled in a push and pull. "Have you had lessons?"

"No," Meghan lied again with a smug smile. "I'm a natural." In truth, she'd had many lessons in the past, but it had been years since she'd danced with someone, and she'd certainly never danced with a woman. Apparently, they were doing something right because the audience was cheering them on so loud, she could barely hear the music. Just before the music stopped, Florence dipped Meghan back and pulled her up again. She was breathing fast as she cupped her neck and pressed their foreheads together.

Meghan stood there for longer than necessary, partly to catch her breath, and partly because Florence's nearness startled her. Their lips were only inches apart, and it would be so easy to kiss her. She hadn't expected this reaction, especially not the flashes of arousal she felt each time her chest heaved against Florence's.

"Thank you for the dance." Florence stepped back and smiled as if nothing had happened, but her mischievous smirk did not go unnoticed.

"No. Thank *you*." Meghan's legs were trembling as she stepped off the podium. "That was fun."

## 14

## FLORENCE

*W*hen the music stopped and the night came to an end, Meghan was still sitting there, talking to a few women she'd met. Florence watched her as the women got up and lingered at her table, finishing their conversation before they left.

It had been a fun day with great music and a happy vibe all around, but Florence was tired, and her muscles ached as she headed for the littered tables.

"Go," Stella, her manager said, tapping her on the shoulder. She took the bag from Florence and started piling up the cups. "You had a late one yesterday. I'll clear the tables and ask Manuel to close up."

"Thank you." Florence hesitated as she shuffled on the spot. "Do you have a moment? There's something I need to tell you."

"Of course." Stella frowned. "What is it?"

"I stayed in a guest's room last night. That woman over there." Florence pointed to Meghan. "Nothing happened," she quickly added. "But she was scared because her friend was away, and she was the only one in the hotel apart from Robert."

"Okay. That's very kind of you, but you know that's not part of your job," Stella said. "You have no responsibility for the guests after your shift ends."

"I know, but I wanted to. She's really nice and...well, I wanted her to be comfortable." Florence paused for a moment as she glanced at Meghan. She was looking up at the hotel as if dreading going in. "I think she has a trauma of some sort, and her friend is away again. I want to walk her up to her room and check it, so she feels safe. I just thought I should tell you first, so you don't think I'm..."

"That you're fraternising with guests." Stella nodded. "Thank you for telling me, and of course that's fine. I can ask security, though."

"No need. I'll gladly do it." Florence shot Stella a grateful smile. It wasn't like Stella was a saint herself; she'd gotten personal with one of the guests over summer, and now she and the woman in question were dating, which was why she often turned a blind eye to holiday romances as long as nothing happened on the hotel grounds. "Thanks, Stella. I'll see you tomorrow." Butterflies fluttered as she headed over to Meghan's table, and she wondered if her hair looked okay. She hadn't looked in a mirror all day, only using her short breaks for a coffee and a quick bite to eat.

"Hi, there." Meghan smiled, but Florence saw a hint of distress in her expression.

"Hey. Did you have a good day?"

"It was lovely. I made so many new friends." Meghan hesitated as she fiddled with the strap of her straw beach bag. "And I really enjoyed our dance."

"Me too. You're a great dancer. We should do it again some time."

Meghan met her eyes, and Florence was sure she detected a little flirtation in her gaze. "I'd like that." Apart from a couple of women who were talking to the DJ, the poolside was quiet. She got up and grabbed her bag. "I'm sorry. I suppose I should leave so you can clear."

"I'm off duty now, but yes, I'm afraid you'll have to leave the poolside," Florence said. "I'll walk you to your room if you want."

"You don't have to do that. It's—"

"It's nothing. Please let me," Florence interrupted her. She put a hand on Meghan's lower back as she led them into the hotel. "I sense that you're still uncomfortable. Are you?"

"A little." Meghan gave her a grateful smile and let out a long sigh. "Thank you. You must think I'm crazy. There are hundreds of women here, and there's nothing to be afraid of."

"That's not the point. Your fear is real to you, so no, I don't think you're crazy." Florence noticed women staring at them as they went into the lift together.

"I bet they're jealous," Meghan said with a nervous chuckle as if reading her mind. "They've been pining after you all day."

Florence laughed and shook her head. "It's more likely to be the other way around. You certainly made yourself popular today." She let Meghan exit the lift first and waited for her to open the door to her room.

"They were just being nice," Meghan said with a shy smile, taking a few careful steps into her room while Florence got on her knees to check under the bed, then went outside to the balcony and into the bathroom. "Like you." She looked at her pensively. "Why *are* you being so nice to me? I know I already asked you, but it's late and I'm sure you're tired."

Florence shrugged. "I like you." Her eyes met Meghan's, and she hoped Meghan could see she meant it. There was a long silence in which neither of them moved or looked away until Meghan finally spoke.

"I like you too," she said in a whisper. "And thank you, for checking the room. It makes all the difference."

"You're welcome." Florence felt like she was drowning in Meghan's big, dark eyes that still carried a hint of unease. "Is Kim coming back tonight?"

"No. She's staying with Andres."

"Will you be okay?"

"I think so. It's about time I get over this..." Meghan's voice trailed away, and she swallowed hard. "This stupid, irrational anxiety." She gestured to the thin wall that let through the noise from the room next door. "There are people here, for God's sake. So many people. Nice women. It's not like they're going to..."

"Going to what?"

"Nothing," Meghan whispered, shaking her head.

Florence put a hand on Meghan's shoulder and winced when she felt her trembling. "Would you like me to stay with you?" When Meghan didn't answer, she pressed on. "You don't have to feel bad about it. I'm very happy to sleep here again so I don't have to commute back and forth, and my manager already knows I spent the night here, so it won't get me in trouble."

"Are you sure?"

"Yes." Florence pointed to the bed. "Can I have my usual side?"

"Of course." Meghan looked visibly relieved. "I have a nice bottle of wine in the fridge that Kim brought from Andres' restaurant. Would you like a nightcap?"

## 15

### MEGHAN

*I*t was cooler than last night, and it was pleasant as they sat on the balcony with a blanket. Meghan was torn between contradicting emotions; shame that she couldn't spend a single night on her own without being afraid, a sense of excitement that Florence was here again, and on top of that, she felt confusion regarding that same excitement. Her anxiety hadn't been an act; she truly was scared of being here by herself, but she'd never expected Florence to offer her company for the second night in a row.

"What Kim said today, about you being my type..." She paused, pondering over how best to explain she wasn't taking advantage of Florence. "It was just a joke. I don't want you to think I've been playing the damsel in distress because..."

"I know. You already told me. You're not into women, and even if you were, that's not why I'm here." Florence put a hand on hers and turned towards her. "Look, you don't have to tell me, of course, but if you'd like to talk about it, I'm here."

Meghan felt her heart race at the question. In any other situation, she'd avoid answering, but Florence made her feel safe and she wanted her to understand why she was behaving in a way that may seem pathetic to some. "I was robbed in a hotel room," she said in a thin voice. "Two years ago, in Paris."

"Oh no..." Florence covered her mouth with her hand as she stared at her. "I'm so sorry that happened to you."

"Yeah, me too." Meghan sighed. "I was travelling on my own, for work. There was a managers' meeting organised by our mother company in a venue somewhere on the outskirts on a Thursday, but I also booked a room in a more central hotel for myself on the Friday and Saturday because I wanted to see the city. The hotel wasn't the best I've stayed in, but it wasn't bad either. I had a lovely time exploring Paris, but when I came back to my hotel room on Saturday night..." She paused and took a couple of deep breaths. "It all went so fast at first. I barely had time to process what was happening. There was a knock on the door, and I assumed it was hotel staff, so I opened it. There were two men, both wearing balaclavas, caps and shades, and one of them held a gun to my head and told me in broken English to be quiet while the other one tied me to a chair and gagged me. Then they searched the room and took anything valuable they could find. My phone, my iPad, my watch, my jewellery and my handbag with my wallet and passport."

"My God, did they..." Florence bit her lip, stopping herself.

"No, they didn't sexually assault me, but I speak a little French, and one of them said to the other that he liked the look of me and that it would be a shame not to take advantage of the situation since they were there anyway. The other man stopped him and told him they didn't have time, but when he turned at the door, he hissed that he'd come back for me later." Meghan held on to her stomach, sick at the memory. "I tried to escape but couldn't free myself, so I sat there for hours, expecting him to come back and to..." Warm tears trickled down her cheeks, but she allowed them to flow as she always felt a bit better after. "I thought he was going to rape me."

Florence pulled her into a tight hug and held her for many minutes. "Who found you?" she asked in a whisper.

"Those men had robbed four other rooms on my floor that night. One of the victims managed to free himself after two hours, and he alerted the reception, who then called the police. The hotel security checked all rooms. They were there before the police arrived." Meghan inched back and gave Florence a small smile. "I've never been so terrified. I had no passport, no phone and no bankcards, so the embassy and the police worked with my travel insurance to me get back home the next day. The hotel offered me their suite as an apology, but I was so scared that I went to the airport instead and spent all night at the bar."

"Did they arrest them?"

"Yes, but not until four months later when they were caught doing the same thing at another hotel. And then, because of the pandemic, I didn't travel after that. I thought I'd be fine by the time we came here. I don't have nightmares anymore, and I'm comfortable at home alone. But clearly, I'm not fine."

"That's understandable." Florence took her hand and squeezed it. "Does Kim know about this?"

"No, I never told her. Only my parents and my therapist know." Meghan swallowed hard. "Perhaps I should have told her, but I don't like talking about it, and as I said, I didn't think I'd be so afraid. I only told you because...well, because you've helped me so much and I want you to understand my fear." She frowned as she was thinking out loud. "Maybe I should check myself into a hostel for the remainder of my stay. Ten people in a dorm should solve the problem. Or I could sleep on the sunbed all day and stay up at night. There must be nightclubs that stay open until dawn."

"Sure there are, but that's ridiculous. You've paid for a decent room, and you won't enjoy your holiday either way," Florence said. "I'll stay with you, or you can stay with me."

"No, absolutely not. It's so sweet, but I could never ask that of you. You have better things to do than make me feel safe, and I'm not your responsibility."

"You didn't ask." Florence looked at her. "And I wouldn't offer if I didn't genuinely want to do it."

## 16

## FLORENCE

*F*lorence woke early to the raised voices of the women in the room next door. They were laughing inside before they ventured out onto the balcony, and she could hear every word, as Meghan's balcony door was open. She turned to Meghan, expecting her to wake up, but she remained fast asleep. A lock of dark hair draped over her face moved ever so slightly each time she breathed out. She looked so peaceful, cocooned in the covers, and Florence wondered what it would feel like to lie there with her, against the heat of her skin.

She hadn't been prepared for what Meghan had told her. Such things didn't happen to people she knew. Apart from the occasional run-by handbag grab in town, she only saw robberies on the news. Florence was glad she knew now, and she didn't regret her staying over. As long as Manuel didn't mind bringing in clothes for her again, it was no trouble, and she loved that she could stay in bed forty minutes longer. Just watching Meghan sleep made her calm and happy, and she wanted her to have a good time and not worry about anything. It made sense now that she'd panicked that first night, when the hotel was entirely deserted. And it also made sense that she was scared last night at the prospect of sleeping here alone.

"Good morning." Meghan stirred and smiled as she woke up. "Did the neighbours wake you?"

"Yes. They're very lively considering it's only seven o'clock," Florence said with a chuckle.

"I don't mind. It's nice to wake up to the sound of laughter." Meghan yawned and sat up. She was wearing that transparent T-shirt again, and her full breasts looked delightful as she stretched. "Do you want coffee? I got some instant at the hotel shop yesterday. It's not the best, but it's nice not having to leave the room before the first one, right?"

"I'd love a coffee but let me make it." Florence got out of bed and turned on the small kettle on the mini fridge. "Did you sleep well?" she asked, turning to Meghan as she scooped instant coffee into two cups.

"Yes. I'm actually feeling quite awake." Meghan got up and joined her. She pulled a pot of coffee creamer out of a grocery bag and handed it to Florence. "Shall we take it outside?"

"Sure."

Florence picked up their coffees while Meghan pulled the blanket from her bed end and put it on the balcony to sit on. She didn't seem self-conscious about her lack of clothes anymore. They'd seen each other enough now to not be precious, and Florence didn't care about wearing the thin T-shirt either.

"This view is much nicer than the view from my balcony," she said, wincing against the sun as she sat down and sipped her coffee.

"I'm glad staying here has at least one perk." Meghan raised a brow at her.

"Not just one. I have more time in the morning when I'm here, and then there's you, of course." Florence felt her cheeks turn red the moment she'd said it.

"Me?" Meghan smiled shyly.

"Yes. I like this, with you. Waking up, drinking coffee, talking…"

"Hmm." Meghan's lips pulled into a goofy grin. "Me too. It's…"

"Good morning. Am I hearing voices?" A woman leaned over the balcony railing and stuck her head around the dividing wall.

"Good morning. Sounds like you're having fun!" Meghan turned and smiled at her. "What's going on?"

"My friend is just being silly," the woman said. "She's trying to make me wear a dress for the first time in my life, and it's not happening." Her eyes widened in shock as she looked from Meghan to Florence and back. "Oh my! So *you* managed to bag yourself the bartender!" She laughed and turned. "Tamara, come see who's here. It's Florence, the bartender."

Her friend, whose head appeared above hers, gasped. "I knew it when I saw you two dancing yesterday. It was the way you looked at each other that gave you away." Tamara gave them a thumbs up. "Good for you, girls!"

"No, it's nothing like that. We're just friends," Meghan was quick to say.

Florence shifted away a little when she realised they were sitting really close, both scarcely dressed. "Yes, we're just friends," she repeated, wondering how her attraction to Meghan could be that obvious.

"Of course. Staff rules and all that. I understand. Don't worry. Our lips are sealed." Tamara winked and shot them a grin. "Well, ladies, enjoy your coffee. We're going to get one downstairs."

They disappeared before Florence had the chance to defend the situation, but it was clear they wouldn't have believed her if she tried. "Sorry about that," she said after their neighbours had closed the balcony door behind them. "I didn't think anyone would draw conclusions."

"It's fine. They can think whatever they want." Meghan shrugged. "It's not like I'm ashamed or anything."

"You're not?"

"Of course not, silly. From what I've gathered, you're quite the catch." The look in Meghan's eyes was flirty as she spoke. "No, scratch that," she corrected herself. "You *are* a catch."

"Oh?"

"Yes," Meghan continued. "If anything, I'm feeling quite smug." She let out a chuckle, and Florence couldn't help but laugh too. "I'm going to walk that poolside today with my head held high, and I'm going to smile and let everyone think that I *did* bag myself the bartender."

# 17

## MEGHAN

*N*ow that Meghan had made some new friends, she was really enjoying herself by the poolside with a dozen or so other early birds, and she felt giddy after her flirtations with Florence. There was definitely chemistry between them—even her neighbours had spotted it—but she wasn't sure what to do with that. Kim was on her way, and she hoped no one would tell her Florence had slept over again. It would only lead to questions she didn't feel like answering. Not today, in this sunny spot that would soon be crammed with smiling, dancing women.

Against all odds, she was kind of sad it was the last day of the Pride event, or 'Paradise Pride' as people called it, because the overall atmosphere was great. She took care in applying sunscreen and left her back until Kim arrived. Knowing Florence was stealing glances at her, she used deliberate, slow strokes, with one leg stretched out in front of her and one leg pulled up before, alternating. She was wearing her nicest turquoise bikini and a light turquoise sarong, and she'd painted her toenails and put on a silver ankle bracelet. It was more effort than she normally made for a day by the pool, especially in the morning, but although she wasn't sure what she wanted from Florence, she was sure of one thing: she liked the attention, and she loved that Florence made her feel attractive and safe. She recognised the sensation of giddiness and the butterflies that wouldn't leave her alone. It had only happened to her one time, and it was a long time ago. *After that girl kissed me.*

"Want me to do your back?" a woman asked her. Holding out her hand, she waited for Meghan to hand over the bottle.

"Oh, I..." Meghan looked up and hesitated. No woman had ever offered to do that.

"I'm not hitting on you. I thought you could do with some help," the woman continued with an amused grin. "I know you have a crush on the bartender. It's not a secret, and I have no intention of coming between whatever is going on with you and her."

"Florence and I are just friends," Meghan said for the second time that morning. She smiled and held up the bottle. "And yes, please. I'd love some help."

"Of course. You're just friends." The woman's tone was mocking as she squirted some lotion into her hand and beckoned Meghan to turn around. "I'm Simi, by the way."

"Meghan." Meghan pulled her hair over one shoulder and leaned forward. "Are you having a good weekend?"

"So good. You never know with these first-time events, but it has definitely been worth the trip." Simi started on her shoulders and worked her way down. "What about you? Someone told me you didn't know the Pride weekend was on—that you're here because of an error in the hotel's system."

"There seems to be an awful lot of talking going on," Meghan said, trying not to sound accusatory.

"We're a tight community. It happens."

"Right." Meghan pondered over that and decided she didn't care what people said about her. She wouldn't get into trouble, but Florence might. "Well, it's true. My friend Kim and I just booked a basic holiday. We had no idea the event was on."

"So...you're straight?"

"Yes." Meghan shrugged. "But I'm having a great time, so who cares?"

"Exactly. Who cares?" Simi laughed as she dropped the bottle of sunscreen on the sunbed and wiped her hands on her tank top. "Well, I'll be at the bar with my friends later, so please join us if you're on your own. Or with your friend," she added when Kim trotted towards them.

"Thank you, I'll come and meet you later," Meghan said, marvelling at how kind everyone was. She'd never felt quite so welcome anywhere.

"Sorry I'm late. It took ages for the shower to turn warm." Kim pointed up to their room.

"That's okay. I haven't been bored for a minute." Meghan smiled at her. "Did you have a good night?"

"Oh, yes. It was amazing. Andres took me to a restaurant by the harbour, and we went for a long walk on the beach. And then we went back to his place for a bath and lots and lots of passionate sex." Kim sighed dreamily. "What about you?"

"I had a great night too," Meghan said. "No passionate sex, though," she joked.

"Are you sure about that?" Kim opened her handbag and took out a napkin. "I found an English phone number on your floor. Who's the lucky guy?"

"I have no idea." Meghan took it and studied it. "It's not mine, that's for sure." It was written on a hotel-branded napkin. Her stomach dropped as she glanced at the bar, where Florence was serving drinks. *It must be hers.*

Kim followed her gaze. "Did she stay over again?"

"She did stay over, so she might have left it behind," Meghan admitted. "We were having drinks and then it got late, so I offered her your bed again."

"Oh." Kim frowned. "I don't mind that she sleeps in my bed or anything, but don't you think it's a bit strange?"

"No. Why would it be strange?"

"Well, you barely know each other and she's into women. She's probably trying it on with you, Megs." Kim held up both hands and chuckled. "I'm sorry to say this, but you can be a bit oblivious sometimes."

"You're wrong. We're friends. I like her."

"You like her, all right. You're blushing when you talk about her," Kim shot back. "Look, most women experiment at some point—at least, that's what I've been told. There's nothing wrong with being curious, but I don't want you to get hurt. Especially if she's taking other ladies' phone numbers."

Meghan felt uneasy at Kim's comment because there was more truth to it than she dared to admit. "I appreciate your concern and you're a good friend, but nothing happened, and nothing *will* happen. It's as simple as that," she said, getting up. "I'm going to get us drinks now, and when I come back, we're going to talk about something else. Okay?"

"Sure." Kim lowered her shades onto her nose and sank back on her sunbed. "Get me a margarita, will you? I'm loving the day drinking."

## 18

## FLORENCE

"Meghan." Florence nudged Manuel out of the way so she could serve Meghan. "What are you having?"

"Two margaritas, please." Meghan leaned on the bar as she fiddled with something in her hands. "You left this in my room," she said after a moment's hesitation. "I figured you might need it."

"What is it?" Florence sighed when she saw it was Amber's number. She'd forgotten all about it. "Oh, yes, that's mine. It must have fallen out of my pocket. I'm sorry, I...I mean, I'm not sorry, but—"

"What could you possibly be sorry for?" Meghan finally looked up at her, and although she was smiling, Florence sensed it wasn't entirely sincere. Why did she feel like she had to apologise for it? It wasn't like they were in a relationship of any kind. It was just harmless flirting. And why did Meghan seem equally uncomfortable discussing it? Was she jealous?

"Nothing." She took the number and tucked it in her pocket. "Anyway, what did you say you wanted?" Forcing a smile, she hoped Meghan wouldn't think she was into someone else, even though it would make no difference when Meghan was straight.

"Two margaritas."

"Of course." Florence didn't dare look her in the eyes as she mixed the cocktails. Why did this suddenly feel so complicated? There was literally nothing complicated about their new friendship, but now it felt too multidimensional to dissect. "Here you go," she said, putting the drinks in front of Meghan. "See you later?"

"Sure," Meghan said politely. "I'll be around."

"Was that just me or was that an awkward moment?" Manuel asked after Meghan left. "I thought you said nothing happened between the two of you."

"That's true, but..."

"But what?" Manuel frowned. "Do you like her?"

"Yes," Florence admitted. She'd rarely enjoyed a woman's company as much as Meghan's, and she was already excited for tonight. "I do like her, but she's straight and a guest. Besides, she's only here for two weeks."

"Yeah, about the straight thing..." Manuel tilted his head as his gaze followed Meghan, who was walking back to Kim with their drinks. "I've been all levels of confused with such a mix of different women here, but I could have sworn she was into you."

"You think so?"

"Yeah. It's the way she looks at you." Manuel shrugged. "So maybe she's not so straight, and as far as your job is concerned, Stella knows about your sleepovers, right?"

"Not exactly. She knows about one sleepover," Florence said.

"Stella knows what?"

Florence jumped at the voice behind her and turned

around. "Oh, hi, Stella. Manuel was just asking if I'd told you about staying over in Meghan's room." She had no intention of mentioning the second night unless she really had to. Or the other nights she planned on keeping Meghan company.

"Yes, she told me, and it's fine," Stella said while she opened the fridge to check the stock levels. How are you guys? I'm not super busy, so I can take over if you need a break."

"I'm good. Everyone prefers to order from Florence, so I haven't exactly been working hard." Manuel tutted. "They're practically throwing themselves at her. I've never felt so invisible in my life."

Stella laughed and tapped the fridge. "Why don't you go and restock, then? We're low on Bacardi, vodka and lemonade." She paused as she scanned the bar. "Oh, and we need more straws and umbrellas. They're in the back of the stockroom, top shelf."

"Will do, boss." Manuel piled the empty bottles into a crate and slipped from behind the bar.

"And you?" Stella turned to Florence. Do you need a break?"

"No, I'm fine," Florence said, needing distraction from her recent exchange with Meghan. "Maybe later."

"Okay, just give me a shout." Stella shot Florence an amused look. "I've never heard Manuel complain about lack of attention."

"I actually wouldn't mind if the attention was on him." Florence lowered her voice as a group of women approached. "It's hard work, and we don't even get tips as it's all-inclusive."

"Yes, if this was a paid resort, my guess is you'd be able to retire tomorrow," Stella joked. "Well, let me know when you need a breather. I'll be over there with Lisa for a little while."

Florence watched Stella join her girlfriend and some friends at the other bar. It was weird to see her boss all giddy around a woman, but Stella and Lisa made a cute pair. The tall, blonde woman had arrived from the UK months ago, and after meeting Stella, it looked like she was here to stay. Well, not at Paradise Hotel, as Lisa was living with Stella now, and Florence admired how they were doing everything in their power to make it work.

"Florence!" two women shouted in unison. "Our favourite bartender!"

"Hello, ladies!" Florence dug through her memory as she greeted them with great enthusiasm. They'd introduced themselves several times, but she couldn't for the life of her remember their names. She'd never been good with names; not like Manuel, who memorised the name of every attractive woman on the premises. But Florence always remembered what people drank, and that was good enough, she supposed. "What are we having? Unicorns, right?"

# 19

## MEGHAN

*I can do this*, Meghan decided. She would go to her room early and get used to being there alone before it got dark. Surely, that would help. Kim had just left to meet with Andres, so she wouldn't question why she was up there. Meghan didn't want to rely on Florence, and it was time that she faced her fears so she wouldn't find herself in this situation again in future. The phone number had been a wake-up call. It had bugged her all day, and that wasn't healthy. If she spent another night with Florence, her irrational jealousy might ruin her holiday, and she didn't want that to happen. The constant speculation as to whose number it was bordered on obsessive. She'd been observing women at the bar, imagining them with Florence, and it made her feel sick.

As she walked to the main building, Florence came up behind her. "Wait!" she said, catching her breath as if she'd been running. "I was just looking for you. The event finishes at nine, so I'll probably be done by nine-thirty. Do you want to grab some dinner with me later?"

Meghan's heart pounded as their eyes met. This woman

had the ability to throw her off her game in seconds. "Don't you have a hot date or something?" she asked, hoping she didn't sound irritated.

"Are you referring to the phone number?" Florence looked slightly uneasy, and she averted her gaze.

"Yes. I assume you're planning on meeting up with whoever gave you their number?" *Oh, God. Now I really do sound jealous.* It wasn't any of her business who Florence went out with. Just because they were flirting a little didn't mean she had the right to claim her, and besides, why would Florence be interested in a straight woman like her? Maybe Kim was right; the flirtations were probably just a game, and it was obvious she flirted with everyone. Maybe getting a straight woman interested in her was a challenge.

"I am, but not until Tuesday." Florence pointed to a stunning blonde who was packing her things into a bag. "It's that woman over there in the yellow bikini. I'm not really that bothered. She kind of cornered me, but I figured, I'm single, so why not?"

"You don't owe me an explanation," Meghan said, but her stomach dropped at the thought of Florence and the blonde together.

"I know I don't. But it still feels—" Florence stopped herself and shook her head. "Never mind. So, tonight? Are you up for some company?"

Meghan hesitated, her resolve already crumbling. Florence's company would enable her to sleep, but it was a bad idea to spend so much time together when she was becoming increasingly infatuated. At the same time, her growing interest was the very reason she wanted to see Florence. Player or no player, deep down she knew something might happen, and what was the harm in that? She was curious, and if this was a way to scratch an itch, would it be so bad if Florence felt the same way? If Florence got to conquer a straight woman and Meghan got to experience a new kind of intimacy... "Sure," she heard herself say. "If you want to, I'd love to see you tonight."

"Okay. I can meet you in town at nine-thirty?"

"Why don't we stay here instead?" Meghan suggested. "I'll get a takeaway. I'm sure you'll be tired after working your ass off all weekend, and if our date tomorrow is still standing, then—" She stopped herself. "I meant drinks or dinner," she corrected herself. "It's not a date."

"Sure, tomorrow, you, me... Of course it's still on. And I would love to have a quiet night with you tonight. You're right. I am a little tired. My body is, anyway," she said, rolling her shoulders. "If you get the food, I'll bring a bottle."

"Okay. Do you have any preferences?"

Florence narrowed her eyes, and her lips pulled into a mischievous smile. "You could wear the T-shirt you sleep in. I like that one."

Meghan laughed. "I was talking about food, and you know it." *This is getting interesting.* Again, there was electric eye contact that confused her as much as it thrilled her. She certainly didn't mind seeing Florence in one of her thin T-shirts either.

"Oh, right. The food. I don't mind, you pick." Florence grinned widely. "I'm sorry, I'll behave myself."

"You don't have to behave." Meghan bit her lip and shook her head with a chuckle. The words had slipped out as a joke, but they both knew there was truth to them.

"Are you sure about that?" Florence paused. "Because if you let me, I *will* misbehave." She lowered her gaze to Meghan's lips. "And I can be very bad."

Meghan didn't reply, as she had no idea what to say to

that. Yes, she wanted Florence to kiss her. She wanted to do a lot of things with Florence, things she'd never considered before, but it was still too soon to admit that out loud. She was shaking on her feet as she clumsily picked up her towel, hugged it in front of her and buried her hands under her armpits. They were trembling, and she didn't want Florence to see how much her comment had affected her.

Florence didn't break the silence either, and Meghan suspected she was enjoying the standoff and seeing her sweat. She arched a brow and tilted her head as she studied Meghan with bemusement. "Well?" she finally asked.

"Let's see how the night goes," Meghan said so softly she could barely hear herself. She had to get to her room as she couldn't cope with Florence's daring stare any longer, and looking up at the hotel, she was relieved to see her neighbours playing music and dancing on their balcony. That would make her more comfortable in her room if she left the doors open while she got ready for whatever the night would bring. "I need a shower. I'll see you up there." She walked off without waiting for a reply and didn't dare look back.

## 20

## FLORENCE

"Hey, Florence. Are you almost done for the day?" The woman who had been making eyes at her for the past couple of hours swooped right in after Meghan had left. Tipsy from the cocktails, she'd already introduced herself twice.

"Hey, Clarissa. Yes, I'm almost done." Florence wiped her forehead. "We're closing soon."

Clarissa sighed and jutted out her bottom lip. "Well, I'm not ready to go to bed. I'm still buzzing and hoping for a different kind of action."

Florence pretended she hadn't registered the undertone in the woman's voice. "There are plenty of places still open in town, even on a Sunday night."

"Good. Want to come with me? My friends and I were thinking of going dancing somewhere."

"Thank you, but I have plans for tonight."

"With the woman who just left? Was that your girlfriend?"

"Who? Meghan?" Florence shook her head. "You're not

the first to ask me that. She's not my girlfriend, but I am seeing her later."

"Oh. I kind of thought so. But hey, no harm in trying, right?" Clarissa looked disappointed but she smiled anyway. "I hope it works out for you."

"Thank you," Florence said, surprising herself. "And have a great night. It looks like you've made friends." The group of women who were hanging around waiting for Clarissa waved at them from across the poolside, and she waved back.

"Yeah. It's been fun. I'll come again next year if it's on. Will this be a regular thing?"

"I'm not sure. It wasn't supposed to be here in the first place—it was kind of a last-minute change of venue—but the organisation was pleased with how it went, so fingers crossed."

"Well, if it's on, I guess I'll see you next year." Clarissa shot her a smile before she turned away. "It was nice to meet you, Florence."

"Everything okay?" Stella asked as she squeezed past Florence behind the bar.

Florence chuckled. "All good. I'm almost done here. Are you leaving?"

"No, I'll close up with you. I'm meeting Lisa and a friend in town later." Stella grabbed a cloth and started wiping the bar. "This has been so much fun. I feel a little sad that it's over."

"Yeah, me too." Florence watched two team members take down the rainbow decorations. The poolside suddenly looked bare without colour, and there was a large gap in between the sun loungers where the DJ booth had been. "Are we full house tomorrow?"

"Not quite, but we'll be on seventy percent occupancy.

What are your plans? You've got two days off, right?"

"Nothing special." Without thinking, Florence glanced up at Meghan's room.

"Are you sure?" Stella looked up too.

"I'm...ehm..." Knowing she was busted, Florence paused. "I'm actually seeing Meghan."

"Our guest?"

"Yes. I know I'm not supposed to, but we've become friends," Florence said hesitantly. "I just want to show her around town. It's nothing more, I swear." *Not yet, anyway.*

Stella turned to Florence and studied her. "Your face says otherwise. You really like her."

"I do," Florence admitted. She sighed. "Am I in trouble now?"

Stella looked up at the balcony again as if hoping to find an answer there. "No," she said after a pause. "Just don't tell anyone about it. And from now on, don't tell me either. I appreciate your honesty, but as long as I don't know what you're up to, I won't have to take disciplinary action." She shrugged. "I haven't exactly set the right example myself with Lisa, but I'd do it all over again a million times, so sometimes it's worth breaking the rules."

"Thank you. You're happy with her, aren't you?"

"So happy." Stella grinned widely. "Lisa's the best thing that ever happened to me. Love changes everything."

"I'm glad it worked out for you. I hope to have what you have one day."

"You'll know when you find the one," Stella said. "And who knows? Maybe it's Meghan. That's why I'm not getting involved." She started piling the used ashtrays onto a trolley. "You're a flirt, Florence. You and I both know it. But you seem different when you talk about her."

"She's straight, though. I think she's just curious, so it's unlikely it will go anywhere."

"Does she give you the impression she's into you?"

"Yes. I mean, I think so," Florence corrected herself. "I don't know her that well, so she might just be playing a game." She thought of Meghan, who was probably under the shower now, and it made her ache inside. At least she wouldn't have to tell Stella she was staying over again; she was delighted with their new no-sharing rule. What would Meghan do if she tried to kiss her? Would she welcome it? Would she feel uncomfortable? Would she kiss her back? *Let's see how the night goes.* Meghan's words kept lingering in her mind.

"Then leave it to her," Stella said. "If it's meant to be, it will be."

## 21

---

## MEGHAN

*M*eghan ran a brush through her hair and dabbed on some lip gloss. Turning in front of the tall, chipped mirror that was glued to the wall in her room, she checked herself out. Now that she had a tan, she looked good in the short, white, linen dress that she'd bought especially for the holiday. She topped off her look with a necklace made of white shells and painted her toenails pale pink, then decided to change her lingerie last-minute. Knowing she was doing this with Florence—a woman—in mind was mindboggling. Did Florence even care if she dressed up? Did she care about lingerie? Or was that just something men appreciated?

*As long as I feel good about how I look,* she thought to herself, swapping her black lace set for a white one. If she was happy with the way she looked, she'd be more confident. Not that she'd ever make a pass at Florence; she was way too terrified to do that. But if Florence did, she wouldn't turn her down. Every time she was near the woman, her body reacted so fiercely she didn't know what to do with herself. She wanted Florence, and she was ready to admit it.

A knock on her door made her jump, and her heart started racing. *She's early.* Rushing to let Florence in, she was surprised to see Kim there instead. Her eyes were red-rimmed, like she'd been crying.

"Hey, what's wrong? Did you and Andres have a fight?" She pulled Kim into a hug and squeezed her tightly before she stepped back to let her in.

Kim shrugged and sniffed. "It wasn't really a fight, but he's definitely hiding something from me. I just know it." She flopped onto her bed. The bed Florence was supposed to sleep in.

*Don't think like that. Kim is your friend, and she needs you.*

"What did he do to make you think that?" Meghan perched on the end of the bed and patted Kim's leg. "Did he say something?"

"No, but that's the point. He kept looking at his phone, and then he said he had to leave for a couple of hours. When I asked him where he was going, he mumbled something about his parents." Kim sighed. "He promised he'd introduce me to them, so why didn't he just invite me along? I'm sure he's seeing someone else."

"Don't suspect the worst. It's probably nothing. Did he say when he was coming back?"

"No. He told me he'd be gone for a couple of hours, but I didn't want to hang around waiting for him in his apartment while he was off with some other woman. Anyway, it became awkward between us because I kept asking questions and he kept dodging answering, so I left before he did."

"I think you're probably making more out of this than there is to it."

"You don't know that. You weren't there. I *know* he's

hiding something. He was so...shifty." Kim wiped her tears and looked Meghan over. "You look nice. Are you going somewhere?"

"No." Meghan winced at another knock, this one playful and rhythmic like the beat to a song.

"Liar. Who's that?" Kim got up to open the door. "Oh, hey, Florence." She ran a hand through her hair and wiped her cheeks again. "Did you come to take Meghan out on a date?"

Despite Kim's distress, Meghan could have killed her in that moment, and Florence looked equally mortified. "It's not a date," Meghan said before Florence had the chance to answer.

"Ehm, no, it's not. I just came to hang here, actually," Florence stammered, holding up the bottle of wine she'd brought. Her other hand was behind her back, like she was hiding something. "But I see you two are in the middle of something. I can come back another time."

"No, please come in." Kim opened the door wider.

"Seriously, it's fine." Florence handed Kim the bottle of wine and stepped back. "Have this. You look like you could do with a drink."

"Wait!" Meghan said and slipped into the hallway after Florence. "Kim, give me a moment, I'll be right back." She closed the door behind her. It was silly to be so secretive, but she didn't feel comfortable talking to Florence in front of Kim. "I'm sorry about this. I didn't know she was going to be here. There was some trouble in paradise."

"Oh. I thought you'd had a fight."

"No, everything is fine between Kim and me. She's just upset."

"Okay. Then you should be there for her." Florence gave

her a reassuring smile, but there was also a hint of disappointment in her expression. "I'll see you tomorrow? Can I have your number so we can meet somewhere?"

"Yes, of course." Meghan took Florence's phone and entered her number. "Message me so I have yours."

Florence struggled as she held her phone and typed with one hand. "Already done. I'm glad you're not alone tonight." She turned in an unnatural way and stood against the hallway wall, waiting for Meghan to return to her room.

"What's that behind your back?" Meghan stepped closer and tried to see behind Florence, but she pressed herself firmer against the wall.

"Nothing."

"Oh, come on. Let me see." She put her arms around Florence's waist, pulled her towards her and smiled when she spotted the flowers. "Aww... Were those for me?"

Florence grinned sheepishly. "I took them from the big bouquet in the entrance hall. They're replacing them tomorrow, so I figured I might as well take some for you." She opened the bag slung over her shoulder and took out a pint glass. "But Kim's here, and I wasn't sure you'd be comfortable with me bringing flowers, and—"

"I love them," Meghan interrupted her as she took the flowers and the glass. She'd let go of Florence, but they were still standing close together. Much closer than she would with a friend. Their bodies almost touched, and the air hung thick between them. She swallowed hard. "Thank you. That's very sweet." She felt warm and giddy and disappointed they wouldn't be able to spend the night together, but she couldn't tell Florence that...could she?

"Beautiful flowers for a beautiful woman." Florence placed a hand on Meghan's shoulder and softly kissed her cheek before she turned away. "I'll see you tomorrow," she said. "I hope Kim will be okay."

Meghan stared after her until she'd rounded the corner, then looked at the flowers she was holding. They were white roses mixed with greenery, and Florence had tied a white ribbon around them. Meghan's cheek was burning where Florence had kissed her, and she felt clammy and out of sorts as she knocked on the door for Kim to let her back in.

Kim stared at the flowers, which wasn't a bad thing, Meghan decided. It might take her mind off her boyfriend troubles for a while.

"You *so* dressed up for her!" Kim's tone wasn't accusing; it was more of a statement. "*And* she brought you flowers. Are you sure you don't fancy her? She's definitely into you. There's no doubt about that."

"I didn't dress up. I had a shower and put on a fresh change of clothes. There's a difference." Meghan went into the bathroom where she checked her reflection in the mirror while she filled the pint glass. She looked flustered.

"I don't buy that." Kim followed her and stood in the doorway. "Fuck. Did I just ruin your night? Were you planning on...?"

"No! No, you're imagining things." Meghan didn't dare admit she'd been hoping for some steamy action with Florence tonight, not even to her best friend. It was something she had to explore by herself before she'd be able to talk about it. She put the flowers in the glass, opened the bottle of wine and filled two plastic cups. "Want to sit outside?"

"Yeah." Kim's gaze shifted to her phone when it lit up. "Andres is calling me."

"Then pick up."

"I don't know. If I do, I let him get away with his shifty behaviour."

"What if he wants to explain himself? What if it was nothing?" Meghan headed out to the balcony with her glass and the bottle. "Take the call. I'll give you privacy," she said, sliding the doors closed behind her.

## 22

## FLORENCE

*A* little disappointed that she wasn't going to spend the night with Meghan, Florence strolled along the promenade. She was glad Meghan wasn't alone, but she'd been looking forward to another night of long conversations and maybe more. What had started out as a gesture of goodwill only two nights ago had become both intriguing and exciting and the highlight of her day. She was missing the flirting and the look on Meghan's face each time she made an innocent pass on her. On second thoughts, it wasn't so innocent anymore, she supposed. Their moment in the hallway earlier had been filled with promise, and she was convinced something would have happened between them if she'd stayed.

It was quieter than usual on a Sunday night, but that didn't stop the bars from blasting out party music, so she headed to the beach, took off her shoes and continued barefoot, wading along the shoreline. She wanted to clear her head, and the evening breeze was soothing. The weekend had been so busy she'd barely had the time to process her growing interest in Meghan, and now she had so many thoughts buzzing through her head it was hard to make sense of it all. It had been years since she'd thought so much of someone; even her exes hadn't made her feel like this.

Was it because she knew it could never be anything more? Was it just the challenge of seducing the only single, straight woman in a resort full of lesbians? She didn't think so. She wasn't that shallow, or was she? Checking her phone, she saw a message from Manuel, and in need of distraction, she decided to make a detour and meet him and some of her colleagues in a bar nearby. She was off tomorrow, so there was no reason she shouldn't, and without a drink or two, there was no chance she'd sleep tonight.

Manuel, who didn't know she had previous plans of staying with Meghan, sent her another message, and then another one. "Come meet me. We've just moved to Pit Stop!"

*Pit Stop.* Florence groaned. It was the one place she couldn't tolerate and somewhere she'd only ever end up in her worst nightmares. The music was too loud, the cocktails were overpriced and disgusting, and the clientele mainly existed of drunk British and German tourists. She watched a ship sail along the horizon and mulled over her options, contemplating whether to join her friends or go home, but it was still early, and she rarely had a free night.

Spiralling across the beach, she reached Pit Stop in no time and looked up at the ugly façade as she made her way up from the beach, panting and wondering why her friends had decided to gather in the biggest tourist trap on the busy strip. Her question was soon answered when she spotted several hotel guests partying along with her colleagues. *They're mingling.* Florence laughed as she walked up to Manuel, who was dancing with two hotel guests from the Pride event. "I see the party's not over yet."

"Nope. We're going to continue until the early hours."

Manuel gestured to the bar. "Want a drink? I'm getting a round of tequila."

"It's fine, I'll get it," Florence said, not quite in the mood to dance yet. "How many?"

Manuel counted internally as he pointed to their colleagues and the women who had tagged along. "Nine plus you and me. Thanks, Flo."

"Coming up." Florence headed for the bar and had a tequila while she waited for the bartender to pour the other shots.

"Hey, you!" Florence turned at a tap on her shoulder and smiled politely when she saw it was Amber, who she was supposed to be meeting on Tuesday. After Meghan's reaction and their talk earlier, it didn't feel right to go out with Amber anymore. She was aware of the woman's intentions, and for once, she had no interest in sleeping with her.

"Hi, Amber. Would you like a shot?" she asked, making up for the fact that she was about to let her down.

"Sure." Amber looked smoking in a red dress and red lipstick, and all men and women were looking her way. "But only if you let me buy you one in return." She inched close as she leaned on the bar and ordered two shots. "How lucky for me that I ran into you. We may not have to wait until Tuesday, after all," she said in a sultry tone. "By the way, I thought you were busy."

"I am... I was." Florence paused. "And about Tuesday..." She ordered one more tequila for Amber and scooted it in her direction. "I'm afraid I'll have to cancel."

Amber pursed her lips and frowned. "Okay, but we have tonight."

"No, I mean you and me." Florence shot her an apologetic look. "I don't want to be any more than just friendly with you. It's not you, it's—"

"Don't you dare say *it's not you, it's me*," Amber said with a chuckle. "Good God, woman. No one's ever turned me down before. No one." She threw back her own shot followed by Florence's and grimaced as she shook her head. "Well, I suppose there's a first time for everything. So, what's the problem? Do you have a girlfriend or something?"

"Something like that," Florence lied, taking a shot too. "Sorry. Come and have a drink with us, though. We're over there."

"Hmm..." Amber looked at the group of happy people and shrugged. "Okay, I suppose I wouldn't mind that. My friend's in our room, and she's got company." She pointed to the shots on the bar. "Want some help with those?"

"Yes, please." Florence took as many as she could carry and left the rest for Amber. From the way Amber brushed past her, she had a feeling the woman wasn't going to give up anytime soon, but they were here now, and keeping Amber company was the least she could do.

## 23

## MEGHAN

*M*eghan sat on her bed and hugged her knees, fighting the tightening knot in her stomach. Kim had left after Andres begged her to come back so they could talk, and now she was alone.

Apparently, as Meghan had predicted, it was all a misunderstanding; Andres had been arranging a surprise for Kim but couldn't tell her what it was, and Meghan was happy for her, but being alone almost choked her. Her neighbours were quiet—she suspected they were either asleep or out on the town—and although there were still plenty of guests in the hotel, she didn't feel safe.

*Come on, Meghan. History won't repeat itself. It's all in your head.* She should have told Kim the truth and asked her to stay, but she couldn't find the words. So why had she told Florence, whom she barely knew?

*What to do now?* She could go for a walk or spend the night in bars, but deep down, she knew this was something she had to overcome, right now, or she'd never be able to travel by herself. She used to love doing that. Before the incident in Paris, she'd backpacked through Southeast Asia and driven through Eastern Europe on her own. Every day had been a surprise; nothing was ever planned. She'd embraced every opportunity and explored places she wouldn't normally visit. She'd made friends, some for life and some she would never see again, but they'd all left a little piece of them in her heart. And now, she couldn't even spend one night alone in a busy hotel in Benidorm without panicking.

She hated the men who had caused her to become this way. They had taken something much more valuable from her than her belongings. They'd taken her sense of security, and her freedom. Flashbacks resurfaced, trapping her in memories of that night. Her instinct to flee when she saw them. The intense fear when she'd felt the gun to her temple. The panic when they'd blindfolded her. Her pleads for mercy and gasps for air as they stuffed a smelly piece of cloth into her mouth and taped it so tight around her neck that she couldn't move her head. The pain in her wrists and her shoulders as they pulled her arms behind her back and taped her to the chair. The darkness, the paralysing agony of not knowing what was going to happen to her. The realisation that she may not even survive. Imagining her parents when the police told them she'd been raped and murdered. The icy touch of a man's hand on her thigh and his disgusting breath as he whispered into her ear. *"What are you wearing underneath that skirt?"* The short burst of relief when he moved his hand away. The noises in the room as they rooted through her things. The man's threat to return before they left. The gun to her temple again, and the other man telling her not to attempt an escape or he'd kill her. And then the silence and the passing of time that seemed to last forever.

The moment the hotel staff came to save her was perhaps the worst of all, as she'd been convinced the same two men had returned. She'd fought them all the way, even though they were only trying to free her. Through her blind panic, she couldn't see they were different people, that they were good people, and their reassuring words had not registered.

Squeezing her eyes shut, Meghan counted to four while she breathed in, held her breath for four counts and did the same while breathing out slowly, then repeated the action over and over until her heart rate slowed. It only helped a little; the ball of anxiety was still present, rolling through her body, through her brain, clouding her logic. No one here would harm her, and the door was locked. Still, her legs trembled as she stood, took the desk chair and wedged it underneath the doorknob.

It didn't help. After fifteen minutes, she was still staring at the door, terrified she'd see the doorknob turn or someone would knock and tip her over the edge. *Fuck fighting it. I can't stay here.* As soon as she'd made the decision, Meghan couldn't get out of there fast enough. She scrambled to find her sandals and didn't bother with a cover-up as she rushed out and sprinted to the end of the corridor. Vaguely aware she looked terrified, she avoided the stares of other people in the lift as they went down, and when the doors finally opened on the ground floor, she squeezed past them and ran outside. She couldn't breathe and tried to inhale deeply, fighting for air.

Finally, she began to calm down. The dizziness set in, and she steadied herself against a palm tree. It took a few minutes before she was able to move. Chasing the delightful noise of a crowd, she followed the boulevard until she reached what looked like an outdoor club. There was lots of laughter, and people were drinking and dancing to pop music. Meghan looked out for a free table or a stool where she could sit and get a grip. Nearing the bar, she spotted a familiar face—a beautiful face—and was so relieved she had to stop herself from tearing straight over and flinging her arms around Florence's neck.

"Meghan! What are you doing here?" Florence rubbed Meghan's shoulder. "You look upset." She studied Meghan's face, then took her into her arms and hugged her tight. "It's okay," she whispered in her ear, running her hand up and down Meghan's back. "It's okay. Just breathe."

Meghan sighed as Florence held her. She loved the smell of her hair and buried her face in her curls. Someone close by was talking, and it took her a while to realise that person was poking her arm.

"Excuse me. We were kind of in the middle of something," a woman said.

"What?" Meghan looked up. It was the pretty blonde who had given her number to Florence. She was slurring her words a little, but she was standing firm with her hands on her hips.

"Please, Amber," Florence said. "Leave us for a while, will you? Can't you see she's upset?"

Another shock hit Meghan. It wasn't fear this time, but it was intense and made her stomach hurt. Florence was here with Amber, and she was interrupting their date. *She must have called her straight after she left Kim and me.* "I'm sorry," she said, covering her mouth with her hand as she stepped back. "I didn't mean to..." Swallowing her words, she looked from Florence to Amber and back, wondering what exactly was going on. She had no right to say anything, but she still felt hurt. "I shouldn't have come here," she finally said and ran off in the direction of the beach. She heard Florence calling after her but ignored her pleas to come back. She didn't want Florence to see her tears. It was all too much. The fear, the memories, the panic attack, her feelings for Florence, the shock of seeing her with someone else, and the sudden pang of jealousy that made her feel sick.

"Meghan! Please stop and talk to me."

Crossing the road without looking, Meghan barely dodged a car and was reeling at how close it had come to hitting her when she reached the other side. Florence was still calling after her, but she kept going until she was too exhausted and overwhelmed with emotion to continue. Coming to a stop on the beach, she covered her face with her hands and cried.

"Meghan..." Florence caught up with her and took her wrist before she had the chance to move away from her. "Hey, whatever you think is going on between me and Amber, I can assure you, you're wrong." She cupped Meghan's face and met her eyes. "Nothing is going on, I promise. I even cancelled our date on Tuesday."

"And met up with her today instead." Meghan sniffed. "It's okay. You didn't do anything wrong."

"I didn't." Florence looked at her intently. "She just happened to be there."

Meghan shook her head. "I meant you can do whatever you want. It's nothing to do with me."

"Come on, Meghan. You know that's not true. We have..." Florence paused. "We have something special, and you know it."

Meghan finally looked up, although the only thing she could manage to say was, "I look like shit."

Florence chuckled and shook her head. "You don't. You look beautiful as always." She ran a hand over Meghan's cheek. "What happened tonight? Why aren't you with Kim?"

"She went back to Andres," Meghan said through sniffs. "And then I had a panic attack and came here. I'm not a stalker, I promise." She shook her head. "I feel ridiculous."

"Hey, I know you're not a stalker and you're never, ever ridiculous." Florence pulled her close, and Meghan closed her eyes and cherished the warm contact. As always, Florence made her feel safe and desired and better about herself.

"So I didn't interrupt your date?" she asked.

"No. I couldn't possibly go on a date, now that..." Florence hesitated. "Now that we are where we are." She smiled. "That doesn't mean I expect anything from you. I know you're not gay, but it wouldn't feel right to see someone else while you're here because I have feelings for you."

Meghan stared at her. "You do?"

"Yes. I'm crushing on you like crazy. Haven't you noticed?"

Meghan shrugged and couldn't help but smile. "I felt the chemistry." She shot Florence a shy look. "It's mutual, but I'm sure you know that too." Seeing Florence's face light up took away some of her anxiety. "And I have no idea why I'm so scared," she added, wiping her cheeks.

"What exactly are you scared of?" Florence asked, wrapping her arms around her neck.

Meghan lost her ability to speak once again. In Florence's firm grip, her body was on fire. The closeness made her weak in every limb, and she desperately wanted to kiss her.

"I don't know," she stammered. "This feels so intense that I'm worried there might not be a way back."

Florence nodded. "Would that be so bad?"

"I..." Meghan's voice trailed off as she inched back and got lost in Florence's eyes. "Fuck. Just kiss me," she whispered. "Please, just kiss me."

## 24

# FLORENCE

*M*eghan's lips were alluring. Her mouth glistened in the moonlight, waiting like a question, and Florence's eyes were fixated on the ever so slight upward curl of her upper lip. It felt intense to her too. Her heart was beating fast, and she was about to burst with anticipation as she leaned closer. "Are you sure?" she whispered.

Meghan let out a soft breath, and her eyes drifted down to Florence's parted lips, her chin tilting towards her. "Yes." Meghan's fingertips grazed the nape of her neck, her expression changing as Florence curled an arm around her waist and pulled her tighter against her. The flicker of desire in her eyes and the shiver Florence felt as she held her told her Meghan was running out of patience.

She pressed her mouth carefully against Meghan's, and the effect shocked her. Cushiony, soft lips fitted perfectly with hers, and they both let out a quiet moan as they stood there, breathing each other's air. She needed time to get used to this, to what it did to her body. Searing heat coursed through her, her legs felt weak, and she could barely stand as Meghan pulled back to look at her.

Meghan smiled. "That wasn't scary. That was really, really..."

To Florence's surprise, Meghan took charge. Cupping Florence's face, she pulled her in and kissed her, harder this time. Parting their lips, they melted into each other's embrace, and Florence moaned as arousal shot through her, making her crave more. She had no idea how long they kissed for, how long their hands roamed, exploring each other's face, neck, back and waist, how long their lips were locked as their quiet moans filled the night air. She could have kissed Meghan for hours, but a whistle from a group of passing men pulled them out of the moment, and Meghan giggled shyly as she licked her lips and stepped back.

"I don't normally kiss in public," she said with a grin. "I guess I got carried away."

"We could continue somewhere private?" Florence suggested, brushing a lock of hair behind Meghan's ear. "In your room if Kim's with her boyfriend. Or...I could just sleep there and keep you company. We don't need to do anything."

Meghan shook her head, took Florence's hand and laced their fingers together. "I don't want to sleep. I want more."

*More.* Florence was on fire, and knowing Meghan wasn't shying away, she wrapped her arms around her again and ran them over her behind. The short, white dress would come off so easily, and all she wanted was to feel Meghan's skin against her own. "Walk with me," she whispered and took her hand.

Meghan looked down at their entwined hands and tightened her grip. They walked in silence, neither of them knowing what to say. Florence had walked this route to work more times than she could count, but as she glanced around, everything felt alien to her. She barely registered the blasting pop music from the party venues nearby, the little overpriced beach hut that sold hot dogs and refreshments, the water-toy rental company that had closed for the night, and the rows of deckchairs, neatly stacked up and chained to each other. It was as if the rush of endorphins had transported her into a bubble in which there was nothing but them and the night ahead. She felt confused, and that made no sense because if anyone should be confused, it was Meghan. But she also felt elated and light-headed, giddy and immensely aroused.

"Do you think this is a bad idea?" Meghan asked, finally breaking the silence.

"Possibly." Florence stopped in her stride and glanced at her. "You may not enjoy being intimate with a woman."

"After that kiss, I doubt it." Meghan met her eyes, and from the way she was looking at her, Florence believed her. "But if that's the case, at least I'll know."

"Yes, that's true." Meghan's sexuality wasn't Florence's biggest concern, but she kept that to herself. They'd become close very quickly, after sharing personal stories and spending nights together, and what she was worried about was her heart. She stared at her, almost forgetting they were on their way to the hotel. Meghan made her lose herself like no woman had before, and as desire pulled them back together, they fell into another kiss. Meghan's need grew in her arms, the pressure of her lips hardened, and she ground into her with her whole body. Florence vaguely registered people passing, some commenting on their steamy embrace, but Meghan didn't stop this time. Instead, she took a tighter hold of Florence and ran her fingers through her hair and down her back, her lips hungry and persistent as sounds of pleasure escaped them.

Florence's body coiled tighter, and heat rushed through her blood. Her hands were about to travel places they shouldn't in public, so she stepped back and held them up. "I won't be able to stop if we continue," she said with a smirk, then put her arm around Meghan's waist and rushed them back to Paradise.

The ride up to the thirteenth floor seemed to take forever. Squashed in the lift with seven people, Florence didn't dare look at Meghan. Their hands touched lightly between them, and Meghan caressed Florence's thigh with the tip of her finger. If sexual tension was visible, the lift would have been covered in a pink fog, but the other hotel guests didn't seem to notice their exchange. Her head filled with fantasies, Florence hooked her index finger with Meghan's and tugged her closer. When everyone got out and they were finally alone during the last part of the ride, Meghan turned to her, and Florence felt her chest rise and fall against her own. They didn't speak as they stared at each other; Meghan's eyes reflected a mixture of arousal and fear, and Florence wondered if she was having second thoughts. Her question was answered when Meghan's lips pulled into a smile.

"In case you're wondering," she said, "I haven't changed my mind."

## 25

---

## MEGHAN

*M*eghan was shaking as she hung the 'do not disturb' sign on the doorknob and closed the door behind her. She could still feel the aftereffect of the kiss and Florence's wandering hands; she ached for Florence to touch her, and to touch her in return.

"We're alone," she said, stating the obvious as she leaned back against the door. Her gaze travelled over Florence. Her tanned legs in the denim shorts she was wearing, her toned arms and her small breasts underneath the tight, white top that hugged her athletic figure. Her wild curls, her piercing, dark eyes and that delicious mouth that had been on hers only minutes ago. Meghan wanted her like she'd never wanted anyone before, but insecurities had her doubting herself. "I have no idea how this works." She suddenly felt terribly self-aware.

"Don't worry about anything." Florence closed the distance between them, leaned into her and dropped her hand to her behind. When she inched her hand under Meghan's dress and squeezed her, Meghan gasped at the flash of arousal that shot between her thighs. "Just tell me if you want me to stop." She brushed Meghan's hair away and kissed her neck down to the dip of her shoulder, then back up to her lips, tugging at them with her own. As their mouths melded again, Florence's other hand moved to Meghan's breast, stroking and kneading it.

"Mmm..." Meghan moaned, the sound of her own pleasure in the quiet room alien to her. Apart from moments ago on the beach, she'd never heard herself do that, not with anyone, but she was so turned on she was about to burst, and her arousal needed an outlet. *She's touching me. Her hand is under my dress. This is happening.* Meghan's mind spun, but a scorching kiss burned away her train of thought. Something staggering was building already. The pressure of Florence's thigh between her legs, her hand on her behind and her hot breath and moist lips on her mouth and neck made Meghan squirm in her grip. She closed her eyes and tilted her head to the side, welcoming every kiss and caress as she slipped her hands underneath Florence's top and marvelled at the sensation. Everything about her was soft. Her lips, her skin, her hair... It was the softness Meghan didn't know she'd craved, the softness she couldn't find with a man. It was overwhelming and exciting and scary, but the good kind of scary. Her last kiss with a woman had been exciting, but it was nothing like this. Perhaps because then it was just a drunken spur of the moment, and she didn't know the woman. This felt real. She wasn't drunk, and it wasn't impulsive. She'd wanted Florence for days, and it wasn't a mistake or a means to satisfy her curiosity, like she'd suspected. This, right now, was what she'd always craved.

Vague thoughts came and went, but her mind went blank once more as Florence sucked at the sensitive skin of her neck, then moved to her jawline before she met her lips in another kiss that slayed her and washed her nerves away.

"I want you," Florence whispered, breathing hard against her lips. "I want you so much."

"I want you too," she said, pulling Florence's top over her head. Meghan's breath hitched as she stared at her breasts in a white sports bra. "You're so beautiful and smooth and... hot," she finally settled on. Yes, Florence was smoking hot, and she drove her wild and delirious and filled her with a carnal need to fuck. Sex had never been that straightforward to her; it was always about pleasing her partners, as she didn't get that much out of it herself and rarely had an orgasm unless it was self-inflicted. She liked foreplay and being intimate with someone, but now, with Florence, all she wanted was to be fucked until she exploded.

Florence smiled as she removed her bra. She dropped it to the floor and stood before Meghan like she wanted to give her time to get used to her. "We can stop if you—"

"No." Meghan traced Florence's shoulders down to her breasts and took in a quick breath when her nipples hardened under her touch. She cupped them and parted her lips in awe at the feeling of another woman's breasts in her hands. They were small and perky and soft and warm. Needing to feel that warm skin against her own, she pulled her dress over her head and tossed it on the floor. She wasn't self-conscious, not with Florence watching her like she wanted to eat her alive. "Do I look like I want to stop?" she asked in a breathy voice.

Florence's gaze intensified as she looked her up and down, taking in her curves enveloped in a delicate white, lacy set. "No. You look like you want me to give you something you've always craved." Her lips pulled into a flirtatious grin before she went in for another kiss and pushed herself against Meghan. "And trust me..." she whispered before running her tongue over Meghan's upper lip, "I will."

"Fuck..." Meghan shivered and fumbled with the button on Florence's shorts, eager to get her out of them.

Florence pushed them down, kicked them off and embraced Meghan while she ground into her and kissed her hard. The friction of her thigh against Meghan's centre alone was enough to send her over the edge.

"Can I touch you?" Florence asked, sliding her hand down Meghan's body.

Meghan nodded and smiled against her mouth, and when Florence slowly traced the inside of her thigh, her agonising need for release made her throb. Florence stopped just before she'd reached the edge of Meghan's panties, drawing a groan of frustration from her.

"Let's get on the bed," she whispered. "I want you to be comfortable."

Meghan dropped down onto the nearest bed and stared up at Florence, who leaned over her with hungry, hazy eyes. Her smile was sexy and confident, and it put Meghan at ease that at least one of them was. She felt a tingle of nerves as Florence reached around her to unclip her bra, but no nerves could stop her. She was so attracted to her that she'd do anything for release. *Anything.*

"Look at you." Florence bit her lip as she removed Meghan's bra and looked her over. "You're gorgeous."

Meghan fought the instinct to cover herself and reached out to trace Florence's shoulders. They were strong, square and defined, with a faint dip. "You're beautiful," she said for the first time in her life, surprised by how comfortably it rolled off her tongue. She was glad she hadn't been drinking and that the bedside light was on because she loved looking at Florence. She wanted to remember everything about tonight.

Florence kissed her lips, then her neck before she

moved back to kiss her way down to Meghan's breasts. She ran her tongue over her nipples, then sucked one into her mouth and bit softly. Meghan moaned and dug her nails into Florence's back, basking in the glorious sensation of teeth and tongue against her hard buds.

"Mmm...you're delicious," Florence mumbled as she continued to explore Meghan's body with her mouth—her ribcage, her belly, her hips... Meghan twisted and turned in ecstasy, weaving her hands into Florence's curls when she moved lower. She kissed the edge of Meghan's panties, then looked up to meet her eyes. "Can I take these off?"

"Yes." Meghan's voice was hoarse, and she felt dizzy from holding her breath in anticipation. Wiggling her hips, she helped Florence slide down her panties and shivered when Florence's hair tickled her inner thighs as she moved between them and spread them apart. Covering her face in her hands to stifle the cries she knew would soon follow, Meghan felt more exposed than ever, and when Florence blew softly on her most intimate parts, she was so sensitive that she gasped like she'd been deprived of air.

Dipping her head, Florence slowly ran her tongue over the length of Meghan's sex, and Meghan's hands slammed into the mattress, clawing at the sheets as she writhed from side to side. Consuming her with long, slow licks, Florence's tongue curled each time she hit the spot while her eyes remained fixed on Meghan's. Vaguely conscious of how she must look, Meghan bit her lip and forced her face to relax, but she couldn't help arching impatiently against Florence's tongue as she felt a climax building. It promised to be spectacular.

Florence must have sensed she was close, as she licked her lips seductively, then crawled up to meet her with a mind-blowing kiss. Skin to skin, mouth to mouth, they sank into each other and fitted together with stunning perfection. Lowering her hand, Florence's fingers slipped between Meghan's folds, gathering her wetness before she inched two fingers inside her.

Meghan's hips shot up, and she groaned and wrapped her legs around her. Florence's mouth was claiming her as much as her fingers, and she loved the feeling. Penetrating her slowly, Florence went deeper and curled her fingers. It seemed intuitive, as if she understood Meghan's body, a seasoned musician playing her like an instrument. She heard her own voice grow louder and louder until she crashed into a high-pitched cry and came hard, every muscle in her body tensing as she held on to Florence so tightly her arms hurt. Her mind went blank, and she closed her eyes. When she opened them again, Florence was stroking her face and smiling at her. It wasn't the smug smile of someone who'd just converted a woman, but a sweet and caring smile, and it brought a lump to her throat.

Florence rolled off her, and Meghan shifted to her side and rested her head on her chest, taking a beat to gather her thoughts and her breath. That wasn't easy with her body still reacting the way it was. Florence was near-naked, her tender touch both soothing and arousing, and she wanted more. Meghan didn't recognise herself, but she decided that was okay for now. Maybe she'd never really known herself, and this was the beginning of a long, new road of discovery. One thing she'd been right about, though; she couldn't go back.

## 26

## FLORENCE

*F*lorence would have given anything to know what was going through Meghan's head as she stroked her hair. She was even more confused than before, as she hadn't expected it to be so intense or to feel so meaningful, and if *she* was confused, she couldn't imagine Meghan's inner turmoil. They'd been lying still for a while, and she hadn't said anything.

"Are you okay?" she asked in a whisper.

"Yes..." Meghan lifted her head off Florence's chest and looked up at her. "I'm okay, I'm just..." She shook her head with a chuckle. "I still can't seem to form a sentence, so you'll have to give me a moment."

"Of course." Florence closed her eyes, and the steady sound of Meghan's breathing in sync with her own and the warm skin against hers brought her comfort. They were curled up in bed together and still, she wanted to be closer. She wanted to be in her head.

"I don't understand," Meghan finally said. "How do you make me feel this way?"

"How do you feel?"

Meghan bit her lip as she hesitated. "You make me feel so...so amazing. So safe and desired. And what we just did has shattered everything I thought to be true about myself and about my future. Frankly, I don't know whether to be ecstatic because I'm getting a glimpse of who I really am or to be upset because I clearly didn't know myself at all. I've wasted so much time having bad sex and mediocre relationships, and now I know why." She shot Florence a small smile. "I can't go back to the way I was."

"Back to being with men?"

"Yes."

"At least I didn't put you off." Florence smiled back at her. "I suspect you might want some time to think, and I would normally ask if you wanted me to leave you alone, but as you're not comfortable being on your own—"

"I don't want to be alone," Meghan interrupted her. "Even if I didn't have panic attacks, I'd still want you to stay —if that is what you want too." Desire flashed across her features as she trailed a finger over Florence's breasts. "This is beautiful, and I want to do it again and again and again."

Florence's core tightened at her words. "Me too. We still have a couple of hours before Kim gets back, right?"

"We have more than enough time." Meghan's fingers continued down her body, and Florence felt her tremble as she rested her hand on her stomach. "I want to touch you. Tell me what you like," she whispered. "Show me."

Florence guided Meghan's hand between her thighs, to where she wanted it, and let out a sigh of delight. Her skin, where Meghan touched her, burned. Meghan shifted onto her elbow to look at her. Her face was still glowing, and her hair was a wild tumble. Slowly, softly, she stroked Florence, tracing the thin strip of hair between her legs.

Meghan's lips parted when she moved lower and felt her wetness.

"That's what you do to me," Florence whispered through heavy breaths. She pulled her in for a kiss and moaned as Meghan explored her. She guided her fingers back up and circled them around her clit, and she felt Meghan's lips pull into a smile against her mouth as her moans became louder. Her touch slayed her, every stroke divine, taking her higher. Handing control over to Meghan, Florence let go of her fingers and weaved her hands through her hair. She arched her back as tightness grew in her core. Her physical reaction to Meghan was astounding; every nerve was screaming out for her. Lifting her hips in search of release, she groaned as Meghan's fingers moved faster, circling and stimulating her right where she needed it. Meghan looked up, her pupils dilated as she stared at Florence like she was the most fascinating thing she'd ever seen.

"Yes..." Florence gave her a nod, then threw her head back as a climax washed over her. She shuddered, twisted and turned, and her nails dug into Meghan's back as she tensed against her. Waves kept coming, and she gasped when Meghan trailed a finger up and down one more time. She barely touched her now, but it felt like lightning.

"Was that...?" Meghan retracted her hand and studied her. "Did you just...?" She blushed as she stroked her cheek.

"Yes." Florence chuckled, then let out a long sigh as she relaxed.

"Wow. I didn't think I could do that."

"You didn't think you could give a woman an orgasm?"

Meghan shook her head, and clearly pleased with herself, she bit her lip and grinned. She was so cute when she did that, and Florence cupped her face to kiss those smiling lips again.

"Was it good?" Meghan asked.

Florence laughed. "It was amazing," she said, brushing a lock of hair behind Meghan's ear. "You have no idea what you do to me." She shivered when Meghan lifted the fingers that had been between her thighs only moments ago and sucked them into her mouth. It immediately caused her libido to fire, even now, right after a screaming orgasm, and she squeezed her legs together. "Fuck."

"I want this," Meghan said, then licked her lips. "I want to know what you taste like."

Florence was pretty sure she'd never seen anything more sensual and realised she was staring, open-mouthed. "You'll have to wait," she said when she found her words again. She ran her hand over Meghan's waist and hip, then shifted and pushed her onto her back. God, she wanted Meghan's mouth on her, but priding herself in being a pleaser, she wanted Meghan first. Pinning her down by her wrists, she steadied herself over her. She knew Meghan liked her taking back control from the way she moaned and wiggled beneath her, and bringing her mouth to her ear, she whispered, "Because it's my turn."

## 27

## MEGHAN

*T*he sound of the door opening made Meghan shoot up in bed, and she covered herself with the sheets when Kim stepped in. "Good morning, sunshine." Kim beamed. "Why are you naked? It wasn't that warm last night." She spoke in a singing tone, something she only did when she was extremely happy.

"Hey." Meghan's heart was racing, and she waited for the moment Kim spotted Florence. "I, ehm... Yes, it was warm, at least in here." She cleared her throat. "Could you give me a moment? I'll just put some clothes on."

"Come on. I've seen you naked plenty of times." Kim picked up a T-shirt and a pair of panties from Meghan's open suitcase on the floor and threw them at her, and as Meghan turned to catch them, she realised there was no one in her bed. Although she was immensely relieved that she wouldn't have to explain herself to Kim, she also felt Florence's absence, and it stung. *She left. I must have slept so deep.* It wasn't strange or rude that Florence had left. She'd probably decided it was best to get out before Kim came back, and Meghan couldn't agree more with that decision.

She needed time to process this on her own before having to discuss it with her friend, but she missed Florence already.

Flashes of last night came back, and she shivered at the memories. They'd made love for hours. Careful and tenderly, raw and intense until they fell asleep in each other's arms. Florence's body draped over her, her fingers inside her, her mouth between her thighs, her hair tickling her skin, lips locked in deep and passionate kisses and her hands and mouth everywhere... The feel of Florence's aroused sex against her fingertips, the taste of her on her tongue and the glorious sensation of making her climax against her lips. Meghan had been insatiable, and the pull for more still hadn't left her body that was aching with arousal.

"Megs? Hey, Meghan?" Kim snapped her fingers in front of her face. "What's wrong with you? Are you still drunk or something?"

"No, I'm fine. Just sleepy, that's all." Meghan pretended to yawn before she put on the T-shirt and panties and finally met Kim's eyes. "How was your night?"

"Well..." Kim dropped a dramatic pause. "I've been waving my hand in front of you since I came in, but since you're not the most observant this morning, I'll just have to rub it in." She held out her hand, palm down, showing off a sparkling diamond ring.

Still processing one steamy flashback after another, it took a while for Meghan to realise it was an engagement ring. She frowned as she stared at it, then shot Kim a wide smile. "Are you getting married?"

Kim nodded and burst into giggles as she hopped from one foot to the other. "Yes! I'm getting married. Andres asked me last night. And to think I was convinced he was up to something shady. He was just picking up my ring!"

"Oh, babe, come here!" Meghan got up and fell around Kim's neck. "Congratulations, I'm so happy for you!" She stepped back and placed her hands on Kim's shoulders. "I can't believe you're getting married, and I haven't even met him."

"But you will tonight, remember? Double date."

"It's not a double date, you promised. But I can't wait to meet your future husband."

Kim started bouncing again and let out a little shriek of joy. "Oh my God. I'm getting married, and I'm so, so excited. Will you be my maid of honour?"

"Of course." Meghan laughed and felt warm inside at seeing Kim's outrageous happiness. "Want to go for breakfast and celebrate by the pool?"

"Let's do it." Kim put on her bikini and gathered her towel and sunscreen, then waited for Meghan to get dressed. "I bet you're keen to see that bartender again. I'm so sorry I interrupted your date last night. That was terribly dramatic of me."

"It wasn't a date," Meghan mumbled. "Besides, she's off today, so she won't be there."

"Oh, you know her schedule now, do you?"

"We're friends," Meghan said. "So, yes, I know her schedule."

"Right." Kim shot her a sceptical look. "There's nothing wrong with wanting to experiment. I get it. You want to kiss a woman because who hasn't? After being around lesbians the whole weekend, your head got filled with all sorts of naughty ideas." She patted Meghan's arm. "And what better place to do that than in another country where no one knows you? Don't worry, I promise you. What happens in Benidorm, stays in Benidorm. This will go no further, ever."

Kim couldn't have been more wrong, but Meghan didn't

tell her that. She didn't tell her that she'd had the most meaningful night of her life with spectacular sex and new, wonderful emotions that were still raging through her. She didn't tell her that she couldn't stop thinking of Florence, and that she longed for her with a fire that was unknown to her, a yearning so deep it possessed her.

"It wasn't a date, we're just friends," she said again, filling her beach bag with anything she could possibly need so she wouldn't have to go back to the room on her own. "How about we take a break from the pool and go to the beach instead? I read about this lovely beach bar, and I wouldn't mind a dip in the sea. It's not far, we can take a taxi." With Florence not being around, a day at the poolside suddenly seemed awfully dull. She needed to get away from Paradise Hotel for a few hours because everything reminded her of Florence, and it took away her ability to think clearly and focus on her friend's happiness.

"I like your, thinking," Kim said. "I deserve somewhere fancier to celebrate my engagement than an all-inclusive hotel."

"Exactly." Meghan checked herself in the mirror and put an arm around Kim as they headed out. "My treat."

## 28

## FLORENCE

*F*lorence watched Manuel attack the toast like he hadn't eaten in years. They were sitting outside the breakfast café under their apartment, waking up in the sun over coffee and scrambled eggs, but she wasn't hungry.

"Here, have mine too," she said, sliding her toast basket across the table. The uninspiring venue was basic and the menu limited, but it was their standard spot in the morning when they both had a day off. Manuel was grilling her relentlessly over last night, but she hadn't given anything away.

"Thanks." Manuel buttered another slice. "Are you sure nothing happened?" he asked again, arching a brow at her.

"I'm sure. I think I'd remember."

"That's interesting. Maybe I can jog your memory." Manuel grinned as he dropped a pause. "Someone saw you kissing on the beach last night."

Florence felt her cheeks burn, and she kept quiet as she hid behind her big mug. *Fuck. I should have been more careful.* It wasn't as much her job she was worried about as Meghan.

She suspected Meghan didn't want anyone to know, and if the staff knew, they might throw them looks or crack jokes, and that would be uncomfortable for her.

"Who told you that?" she asked, sipping her coffee.

"One of the guests who was out with us last night. She said it looked pretty intense."

"Right." Florence sighed. "Did she tell anyone else?"

"I'm not sure. Maybe her friends, but they're all flying back today, so it doesn't matter." Manuel's grin widened. "Hey, don't worry. I'll keep it to myself."

"Good. I'd really appreciate that." Florence took a small bite of her eggs and dropped her fork. She couldn't eat, she couldn't think, and she couldn't function. The only thing on her mind was Meghan, and she didn't understand how one night could have such an impact on her sanity.

Manuel finished his eggs, then pointed to Florence's plate. "Aren't you going to eat those either?"

"No. You can have them." She pushed the plate towards him and sat back.

"So, now that you know I know, are you still not going to tell me?"

"It's private." Florence had no intention of telling him anything. In ten days, Meghan would return to the UK and that was that. She'd miss her, and she'd probably need some time to get over her, even though they hadn't known each other for long. It would be crazy to think that a holiday romance could ever work out in real life. She saw it regularly with hotel guests—the tears as they hugged each other goodbye while they were waiting for their separate tour operators to pick them up and take them to the airport. Sometimes it worked out, she supposed. If they lived in the same country, and their circumstances were right. But more often than not, it ended in pain, and that was exactly what was going to happen to her and Meghan.

"You're in love," Manuel said, so casually it sounded like a joke.

"I'm not in love," Florence shot back at him. "That's ridiculous. I barely know her."

"Then you have a crush on her, or whatever it's called when people can't eat or sleep. I have a sister. I know the signs." Manuel pointed to her plate that he'd almost cleared. "You love breakfast, but you haven't touched your food and you have a weird stare," he said. "It's kind of creepy, like I'm transparent and you're seeing right through me when I'm talking."

"I can see you perfectly fine." Florence waved at the waiter and held up her coffee cup for a refill. She hadn't slept much as she'd left early in case Kim returned, and back in bed at home, she wasn't able to sleep at all. "Anyway, what you just said ... It sounds like you've never been in love. Surely, you must have fallen for someone at some point in your life."

Manuel shrugged. "I don't think so. I've never been like you are now, that's for sure." He chuckled, then added, "Thank God. Shoot me if I ever become a love zombie."

"What about relationships?" Florence asked, embracing the opportunity to shift the topic to him.

"Never been in one." He finished his last bite, then burped loudly.

"Gross. No wonder." Florence rolled her eyes and laughed. "Do you do that in front of women you date?"

"Nah. Mainly just in front of you." Manuel laughed too. "Look, I don't really date, unless picking up women in a bar counts as a date?"

Florence grimaced. "Jesus, you're such a caveman. I saw two women coming out of your room this morning, by the way."

"I don't care if you saw them, because unlike you, I have nothing to hide." He shot her a smug look. "So, call me a caveman all you want, but at least I have no drama. I have no trouble getting laid and women come to me, so I don't need to bother all that much. The best thing about sleeping with tourists is that they leave again."

"Hmm..." Florence glanced up and thanked the waiter when he topped up her coffee. She was no saint herself; she regularly slept with tourists, but she was nowhere near as bad as Manuel, and after meeting Meghan, she felt sad at the thought of saying goodbye.

"You're doing it again," he said. "That look."

Florence made a point of looking him in the eyes, but she was aware that she was acting out of character. The café was on a busy road, and they'd normally check out women together over breakfast, but she had no interest in that today. She hadn't had any interest in women in general, not even during the Pride event.

"Okay, I do have a crush on her," she finally admitted. "But it's pointless." She didn't even know how Meghan felt this morning. Perhaps she regretted it, or perhaps she would decide being with women wasn't for her, after all.

"Why is it pointless? Sure, she'll go back to London, and even when you're back there too, you may not ever see her again. But you enjoy being with her, so why can't that be enough for now? If anything, make some memories together. Call her, see what she's up to and have a good time. Sitting here and staring into space won't get you anywhere, I can tell you that."

Florence let out a deep sigh. Manuel made everything

sound so simple and maybe it was. Either way, she needed to know how Meghan felt because she couldn't wait until tonight.

"Fine," she said, picking up her phone. "I'll message her."

## 29

---

## MEGHAN

"I love this place." Kim took the iced coffee Meghan handed her and sipped it as she sank back on her sun lounger. The bar on the small beach a ten-minute drive from the city centre was comfortable and stylish with white furniture, white parasols and sun loungers, and white daybeds under straw canopies surrounded by light, linen curtains. As it was a private beach, it wasn't overly busy, and it would have even been romantic if it wasn't for the DJ belting out mellow house tunes at eleven in the morning.

"Yeah, I'm pleasantly surprised too." Meghan sat down in the lounger next to her and adjusted their parasol, so she'd be in the shade. She was supposed to meet Florence for dinner tonight, and she didn't want to be sunburned. "This iced coffee is excellent." Staring out over the sea, she laughed when a speedboat passed, dragging screaming tourists on an inflatable behind it. They barely held on, and it kept zigzagging until finally one of them slipped off. "You want to give it a go?" she asked. "We can book a ride at the bar." She wouldn't normally be tempted, but screaming felt like the only way to get rid of some of the pent-up energy inside her. She'd been fidgety and absent over breakfast and on the way here, and now she didn't know what to do with herself.

"No, I'm good," Kim said, lowering her shades to check out the drifting woman who kept disappearing behind waves. "It looks rough, and I don't want to get bruised. Andres is taking me out for dinner tonight." She turned to Meghan. "You're welcome to join us."

Meghan smiled and shook her head. "You two lovebirds have fun. I'm meeting him tomorrow, and anyway, I'm seeing Florence tonight." She tried not to grin as she said her name out loud, because since this morning, 'Florence' was officially the most beautiful name in the world.

"Oh, yes, your date. I forgot about that." Kim shot her a knowing look. "So, is tonight the night? Are you going to kiss her?"

Meghan shivered at that thought. They'd done a lot more than kissing, but yes, she couldn't wait to kiss her again. Florence's lips were so soft, and the way she held her while she kissed her was... She closed her eyes for a moment, composing herself. "Stop it, Kim," she said, looking away as flashes of arousal hit her, one after another. It was intense; she felt like she was about to explode if she didn't find some form of relief.

"You're blushing," Kim teased. "You're so blushing and you know it."

Meghan shook her head with a chuckle. She wished she could tell her best friend about her night, but now that it was real, now that it had happened, she was terrified of anyone knowing. *Why is that?* At the same time, she didn't want to deny it entirely either, so she changed the subject. "Let's talk wedding plans," she said, knowing that was the only way to shut Kim up. "Where are you guys getting married? Here or in the UK? Or have you not decided yet?"

"Here, of course." Kim gestured to their surroundings and smiled. "In summer, on the beach. It's much more charming than having it in some sombre hotel in the UK, and the flights are cheap, so I'm sure most of my family and friends would be up for making the trip. In fact, this place seems great, but Andres has some venues he wants to show me."

"On the beach sounds perfect. And what about your life? Where are you going to live?" When Kim shrugged, Meghan placed a hand on her arm and smiled. "I'm asking too many questions, aren't I? You haven't even had time to think about any of that."

"No, I haven't, and there's a lot we need to decide on," Kim said. "But we have time to figure things out before the wedding. We were thinking May or June, so that's still a while away, but I'm sure the time will fly by." She hesitated. "If I'm totally honest, I'd like to live here for a couple of years. It crossed my mind even before Andres proposed."

"I'd be sad if you left, but I get it. I wouldn't mind living in the sun either. If I'd be able to find work out here, I might even consider it at some point."

"Work...yes, that's an issue for sure. The salaries are much lower here than in London, but I suppose the rents are lower too." Kim sighed as she brought a hand to her temple. "Oh, God, I hadn't thought about that. And then there's the living arrangement," she continued. "Andres' place is okay, but it's a typical small bachelor's pad, and I'm in a shared apartment, so that's not ideal either, and—"

"Hey, deep breaths," Meghan interrupted her. "There's no need to stress about anything. Just take the time to talk while you're here and you'll figure it out. You could try different things together, right? Just because you're getting married doesn't mean there's pressure to have the house and the car and the kid straight away. The only pressure is the pressure you put on yourself, so don't do that."

"That's true…" Kim took her hand and squeezed it. "Will you please help me? You're good at organising, and I could really benefit from your management skills."

"Of course I'll help you. Once you both know what you want, I'll help you make a plan and—" Meghan stopped herself when Florence's name lit up on her phone. "Excuse me for a moment, I just need to answer this," she said, fighting the smirk she felt spreading over her face as she read it.

*Hey, beautiful. I hope you're okay after last night. Sorry I snuck out. I didn't want to put you in a difficult position in case Kim came back early. I'd love to see you tonight, but I understand if you need time to yourself. Let me know. I'm thinking of you.*

"I know that look." Kim leaned in to catch a glimpse of her screen, but Meghan turned it away. "Oh, come on. Let me see."

"Private," Meghan mumbled, reading the message again and again. Then she got up and walked away to type a reply. Suddenly shaky on her legs, it was hard to walk with a storm brewing inside. The butterflies were intense, her mind was churning, and her hands were trembling as she typed a reply.

*Hey! Last night was amazing. I'm thinking of you too and I would love to see you later. It's a date .*

## 30

## FLORENCE

*F*lorence could see Meghan was nervous as she got out of the taxi. She looked stunning in black-and-white polka-dot shorts and a low-cut black top. Her brown hair hung loosely around her shoulders, and her left wrist was graced with a few silver bangles. She glanced over the terrace in front of the restaurant, and her face lit up when she spotted Florence.

"Hello, am I late?"

"No, I'm early." Florence got up to greet her. She wasn't sure what Meghan was comfortable with, so she settled for a kiss on her cheek before she pulled out a chair for her.

"Thanks." Meghan blushed profusely as she sat down. "This is..." She chuckled. "Forgive me. I'm just getting used to a woman pulling out a chair for me."

"I'm sorry. Was that too much?" Florence winced. "I wasn't thinking, I—"

"No, I like it." Meghan shot her a shy smile. "This is nice. Do you come here often?" Rolling her eyes, she laughed again. "God, that was a lame question."

"Not lame question, and I do, actually. I have some

friends who live nearby, so we tend to meet up here." The Spanish restaurant Florence had chosen wasn't fancy, but it had a lovely big terrace, great food and friendly service. It was also just outside the city centre in a quiet residential neighbourhood, void of drunk tourists, which was another bonus. "Do you like traditional Spanish food?"

"Of course. Who doesn't? I haven't had much Spanish food since I arrived, though, apart from tapas with you." Meghan kept shifting her napkin on her lap as if she wasn't quite sure what to do with herself.

"Was Kim okay?" Florence asked, giving her a chance to change the subject.

"Yes, she was fine. More than fine. She's getting married to her boyfriend. He proposed to her last night."

"Really? That's great. I thought they'd had a fight."

"It was just a misunderstanding. She came back this morning with an engagement ring on her finger, and we celebrated at a beach club all day." Meghan touched her cheeks. "I tried not to get sunburnt but failed."

Florence looked her over and shook her head. "You're absolutely stunning."

"Thank you. So are you." Meghan looked at her, and their eye contact was electric. Yes, she was nervous, but Florence clearly detected that same desire as last night. "I've never seen you in..." She paused. "I've never seen you dressed up. You look really nice."

"Thanks." Jeans and a white linen shirt were as far as Florence went when it came to dressing up, but she felt good about how she looked tonight. Even her hair was behaving, which was a welcome bonus. Although people rarely saw a difference in how her curls fell around her face, *she* did, and she was grateful for a good hair day and an abundance of energy, even after a long week of hard work and very little sleep. "So, you had fun today?" she asked.

"Yes, it was fun. I was quite distracted, though, after your message, so Kim was constantly on my case. She doesn't know anything about what happened last night, but she knows I'm out with you tonight. She thinks I have a crush on you."

"But you do. You told me so last night," Florence said with a grin.

"I do." Meghan buried her face in her hands and laughed. "Oh, God. You make me shy. I swear, I'm never shy around people, but with you, it's like I don't know how to be myself." She looked up to meet Florence's eyes again. "It's a date, and that's kind of a big deal, and I—"

"Don't overthink things," Florence said, placing a hand on Meghan's. "It's a drink between friends, and we just happen to like each other more than friends normally do. Does that help?"

"Not really." Meghan laughed, then lowered her voice. "You just look really hot, and I don't know how to deal with the situation because I can't stop staring at you like some weirdo." She seemed relieved when the waiter brought their menus, and she ordered a white wine before she continued. "You just pulled the chair out for me, and you're looking at me like you genuinely like me, and I need to get used to that."

"I more than like you, Meghan." Florence tilted her head and regarded her. "Has no one pulled out a chair for you before?"

"Honestly, no." Meghan shrugged. "When I'm with you, I feel like I'm the only one for you, and that's special to me." She paused. "And at the same time, I can't stop overthinking things. I've been thinking and thinking all day, and that isn't something I normally do."

"What are you thinking about?" Florence asked. She had a pretty good idea, but she needed to hear her say it.

"Where do I start? Just everything..." Meghan said. "What am I doing? What are *we* doing? Who am I? Who was I? Who will I be? Why have I never tried this before? Am I bisexual? Or am I gay? And if I am, have I wasted the past two decades of my life? What will my friends think? My family? My colleagues? What about that family I always wanted? Will my future look different now? I don't want to tell Kim yet, but if I can't even tell my best friend, then how do I tell others?" She sighed. "Something along those lines."

"That's a lot." Florence took her hand this time and squeezed it gently. "As I said, if you need time, we don't have to do this."

"No. I want to see you. If there's one thing I'm sure of, it's that I want to be with you, right here and right now." Meghan squeezed back, then glanced around as if she was suddenly worried people were watching her. Letting go, she inched away and thanked the waiter, who brought her wine. "Anyway, there's no point discussing my confusion. It will only confuse me more. How about we order food?"

# 31

## MEGHAN

*T*he sun had set, and by her second drink in, Meghan finally found the strength to bring up one of the questions that had been on her mind. They had talked and laughed over delicious tapas, and she'd made sure to steer away from serious topics, but she was ready now. Everything was easier in the dark, especially after some liquid courage.

"How did you feel when you realised you were bisexual?" she asked. "You made it sound so simple when we spoke the first night you stayed over. You talked about it as if it was merely a realisation, but aside from breaking up with your boyfriend at the time, surely, it couldn't have been easy."

Florence shook her head. "No, it wasn't easy, and I never meant to imply that it was. I asked myself the same questions you're asking yourself now because I needed to know who I was. But no matter how much I thought about it, I always ended up with the same counter question: Does it really matter? Does it matter if I'm straight or bi or gay? Will it impact on my happiness? I didn't think it would, so I decided not to label myself and embrace every attraction I felt." She shrugged. "And now, I don't think about it at all. I'm attracted to a person and that's that."

"Again, you make it sound so simple." Meghan gave her a small smile.

"It took me some time to get here, and it's different for everyone. It's natural to be confused."

Meghan nodded. "Will you stay with me tonight?" She brushed Florence's foot under the table.

"To help you figure things out?" Florence shot her a wink.

"Yes. I'll definitely need more practice before I can make up my mind," Meghan said playfully. "That's *my* process. Different for everyone, right?" She felt more at ease now, and she'd almost lost her sense of self-consciousness. Almost. She still felt like people were looking at them, especially when Florence touched her, but she knew it was all in her head. Who cared if two women were on a date nowadays? She didn't. Her family and friends didn't; at least, she didn't think so. Last night on the beach, she hadn't cared if people saw her kissing a woman. She'd been in her own little world, swept away in the wondrous, life-changing moment, but her world was back to normal, and bigger today. It involved others, both strangers and people close to her. "Do you think I should tell someone?" she asked, her expression turning serious.

"Tell them what exactly?"

"I don't know..." Meghan hesitated. "That I have a crush on a woman. And that I think I might be a little gay or something."

"A little gay or something..." Florence smiled and reached under the table to stroke her thigh. "Yup," she said when Meghan took in a quick breath at her caress. "Definitely a little gay." She shook her head. "I'm sorry, I shouldn't be joking about this. I know it's not easy for you."

"It's okay." Meghan laughed and noted it didn't take much for Florence to set her on fire.

"Anyway, to answer your question," Florence continued, "I think you should do what feels right. If you want to talk about it with someone other than me, do so. If you don't, keep it to yourself until you've got your thoughts and feelings in order." She paused "However, for me, it was good to discuss it with friends because it made it real. My friends weren't surprised, and they didn't judge me, and talking to them helped me with the process."

"Right." Meghan thought of Kim and frowned. Kim wouldn't be surprised if she'd told her she'd kissed Florence, but she'd certainly raise a brow if she admitted to her feelings.

"Either way," Florence said, "I'll be here for you, and you can call me anytime if you want to talk."

"Thank you." Meghan shot her a grateful glance. "You're wise for a twenty-five-year-old."

"Hey, don't throw the age card on the table. I am who I am, and age has nothing to do with it." Florence narrowed her eyes as she regarded her. "Is my age a problem to you?"

"No." Meghan shrugged. "Well, you are almost ten years younger, but..."

"But it's just a holiday fling, so it doesn't matter?" Florence finished her sentence. She didn't sound accusing, but Meghan could tell by her expression that it bothered her.

"No, I didn't mean it like that. I—" Meghan stopped herself because she hadn't thought about Florence in any other context than the here and now. "I don't know if it would be a problem to me. I don't know anything right now." She leaned closer and lowered her voice. "How do *you* feel about us?"

"Complete honesty..." Florence picked up one of the last pardon peppers in the bowl, then dropped it back. "This feels right to me, so I would love more, and not just while you're here. I'd like to explore where it could lead." She cleared her throat. "But I'm also realistic, and I know you're not ready for that. And yes, I'm a lot younger than you. Also, I'm just a simple bartender and you're a casino boss. We're at different stages in our lives."

"I'm not a boss. I manage a small casino," Meghan protested. "Work has nothing to do with this. I don't care what you do for a living."

"But age could be a dealbreaker?" Florence asked.

"I haven't thought that far."

Florence nodded. "That's okay, I don't expect you to have your thoughts in order. This is a lot. But I want you to know how I feel. I'll miss you when you're gone."

"I'll miss you too," Meghan said, and she meant it. "But I can't make any promises."

"I know. Let's just be together while you're here. We don't need to think ahead." Florence put on a brave face and smiled. "Do you want dessert?"

"No. Not unless you do." Meghan's appetite still wasn't back. The constant butterflies made it hard to eat, and anticipating their night ahead, she couldn't wait to get Florence out of that white shirt.

"I'm good." Florence asked the waiter for their bill. Clearly on the same wavelength, her eyes sparkled with mischief as she turned back to Meghan. "We could go to the hotel," she suggested, looking her up and down as if undressing her with her eyes. "I wouldn't mind having *you* for dessert."

## 32

---

# FLORENCE

"*A*re you sure you don't want to stay here and wait for Kim?"

Meghan shook her head. "I'm sure. I already messaged her with an excuse. She won't mind being on her own for a while, and she can always hang around the restaurant while Andres works." She smiled. "It's your day off, so I'd love to do something together. I'm meeting Kim and Andres and one of his friends for dinner tonight, though, but that's not until seven."

"Great." Florence felt her stomach rumble. She hadn't been able to eat much last night, and her body was screaming out for food. "How about breakfast?" she suggested.

"Perfect. I'm actually hungry for the first time in days." Meghan ran a brush through her hair, then ruffled a hand through it. She was wearing an elegant navy dress Florence hadn't seen before and she looked beautiful with white leather sandals and little pearl earrings. "Do you have a favourite breakfast place?"

"I do have a regular, but it's under my apartment, so it's

probably best if we go somewhere else." Florence stared at Meghan's reflection in the mirror. "I'll be all, over you when you're looking like that." She bit her lip and winked. "Beach or town?"

"You decide." Meghan turned away from the mirror to look at her with a dazzling smile, then closed the distance between them and wrapped her arms around Florence's neck. "Anywhere a little private is good for me."

"Then beach it is." Florence pulled her close and kissed her. She couldn't get enough of those soft, full lips and although she'd gladly just stay here and go back to bed, there was also something to say for being out and about in the daylight with Meghan because they hadn't had that chance yet. This was an opportunity to talk more, and she was looking forward to getting to know her better. "Are you up for taking a bus?"

"Of course." Meghan grinned. "What, you don't think I take public transport in London?"

"Well, you are a casino boss. Don't you have a white limo or something?" Florence joked. "With some hot women in the back?" She held the door open for Meghan, wishing she had a car or any other form of private transportation to show her around. It wasn't very gallant to make her go on a bus, but Meghan didn't seem to mind.

"Yeah, lots of hot women," Meghan shot back at her, then added, "In bikinis. We drink Champagne straight from the bottle, and I eat sushi from their breasts."

"Now that's a sexy picture you're painting." Florence pushed her against the wall in the lift and kissed her again. Their playful and sexy interaction had her hormones raging, and running her hands under Meghan's dress, it was hard to hold back as she felt her tense under her touch. "I wouldn't mind being in the back of a limo with you," she whispered, moving her mouth to Meghan's neck. "Do you know what I would do to you?"

"What?"

The lift abruptly came to a halt, and it shook so hard that Florence shrieked as she jumped back. "Fuck. What was that?" Her eyes darted to the operating panel, and then she spotted the red emergency button above it. *Did I just push Meghan against it?* They waited in silence, but nothing happened.

"I think the lift broke," Meghan said, straightening her dress.

"No. We caused it." Florence pointed to the red button.

Meghan gasped. "Oh, God. I did wonder what was pressing into my back. Her gaze shifted around. "Are there cameras in here?" She winced as she nodded upwards, to the opposite corner. "We're busted."

"Security cameras rarely work," Florence said nervously while she waited for someone to come and save them. "Is it warm in here? It feels warm." She opened a couple of buttons on her shirt and noted her heart was racing. They were stuck, there was no way out right now, and that made her incredibly uncomfortable. "We need to get out of here."

"Someone will come soon enough," Meghan said, placing a hand on her shoulder. "Hey, are you okay?"

"Yeah, I'm fine. Why?" Turning away from Meghan and trying to prise open the doors, Florence's breath quickened. "Why won't they open? Aren't they supposed to give way just a little so we can get oxygen? Isn't that what they do in the movies?"

"There's a vent in the ceiling. We won't run out of oxygen, no matter how long it takes." Meghan took her face in her hands and forced her to look at her. "Don't panic, Florence. Just breathe. It's really important that you stay calm right now. Nothing is going to happen. You're safe, I promise." She glanced over the operating board and pressed 'call'. It rang a couple of times, but no one answered.

Half kicking herself for not coming up with that idea herself, even though she was having a serious meltdown, Florence pressed the button again and again. "Why are they not picking up?"

"I don't know. Maybe the security guard went for a break? It could be anything." Meghan took her phone out of her purse. "I'll call reception from my phone, but to be honest, they're probably already onto it." She locked her eyes with Florence's. "Please sit down on the floor and try to breathe. I've got this. We'll be out of here in no time."

Florence nodded and sank down in a corner. She felt like she was suffocating and there was no way they'd ever get out of there. *The lift might drop, and what if the lights go out?* "I can't breathe," she whispered, leaning forward to tug at the door.

"Stay with me, Florence. You're having a panic attack," Meghan said, lifting Florence's chin and turning her face towards her. "The phone is ringing—they'll pick up soon. Breathe in while you count to four..." She nodded when Florence did so. "Good. now hold it for four counts and then breathe out over four counts. Keep doing that while I get help. Can you do that?"

Florence tried to concentrate, but Meghan's voice fizzled out and dizziness took over. She felt like the lift was spinning. *Are we falling?* That was her last thought before her mind went blank.

## 33

# MEGHAN

"She'll be fine. Just make sure she hydrates and gets some rest." Stella, the poolside manager, put a blanket around Florence's shoulders and rubbed her back. They'd moved her into a spacious room behind the reception desk that was filled with files, cardboard boxes and messy stationary cupboards.

"Thank you." Meghan already suspected Florence had fainted because of her panic attack, but she was relieved that Stella, who was a qualified first-aider, agreed with her. Florence had only been out for about twenty seconds, and by the time she came around, security had sent the lift down to the ground floor. "I'll take her home."

"I'm fine," Florence protested. "Seriously, I don't need to rest. I've just got a headache, but that will go away."

"I still think you should see a doctor, just in case. Has this happened before?" Stella asked.

"What? Me being stuck in a lift?"

"You know what I mean." Stella looked at her pensively. "The panic attack. Are you claustrophobic?"

Florence shook her head and shrugged. "I don't love

small spaces, but I rarely use lifts and I've never been stuck in one, so I've never thought about it much. As soon as it stopped, though, I felt like the walls were closing in on me and I was desperate to get out, so yeah, I suppose I may be claustrophobic."

"You're part of the hospitality team, right?" the security guard asked. He was big and tall with broad shoulders and a bald, sunburnt head. "So you have no reason to go up there. The lift is only for guests, maintenance and housekeeping. Why were you up there? And why did you press the emergency button?"

"Not now, Sergei," Stella said as her eyes shifted from Florence to Meghan and back. "We can talk about this later, but Florence needs to get some rest first."

"It was me." Meghan shot Sergei and apologetic look. "I pressed it by accident."

"You have to press it pretty hard for the lift to stop."

"I guess I did. I fell against it. I'm sorry." Meghan gave him her most innocent look. She was not going to have Florence take the blame for any of this. "Florence was kind enough to return my purse to my room. I left it downstairs after breakfast." She sincerely hoped Florence was right about the cameras not working because if Sergei saw the footage, it wouldn't look good for her.

"There. See? There's always a reason." Stella smiled at Sergei, but Meghan also saw a flicker of worry in her eyes. "Let's leave it at that, shall we? The lift is up and running again and everyone is fine. I have to go back to work, and Florence needs to rest."

Sergei hesitated for a moment, then nodded. He clearly took his job very seriously. Although it was nice to know the security guard didn't just come in with the purpose of falling asleep in front of the cameras, he was being awfully strict about the matter. He stepped back and looked Florence over once more. "You're not wearing your uniform."

"Her shift hadn't started yet," Stella lied. "And *I* asked her to bring up Meghan's purse. I know that's not the protocol, but sometimes it's easier and quicker than going through reception and housekeeping, as it can take up to an hour before guests finally have their belongings back." She tilted her head and raised a brow at him. "You know that."

Sergei nodded again, and he finally looked like he was bored with interrogating them. "Okay. Have a good day, everyone. And stay away from the big, red button from now on."

"I will." Meghan helped Florence up. "Can you walk?"

"Yes, I'm fine." Florence put on a brave face, but she still seemed unsteady on her legs.

"Come on, let's get you home." Meghan put an arm around her waist.

"That's very kind of you, but I'll drive her back," Stella said, stopping them. "I can't have anyone see you doing that." She took a deep breath before she continued. "Look, I have no idea what happened in that lift, and I don't want to know, okay? But here's a word of warning. Whatever you two are up to, it can't happen on the hotel premises. What you do outside the hotel grounds is your business as far as I'm concerned, but not here."

Florence nodded. "I know. I'm sorry." She turned to Meghan and squeezed her hand. Will you come and find me later? I'll message you my address."

"Of course." Meghan was still shaken herself as she headed for the breakfast area to get a coffee. She'd rather get in a taxi and ask the driver to follow them, but she suspected that might be pushing it with Stella. Apart from her own panic attacks, she'd never witnessed anyone else having one and she'd been terrified when Florence passed out. She knew what it felt like, and she feared Florence might not ever set a foot in a lift or a small space again. Meghan thought about that as she helped herself to a coffee and sat on the terrace. A voice roaring through the speakers announced an ab-tastic class in the pool and she saw Manuel, Florence's colleague and housemate, head for the pool in a pair of ridiculously small, red Speedos. As soon as the music started, he addressed the guests and gestured for them to join him in the pool for a workout.

It was amazing how many of them got in, and even some of those who hesitated were persuaded by his comical enthusiasm. It was a brave thing to do. Meghan couldn't imagine herself doing that; she'd be terrified no one would join in, and addressing crowds wasn't her thing either. Florence was never afraid to yell through the microphone; from what she'd told her, she wasn't afraid of anything. Meghan stretched her legs in front of her and sank into thought as she watched the class. It seemed like Fearless Florence wasn't so fearless after all...

## 34

### FLORENCE

"*H*ow are you feeling?" Stella glanced at Florence sideways as they drove out of the car park. "Still dizzy?"

"No, just a headache." Florence blew out her cheeks as she opened the window. "I had no idea I was claustrophobic."

"I'm sorry that happened to you. But as Sergei said, you have no business being in that lift, especially when you're off duty, so you won't be using it again." Stella paused. "You can't go up there anymore, Florence. I sincerely hope he doesn't look at the security footage because that could get me in trouble too."

"I didn't think the cameras worked," Florence said sheepishly. She met Stella's gaze and was relieved not to see anger in it. "I'm so, so sorry, and thank you for covering for me. I wasn't thinking."

"I figured as much. I was willing to turn a blind eye, but I can't have you making out in lifts at work, so you'll have to take this elsewhere."

Florence nodded. "Are you going to give me an official warning?"

"No. We're going to pretend it never happened and hope for the best," Stella said. "You only have seven weeks left on your seasonal contract, so don't screw it up now that you're almost done. You're good at your job, and I'd love to have you back next year." She shrugged. "And between you and me, yes, there's a big chance the cameras are out of order. They're always talking about repairing them in budget meetings."

"I promise I won't screw it up." Florence stuck her head out of the window and closed her eyes. "I wasn't just messing around. I really like her."

"It seems she likes you too. How long is she staying?"

"She's got nine days left."

"And how do you feel about that?" Stella asked.

"I wish we had more time to see where it could lead. It feels special," Florence said honestly. "I'm worried it will fizzle out after she leaves, or that she will change her mind when she's back in London." She pointed to the main boulevard. "Left here and right at the third set of traffic lights."

Stella followed Florence's instructions. "She lives in London? That's convenient."

"Yes, but as I said, it's been a bit of a whirlwind, and I'm not sure how she'll feel when she gets home. She's never been with a woman before, and I'm quite a bit younger, so I wouldn't blame her if she doesn't want more."

"Oh... Right, I get that you're a bit worried." Stella frowned and bit her lip as if she was mulling over something before she continued. "Would you like to take some time off?"

"Are you serious?"

"Absolutely. High season is over, and I'm sure there are

lots of people on the team who would love overtime now it's not so busy anymore."

"Huh. I thought you might give me a disciplinary or worse, but instead you're offering me time off..." Florence chirped up. The thought of more time with Meghan instantly made her feel better. "I'd love that. Thank you so much."

"Good. Email me the dates so I have it on record and enjoy your time with her," Stella said. "I really hope it works out for you. I know how it feels and I can relate."

"I really appreciate that. How are you and Lisa?" It felt a little strange to ask her manager such a question, as they rarely got personal with each other.

"We're good." Stella smirked. "We're very, very good, and Lisa's here to stay. She's got a job she loves, she's living with me, we share two adorable little puppies, and we're happy."

"That's amazing." With all the gossip going on at work, Florence already knew this, but she kept that to herself. "So, she's the one?"

"Yes. No doubt about it," Stella said resolutely.

"How did you know?" Florence asked. "How did you know she was the one?"

"She made me incredibly happy, and I couldn't stand the thought of being without her. This might sound cliché, but when I see her, I feel like the sun comes up. She warms me from the inside out."

"That's so sweet." Florence pointed to the right as they neared her street. "This one."

"You live close to work." Stella took the turn and drove to the end of the street until Florence gestured to her apartment. "And you have a café right underneath." She laughed as she spotted the closed shutters opposite. "And a strip club nearby. How convenient."

Florence laughed too. "Yes. I share the apartment with another woman who's never home—she's a flight attendant —and with Manuel."

"Manuel from work?" Stella shot her a humorous look. "That must be interesting."

"It can get a little noisy when he brings girls home, or when he has poker nights with his friends, or when he's grunting while working out, but all in all, it's not so bad. He's a good guy." Florence opened the door but stayed where she was for the moment. "Please don't tell him about the lift, though. It might sound weird, but I'd rather people didn't know."

"Of course. This stays between us. I hope your headache goes away soon. Take it easy and have fun with Meghan."

"I will." Florence got out of the car and smiled back at Stella. "Seriously, thank you. You're an amazing boss."

## 35

## MEGHAN

*M*eghan looked up at the three-storey building and smiled when she saw Florence sitting on her balcony. "Room service!" she yelled, holding up the tray of coffees and the bags containing takeaway breakfast.

"Hey! I'll buzz you in!" Florence disappeared inside and seconds later, the door opened. The hallway was warm and stuffy, and the old building needed work, but the location was central, and Meghan liked the cheery, no-nonsense café underneath with its busy terrace and local clientele. Walking up the second flight of stairs, she saw Florence waiting for her in the doorway, dressed in a pair of jersey shorts and an old T-shirt that was torn at the edges.

"Sorry about my outfit. It's what I put on when I come home, and I wasn't thinking."

Staring down at Florence's legs, Meghan didn't mind her skimpy outfit at all. "I like it." Still sensing vulnerability in Florence's demeanour, Meghan inched closer and gave her a long, clumsy hug while she balanced the coffee tray. "How are you feeling?"

"Much better, thank you." Florence took the breakfast bags from her, walked ahead into the kitchen, and put them on the counter. "Sorry about the mess. I decided early on that I wasn't going to clean up after Manuel, so I've just learned to live with his mess. As long as he takes the trash outside twice a week and does his own dishes, I can cope with the clutter. Luckily, we have a cleaner who comes in on Fridays, otherwise I don't think we would last," she added with a chuckle.

"The perks of living with a bachelor." Meghan handed her a coffee and glanced around the kitchen. The drying rack was overflowing with plates, cups and cutlery, empty beer cans were spilling out of the bin, and the counter was full of cereal boxes and protein powders. There was a small breakfast table with a checked cloth and a dead plant, and three chairs, one of which had a leg missing. "It's not so bad, though."

"Wait till you see the living room." Florence unpacked their breakfast and plated the croissants, scrambled eggs and salmon. "Yum. Thank you so much for this. You really didn't have to do that."

"You just fainted. You need to eat." Meghan placed a soft kiss on her cheek and lingered against her. Their interaction was easy today; natural even, as if they'd known each other much longer.

"Mmm... I like being taken care of." Florence's goofy grin spread wide, and she turned to kiss Meghan on the tip of her nose, then beckoned her to follow.

"I see what you mean," Meghan said, taking in the living room. She burst into laughter at the sight of numerous mats, dumbbells, rubber bands and other workout gear scattered over the floor. A huge, cracked mirror was propped against one wall, and training schedules were stuck to the wall above the sofa with duct tape. "I assume this isn't your stuff either?"

"No." Florence laughed and rolled her eyes. "Manuel is so vain, he works out in front of the mirror every day, then spends another ten minutes there, checking out the result." She walked out to the balcony and put the food on a small folding table, then fetched two chairs from inside. "Let's eat here. It's much nicer."

Meghan sat down opposite her and leaned over the railing facing the street. As she glanced down, she could see a small strip of beach in between buildings. "You have an ocean view. That's pretty special."

"Yes, we have a tiny sliver of ocean view, and we also look out onto a strip club." Florence pointed to a large sign on the ground floor of the building opposite, which read 'Diamond Club'. The club was closed, and the security booth in front of the entrance was covered in white graffiti. "It opens at eight in the evening if you're interested in going. I thought since you're a casino boss..."

"Don't tempt me," Meghan joked. "Have you been there?"

"Nope. Manuel went once when we first moved in, and even he didn't want to go back." Florence took a bite of her croissant and moaned. "This is good. I actually really needed food."

Meghan noted that although Florence seemed back to her normal self, she occasionally shivered as if she was cold. "Are you sure you're okay?" she asked. "You gave me quite the fright."

"Yeah. Mostly, I just feel embarrassed." Florence looked away. "It came out of nowhere."

"Don't be embarrassed." Meghan reached over the table

and took her hand. "Do you think I should be embarrassed about my panic attacks?"

"No..." Florence's eyes widened as she shook her head. "No, not at all. That's not what I meant."

"Well, then. You shouldn't be embarrassed either. I'm going to tell you what you told me. Your fear is real to you and therefore very valid. Now that you know that being stuck in a lift—or any small space, for that matter—will cause a reaction, you can choose to fight it, or you can avoid situations like that in future." Meghan shrugged. "I thought I was ready to face my fears, but I wasn't."

Florence gave her a small smile. "I think for now, I'll just avoid lifts too. It's not like it's going to get in the way of how I live my life." She hesitated. "In a strange way, I'm glad it happened when it did because you were with me, and I don't know what I would have done without you. I also think I have an idea of how you feel now, when you're alone in a hotel room. It's horrible, and I wish I could make that better for you."

"But you *have* made it better." Meghan got up, walked around the table and gave Florence a hug from behind. Holding her tightly, she buried her face in her neck and breathed in her scent. Her hair smelled of her shampoo, which Florence had used this morning, and her skin carried a vague hint of sunshine. Meghan loved her scent and wished she could bathe in it. "I miss you already even though I'm still here," she whispered. She hadn't planned on saying those words, but she felt them.

Florence squeezed her arms tightly and pulled her closer. "I've been thinking about that too." She got up to hug Meghan back, and Meghan's heart swelled with warmth. "Stella gave me some time off, so if you'd like to spend the week with me, I'm free," she said, resting her chin on

Meghan's shoulder. "I know you're here with Kim, and you probably have plans, but if there's any chance you—"

"Yes," Meghan interrupted her. "I'd love that. I want to spend as much time with you as I can. I'll talk to Kim and make up an excuse. Andres is taking some time off too, now that they're making wedding plans, so I think I can make it work."

"Really?" Florence inched back to look at her. "That's great. Anywhere you'd like to go or something you'd like to do?"

"Honestly, I don't care as long as I'm with you." Meghan smirked as she gestured at the view. "Even the Diamond Club would work for me."

## 36

## FLORENCE

*M*eghan's knuckles turned white as she clung to Florence's bedframe. She was on her knees, facing the wall, loudly moaning each time Florence thrust into her from behind. She looked so sexy that Florence had trouble holding back, but she wanted this to last. The bed was shaking and banging against the wall, no doubt reaching the neighbours. It was the best kind of noise, the noise that sent her to the brink of a climax herself, just knowing Meghan was enjoying this very, very much.

After breakfast, they'd fallen into her bed, and she'd carefully approached the subject of sex toys. Florence loved her strap-on, but she'd been apprehensive to bring it up. Still, Meghan had insisted she should show her everything, and there had been no hesitation from her side when Florence finally took it out of her bedside drawer.

"I want that," Meghan said, and what followed was a kiss so heated that neither of them was interested in wasting time on foreplay. They'd ripped each other's clothes off, and the look Meghan had given her when she asked her to turn around was something Florence would never forget.

Meghan wasn't shy in the bedroom like she'd been the first night. Now that they were used to each other, she was wild and adventurous, like she was eager to try everything all at once.

Intense flashes of arousal shot between Florence's thighs as she watched the vibrating shaft slip in and out of Meghan, who dropped her face into the pillows to stifle her cries. Florence's hands were on Meghan's hips, her fingers digging into her skin, and her thighs were burning from the strenuous position. The way Meghan moved along, sensually rolling her body, was an incredible sight, and Florence thrust deeper when Meghan's breathing became erratic.

"Yes." Meghan pushed against her. "Yes!"

"You like that?"

"Yes. That's ...ama—" Meghan could hardly speak through her short breaths.

Sensing she was close, Florence moved faster, deeper, harder as she felt her own climax building from the friction and the vibrations against her clit. "Come with me, baby," she said, moving her fingers between Meghan's legs and running them through her wetness. Meghan cried out at her touch and started shaking when she circled her most sensitive spot. Unable to hold back any longer, Florence closed her eyes as waves of delight radiated from her core. They crashed together, their joint voices filling the room with the sound of ecstasy. Their damp bodies were slippery when Florence collapsed on top of Meghan and took her hands.

"Jesus." Meghan sighed as Florence kissed her neck. She was still out of breath, quivering with aftershocks. "Where have you been all my life?"

"Practising for when I finally got to meet you." Florence chuckled as she pulled out and rolled off her. "Come here," she said, taking Meghan into her arms. She nuzzled her neck, cherishing their closeness.

"I love this," Meghan whispered. "Not just the sex, but this. I wish I didn't have to go out tonight. I'd rather stay here with you."

"I'm sure you'll have fun with Kim."

"I will. And I want to meet Andres, but Kim's got this stupid idea in her head that she wants to set me up with one of his friends. Obviously, I'm not interested," she hastily added. "But Kim doesn't know that we're..." She hesitated. "That you and I are doing this."

Florence felt a pang of jealousy, but she pushed it to the background. "So, is it a double date?"

"Not as far as I'm concerned," Meghan said. "I already told Kim I have no desire to be set up, but she insisted." She stroked Florence's hair and kissed her forehead. "We could meet up after? If you want to spend the night with me."

"Of course. I won't let you be on your own."

"You know I'm not just asking because I'm afraid to be alone, right? I love falling asleep in your arms and waking up with you. And if you'd prefer to have some time to yourself, I'll find a way to get through the night. I don't want you to feel pressured to keep me company and—"

"Shhh..." Florence kissed her. "I want to spend every free minute with you, but I can't stay in your hotel room after the lift incident. Maybe you could come here after the double date?" Florence immediately regretted calling it that, as it sounded like a stab.

"Please, Florence, it's not a date." Meghan inched back to meet her eyes. "Are you jealous?"

Florence pursed her lips and stared at her. "A little," she admitted.

"Why?" Meghan asked. "Can't you see I'm crazy about you?"

"But you've been with men all your life. That must be more comfortable for you. I bet he's handsome, and what if you do like him?"

"I won't." Meghan sighed. "I'd much rather bring you, but then I'll have to tell Kim, and I'm not—"

"I know, I'm sorry." Florence groaned as her eyes flicked to the ceiling. "Why am I being so dramatic? I promise you, I'm not a jealous person by nature and I normally wouldn't care."

"I like that you care." Meghan smiled. "Want to hear something that will make you feel better?" She raised a brow and dropped a pause for dramatic effect. "His name is Tiger."

Despite the feeling of unease in her stomach, Florence couldn't help but laugh. "Okay... That's funny."

"Yeah." Meghan laughed too. "You're not the only one to be jealous, by the way. I was so upset when I saw you with that woman at Pit Stop. It was awful. It felt like my gut was twisting and trying to escape through my throat. So I know what it feels like, but I'm not ready to tell Kim."

"I'm sorry I made you feel that way, and once again, I have zero interest in Amber." Florence stroked Meghan's face, wallowing in the warmth of her skin. It was a little unsettling that they were already having conversations like this. Jealousy was too serious an emotion to fight since they weren't even in a relationship, and she already knew she'd be a mess when Meghan left and went back to her own life. "I don't expect you to tell Kim. I don't expect you to tell anyone," she continued. "Just have a lovely time tonight and come back here whenever you're done, no matter how late."

## 37

## MEGHAN

"Finally, we meet. Kim has told me so much about you." Andres hugged Meghan tightly, then turned to his friend. "This is Tiger. He's British, but he lives here. We work together."

"It's so nice to meet you both." Meghan reached out to shake Tiger's hand, but he too, pulled her into a hug. Tiger lived up to his name. He was tall with broad, muscular shoulders, and as he squashed her in his grip, she saw that one of his arms was covered in a tiger-striped tattoo. He smelled of cheap aftershave and had way too much gel in his combed-back hair, but he wasn't unattractive, she supposed.

"That's how we do it here," he said as he stepped back and shot her a wink. "Hugs and kisses only."

"Nothing wrong with getting a good hug from a handsome guy, right, Megs?" Kim giggled as she sat down next to Andres.

Meghan didn't reply to Kim's comment, but she shot her a warning look. Clearly, the message hadn't sunk in, and in Kim's eyes, this was still very much a double date. The table was small, the chairs squashed close together, and Tiger took advantage of the situation and draped an arm over the backrest of her chair. *Here we go.*

"Congratulations on your engagement," Meghan said to Andres, diverting the conversation away from hugs and kisses. She'd seen more pictures of Andres than she could count, but he looked better in real life. Kinder, she thought. He was tall, like Tiger, and it was sweet how Kim, who was much shorter, nestled herself in the crook of his arm. "You look really happy together."

"Thank you. We are." Andres shot Kim a loving, sideways smile. "I can't wait for Kim to be my wife." He turned back to Meghan. "And I hear you're going to be the maid of honour. Tiger will be my best man, so we thought it might be nice if you two got to know each other."

"Sure, why not?" Meghan inched away when Tiger moved closer.

"I could show you around town," he offered. "Kim told me you're on your own at night, so I'm happy to entertain you."

"Or we could meet up with the four of us?" Kim suggested when Meghan didn't answer. "Andres and I are seeing his parents tomorrow and his brother the night after, but I'm sure we can squeeze in a night or two before we leave. We could get together to plan the wedding." She shot Meghan a smile. "I feel bad for leaving you on your own."

"Don't feel bad. You really don't need to entertain me." Meghan shrugged. "I like having evenings to myself, and I haven't been bored once."

"Still, wouldn't it be nice to hang out with a local?"

"There's a concert in town," Tiger chipped in. "Tomorrow. I'd like to take you there."

Meghan ground her teeth and forced a smile. She could

feel Kim's eyes on her and made sure not to look her way. She was annoyed with her friend for trying to set her up even though she'd been clear she wasn't interested, but she couldn't really blame Kim either. Kim had no idea what had been going on with Florence. She was oblivious to Meghan's inner turmoil and all the new feelings that consumed her. If she'd never met Florence, she may have been open to a fling with a handsome man, even if that man had a ridiculous name. But she *had* met Florence, and that had changed everything. It had changed her past into a question, her present into the most confusing situation of her life, and her future into an uncertainty because the desire she felt was real and potent, and it wasn't going to go away.

"That's very nice of you, but I have plans tomorrow," she said.

"Okay, what about the day after?"

"I'm..." Meghan let out a long sigh. "Look, I'm very sorry," she said. "I'm sure you're a super nice guy, and I'm happy to get to know you better if we're going to help out with the wedding, but I don't have much time while I'm here."

"What? Why?" Kim narrowed her eyes at her. "Why are you so busy all of a sudden?"

Meghan wanted to kick her under the table to make her change the subject. Why was she pressuring her? Couldn't Kim see that she had no interest in Tiger? "I'm meeting Florence," she said, at a loss for another excuse.

"The bartender?" Kim laughed. "Again? Didn't you go out with her last night? Come on, Meghan. I've known you for years, and even though you might be a bit curious, there's no way you're gay, so why waste your time?"

"She's not a waste of time," Meghan shot back at her,

sharper than she'd intended. "I like her, so I want to hang out. What's so funny about that?"

"Okay, okay." Kim held up a hand. "I was only trying to help. You're single, and Tiger's single, so I figured you two might hit it off but do what you want. It just seems pointless to hang out with someone you'll never see again, that's all." She turned to Tiger, who looked confused, mostly, and Meghan suspected he wasn't used to being rejected by women. "She's befriended this lesbian bartender."

"She's bisexual," Meghan corrected her.

"Whatever, it's all the same."

"It's not." Irritated that Kim was making lightly of something she'd been conflicted over for days, she picked up the menu, hoping they'd get the hint that she was done talking about Florence.

"Is she into you?" Andres asked. "You're a beautiful woman, and if she's—"

"No." Meghan's core tightened as steamy memories attacked her again. It was hard to think of anything else. When she was with Florence, she wanted her, and when she wasn't, she wanted her just as much. "We're just friends," she said, feeling like a coward. She was a thirty-four-year-old woman, a grown-up, and she didn't even have the guts to tell her best friend the truth. She looked from Kim to Andres and back. "Now, can we stop talking about me, please? We're here to celebrate your engagement, and I'd like to order us a bottle of Champagne."

## 38

# FLORENCE

"Spot me, will you? Can you add eight kilos to the bar?"

"Eight? Are you sure?" Florence groaned as she added weights and lifted the barbell into Manuel's outstretched hands. "Fuck, that's heavy." His new home gym equipment had just arrived—a bench press that took up a third of the living room—and he was eager to test it.

"I can handle it." Manuel blew out his cheeks and did four reps, then nodded for Florence to put it back on the stand. He breathed hard and shook out his arms. "Four more kilos."

Florence raised a brow but did as he asked. It was almost too heavy for her to lift, and her arms ached just watching him. "Seventy kilos in total. That's impressive."

"Just wait till you come back next year. I'll be doing competitions."

"What competitions? Mr. Benidorm?" she joked. "In that case, you might have to get a spray tan. I don't think you're quite orange enough."

Manuel chuckled and got up to stretch. "Nothing wrong

with Mr. Benidorm. It's a renowned bodybuilding contest." He flexed his arms, admiring himself in the mirror, then headed for the kitchen.

"Right." Florence followed him and saw he was making a protein shake. "No beer for you?"

"Not right now. I have to feed these bad boys." He patted his arm, then added a pint of water and a slug of boxed egg white to the brown powder he'd scooped into his mixer. "Want one?"

"Gross. I'll have a beer instead." Florence opened the fridge and took one out. "Are you not going out tonight?"

"Later." Manuel turned to her and frowned. "What are you doing home by yourself? You're hardly ever home at night."

"Meghan's gone on a double date," Florence mumbled. "Well, not a real one. Her friend, Kim, set her up, so she's going with Kim's fiancé and someone called Tiger, believe it or not. She has no interest in him, but I don't like it, and I don't know what to do with myself." She sighed "I bet he's all over her by now."

"Who are you and what have you done to my friend?" Manuel stared at her like she was some rare species he'd never seen. "You're saying Meghan's having dinner with her friend, her friend's fiancé and some random guy she has no interest in. That sounds totally acceptable to me. It's not like they're on a romantic date."

"Yes, well, it still bugs me."

"Oh boy, you're in trouble." Manuel snickered. "There is going to be drama when she leaves, and I don't do drama."

"I won't bug you with it. It's not your problem." Florence picked at the label on her bottle. "Do you think he's flirting with her?"

"With Meghan? Undoubtedly. She's hot, so yeah, I would. I mean if I were *him*," he quickly corrected himself.

"Great. That makes me feel better," Florence said sarcastically. She glanced at her phone. It was only eight o'clock, but it felt like midnight. "So, what are your plans later?"

"I was going to meet some friends in town, but I've changed my mind." Manuel patted her shoulder. "I think I'll keep you company." He downed his protein shake straight from the mixer cup and put it back on the counter with a slam. "You're acting weird, so I want to keep an eye on you," he joked, then opened the fridge and took out a cold beer.

"Thanks. That's sweet." Florence glanced at him as they headed to the balcony. "Why are you being so nice to me?"

"What do you mean? I'm always nice to you."

"No, you're not." Florence sat in her usual chair and propped her feet up on the balcony railing. Manuel was always about Manuel, and although they were great friends, she wasn't used to him being so supportive. "You love making fun of me."

"But not right now. You're fragile." Manuel met her eyes with a smile. "Look, Meghan likes you. I saw it with my own eyes at work, so why are you so worried?" He paused. "You're cool and beautiful and fun to be around, and she knows that too."

Florence chuckled. "Was that a compliment?" She poked him playfully when she saw him blush. "Do you think I'm beautiful?"

"Sure, I do." He took a slug of his beer and leaned over the railing, his eyes darting to the strip club that was in the process of opening for the night. "But not in a hot kind of way. I don't want to sleep with you if that's what you think. You're more like a little sister to me."

"We're the same age," Florence said dryly.

"But you're little in size. I could throw you over my shoulder."

"Please don't." Florence laughed. "So, you think she's just as much into me as I'm into her?"

"For the third time, yes, I do." Manuel ruffled a hand through her hair and tapped her head. "Will you please stop overthinking? Just stop thinking in general. It's not good for you."

"Fuck off." She pounded his hard abs with her fist, then screeched when he picked her up like she weighed nothing and threw her over his shoulder, making her beer spill all over them both. "Put me down, you idiot! Seriously, Manuel!"

"Nah," he said cheerfully. "I'm going to do some squats now, and you're the perfect weight to work out with."

## 39

# MEGHAN

"*A*ndres is driving. We'll drop you off at the hotel." Kim got up and took Andres' hand. "Right, love?"

"No need, I'm fine," Meghan said. Despite the challenging start, the night had been fun, and she liked Andres very much. Even Tiger wasn't so bad; although he had tried it on a few times, he'd eventually given up.

"I wouldn't dream of letting you go back by yourself." Andres dangled his car keys from his index finger.

"I mean it. I'd like to walk. The beach is nice at night." Meghan lingered by the table, hoping they would leave so she could head in the opposite direction, to Florence's apartment.

"Then I'll walk with you. I'm going the same way." Tiger held up a hand. "Don't worry, I got the message. You're not into me, it's fine. But I'm still a gentleman, and a gentleman never lets a lady walk home in the dark."

"Great idea. Why don't you two head back together?" Kim hugged Meghan goodbye, and that hopeful sparkle in her eyes was back. Meghan knew what she was thinking:

maybe if she and Tiger spent some time alone, he'd grow on her, and then they'd fall in love, and they could all hang out together, get married, have babies at the same time and live happily ever after in Spain. Okay, maybe not to that extent, but she was positive there was a hint of selfishness to Kim's eagerness. "Tiger's right. It's dark, and I don't want you wandering around alone."

Meghan suppressed a groan. This was Benidorm, not some shady neighbourhood on the outskirts of London. "Fine," she said. "Walk with me." She could always shake him off and jump into a taxi later, but for now, she couldn't see a way out.

Kim's eyes widened in excitement, and she gave her another hug. "Give him a chance," she whispered in her ear. "He's a nice guy." She stepped back and rubbed Meghan's arm. "See you tomorrow for a late breakfast?"

"Tomorrow?" Meghan hesitated. She didn't want to rush back early tomorrow just so she could pretend she'd slept in her room. "Can I message you to confirm?" Kim opened her mouth, no doubt about to ask a million questions, so she quickly added, "Just in case...you know..." She glanced sideways at Tiger, who was talking to Andres by his car. It was a stupid thing to say; she was only buying time, but it was too late to come back from it.

"Of course." Kim bounced on the spot and pumped a balled fist. "I knew you'd like him, although you have a weird way of showing it." She lowered her voice. "Have fun, Megs. I get why you wanted to walk now. You need to work on your moves, though. You haven't exactly been flirting with him."

Meghan nodded and smiled half-heartedly, then waved Kim goodbye and waited for Tiger to join her. "Over the beach?" she asked.

"Yes, I love the beach. It's the very reason I relocated here." Tiger put a protective arm around Meghan, and although it irritated her, she waited until Andres drove off before she inched away.

"I'm sorry," she said, "but I'm not heading for the hotel. I only said that to get Kim off my back."

"Oh." Tiger stopped at the zebra crossing and turned to her. "Then where are you going?"

Meghan sighed and shiftily looked to the sky. Her heart was pounding, and her palms felt clammy. If she told him the truth, he might tell Andres, and Andres would tell Kim. And if Kim knew, she'd have to tell her everything. "I'm spending the night with Florence," she eventually said, taking a chance. Her shoulders dropped in relief as if uttering the words had physically deflated her. "The woman Kim mentioned earlier. The bartender."

"Why didn't you just say so right away?"

"Because I don't know what I'm doing," Meghan said honestly. "I'm only just starting to figure out this part of me, and I'm not ready to share it with anyone."

"But you're telling *me*?"

"I didn't have much choice, did I?" Meghan shrugged. "I couldn't just walk off. That would be rude. Besides, it's easier to confide in a stranger."

Tiger nodded. "Thank you for being honest." He pulled her back, as people were waiting to cross the road, and continued behind a parked car. "So, are you in love with her or something?"

"I'm not really sure. I just know that I want to be with her. I need to be with her. It's like a strange pull has taken over every nerve in my body and every cell in my brain, and I'm acting on impulse alone." Meghan didn't expect him to understand, the way she was prattling on, but it felt good to say it out loud. "I can't think straight."

"Wow. That's deep." Tiger raised his brows. "And you're not going to tell Kim? I thought you guys were super close."

"I will tell her eventually, but I need time to figure this out on my own first." Meghan met his eyes. "Are you going to tell Andres?"

"No. Why would I do that?" A hint of offence flickered in Tiger's eyes as he furrowed his brows.

"Because he's your best friend."

"He is, but you're telling me this in confidence, and I'm not an arsehole."

"No...you're not." Meghan gave him a smile. "Thank you. I really appreciate it, but you don't have to lie for me either."

"I see it more as helping out a new friend. Seriously, it's fine." He winked and pulled his phone out of his pocket. "Here, take my number. I'll be your alibi until you tell Kim."

Meghan stared at him for a long moment before she flung her arms around his neck. "Really?"

"Yes." Tiger patted her back, then gently pushed her away. "Just don't squeeze me so hard. You're hot, and I'm only human." He grinned. "I'm not going to lie. When I saw you arrive at the restaurant, I was seriously keen on taking you out."

"I'm sure you'll find someone else to take out." Meghan reached out to squeeze his biceps. "Women must be lining up for this." She smiled as she entered her number and waited for him to send her his. "So, friends?"

"Friends," he said. "Message me when you're desperate for an excuse." He waved his phone at her before he slipped it back into his pocket. "Does your girl live far? Do you want me to walk you to her place?"

*Your girl.* Meghan winced at his words. It was strange to

hear him say it—and something she might have to get used to. "Thank you, but as you know, it's perfectly safe." She smiled and gave him another grateful glance as she held her hands in a praying position in front of her chest. "Thank you, again. I'll make it up to you one day."

## 40

## FLORENCE

"Tiger is your alibi?" Florence turned Meghan's way as they walked. Her mind was spinning as she processed what Meghan told her. It was only ten o'clock when Meghan showed up, so she'd met her outside and suggested they'd go for a walk. The little beach bar on a concrete platform overlooking the sea was closing soon, but Florence's uncle owned it, and he didn't mind her hanging out there while the staff was winding down over after-work drinks. "Let me get this straight. You're pretending you're with Tiger so you can spend time with me?"

"Yes." Meghan fell silent as she chewed her cheek. "I don't feel good about lying to Kim, but you should have heard her. She was so pushy with Tiger. And she wanted to have breakfast with me tomorrow morning, and I didn't know what to say, so I may have indicated that I like him. I explained everything to him, and he said I could use him as an excuse to see you."

Florence took her hand as they crossed the road to the beach. "That's nice of him." She should have felt relieved, but the fact that Meghan was lying to her best friend didn't

LISE GOLD

sit right. "You'll never be able to keep this up the whole week, though."

"Possibly, but at least it will buy me some time."

"I don't want to claim you," Florence said. "I don't want you to lie for me. Just do what you need to do. I'm not going anywhere."

Meghan shook her head. "No. You took time off for me, and I want to see you." She put an arm around Florence's waist, and Florence melted.

She led them along the shore to where the strip of beach became narrower. She was dating a woman who used a man as an excuse to see her. Was she losing herself? Was she being untrue to herself just by taking part in this?

"I just worry about your relationship with Kim in the long run, but I suppose that's none of my business," she said, knowing deep down that wasn't the real reason why it felt wrong to her. Out and proud, she'd always vowed never to be anyone's secret after a difficult short-term relationship with a closeted woman, but here she was, hiding behind Tiger, who would supposedly be 'dating' Meghan for the rest of her stay.

"Does it bother you?" Meghan asked. "I sense something..." She paused. "I don't know. I feel like you're annoyed about the situation."

"No," Florence lied. "I'm fine—as long as we can be together." Realistically, she knew the chances of this working out were small to begin with, and remembering Manuel's words to have fun and make memories while it lasted, she shook off her unease and focused on the good. They'd only just met; it wasn't serious. Meghan was everything she'd ever wanted, and although it wouldn't be forever, she had her for now. Maybe that was good enough. "Do you feel like a nightcap?" she asked, pointing to the bar, which had just turned off its lights for the night.

"Sure. Can we go there? It looks like it's closed."

"I can, and you're with me." Florence winked. "It's so much better without all the tourists."

She walked ahead up the steps and knocked on the door. The owner looked irritated when he first opened it, only to break out into laughter when he saw her. "Florence, come here." He crushed her into a hug and greeted Meghan, then gestured for them to walk through the venue. "I see you have a lady friend with you. How about a bottle of rioja?"

"Thank you, Uncle Edgar, that would be lovely," Florence said, pulling her bank card out of her back pocket.

"No, no, no, no, no. I don't want your money. Go out there and enjoy yourselves," he insisted, pushing a bottle and two glasses into her hands. "Anything for my favourite niece. Is this a romantic occasion?"

"It might be," Florence said sheepishly, then thanked him for the wine.

"Very well, we won't disturb you. Have fun, ladies."

"That's your uncle?" Meghan whispered as they passed a handful of staff members drinking at the bar.

"Yes, my mother's brother. I didn't want to tell you upfront because I thought you might freak out if I mentioned family." Florence chuckled. "But he's more like a friend to me, so don't worry. It's super casual."

"He seems sweet." Meghan followed her outside to the back terrace and closed the door behind them. "And wow, this is so lovely." She looked out over the horizon that was sparkling in the moonlight. "And so quiet."

"It is, right? Just the rustling of the waves and the chatter of staff inside. They won't bother us and my uncle won't either." Florence opened the bottle and poured them wine.

She liked coming here; sometimes she'd sit outside talking to her uncle until the sun came up.

"I didn't know you were such a romantic," Meghan said, looking her over with a raised brow.

"I wouldn't call myself a romantic, but I want you to enjoy yourself so you'll come back." Florence held up her glass. "Can we toast to a reunion?"

"Yes." Meghan clinked her glass against Florence's, took a sip and hesitated before she continued. "Actually, I was hoping I'd see you in London first."

Florence's heart warmed at Meghan's comment. "Me too." She paused. "Does that mean you see this going somewhere beyond your holiday?"

"I hope so." Meghan gave her a shy smile as she steadied her cheek in the palm of her hand. "I'm hoping I will have come to terms with...well, with this by the time you move to London for the winter."

"Six weeks isn't long."

"No, it's not. And some time apart is probably good, so I can clear my head."

Florence nodded. "What do you want to do? When you're in London, I mean. Do you want to be in contact? Or do you need space?"

"I don't know." Meghan paused. "I'm sorry, I wish I could give you answers, but right now, I don't know anything." She sighed. "I'm comfortable here because we're alone, and I'm fine when we go somewhere out of the city centre, but as soon as I'm anywhere crowded or close to the hotel, I'm constantly looking over my shoulder, worried I'll see Kim."

"That's why I brought you here," Florence said.

"Thank you. It's ridiculous, but..."

"Hey, it's okay."

Meghan nodded. "Have you ever dated someone who wasn't out?"

"Yes, once." Florence's mind drifted to the woman she hadn't thought about for a while. She'd banned her from her memory because she felt guilty for breaking up with her for exactly that reason: she wasn't out. After a few months, she was tired of only meeting in the woman's home and late at night in obscure bars. They could never do something fun and in the open together, and when Florence started doubting her girlfriend would ever come out, she'd taken the decision to move on.

"But I don't want to talk about past relationships," she said, painting on a smile. "Let's just focus on us, right here and right now."

# 41

## MEGHAN

"This is a nice beach. Do you come here often?" Meghan sat down on the blanket they'd brought and opened the bottle of red wine from Florence's backpack. It was quiet, apart from a few couples dotted around, but they were far away, doing their own, romantic thing. The sand was soft and dry, like flour under her bare feet. With the dunes behind them and the dark water ahead, it felt as if they were far from civilisation, even though it was only a twenty-minute bus ride away from the city.

"I haven't been here in a while," Florence said. "But it's nice, isn't it? Because it's so hidden, only locals come here— well, and the occasional tourist who happens to stumble upon it when they've chartered a boat." She took off her sneakers and poured the wine. "I like London, but the best thing about living on the Spanish coast is that there's always a new beach to discover."

"I see why you like it." Meghan took the glass from her. "Where do you live when you're in London?"

"Wherever I can get a room closest to a central Tube line." Florence shrugged. "They're not always the most inspiring places to live, but I never spend much time at home anyway, so it doesn't really matter." She smiled at Meghan. "I bet your apartment is nice. You must have your shit together, casino boss."

Meghan chuckled. "It's okay, but I could probably find something nicer if I took the time to look around. And, no, I don't live in a penthouse with glass tables, an art-deco cocktail bar and a safe room, in case you're wondering. It's just a one-bedroom apartment in Olympia, nothing special."

"I *was* wondering about that, actually." Florence shot her a wink. "Would you have a problem dating someone who was still finding their way in life? Someone who didn't have the stability you have?"

"You mean someone like you?" Meghan tilted her head as she regarded Florence. The word 'dating' was loaded, and it confused her, as she found it hard to picture herself officially dating a woman out in the open. Introducing a woman to her family, bringing her home for Christmas, building a life together and being a couple seemed so far from her bed. "In my opinion, you've got it all figured out," she said, shaking off her thoughts. "Summers here, winters in the UK, doing something you enjoy... What's wrong with that?"

"True. I enjoy what I do," Florence said. "But sometimes I think it would be nice to have a real home. My life is always temporary, wherever I am. I don't even know what job I'll be doing this winter until my agency decides where to place me."

"Monotony isn't everything either," Meghan said. "The same office and the same people day in, day out. Don't get me wrong, I like my job and my colleagues, but it can get a little boring from time to—" She stalled when she heard familiar laughter. "Wait, I recognise that voice." Raising a finger to her lips, she ushered Florence to be quiet. Was she mistaken or was that Kim? It couldn't be...

"Oh, Andres, this is so romantic," she heard Kim say, and her stomach dropped. "Why have you not brought me here before?" Their voices were coming from the dunes behind them, and as she looked over her shoulder, she saw two dark silhouettes descending.

"Fuck," she whispered, then turned her back to them so they wouldn't recognise her face.

"Just relax," Florence whispered back. "It's dark, they won't even see it's you. Stay quiet and they'll probably just walk past us."

Deep down, Meghan knew Florence was right, but she couldn't think through her anxiety. In a reflex, she got up and ran in the opposite direction without waiting for her. She ran and ran, until she was out of breath, then sank down in the sand, feeling horrible for leaving her behind. After a few minutes, she saw Florence approaching in the distance, carrying the blanket, the wine bottle, and their glasses as well as her backpack with their shoes.

"I'm so sorry," she said, taking their glasses when Florence finally caught up with her. "That was a silly thing to do."

"A little." A hint of irritation flashed across Florence's face, but she smiled dryly and knelt to rub Meghan's shoulder. "Are you okay?"

"Yeah." Meghan frowned as doom scenarios ran through her mind. "Wait. They're not coming this way, are they?"

"No. they went the opposite direction." A silence fell between them as Florence settled on the sand. "Would it be so terrible if she saw us together? She knows we're friends, right? Or are you ashamed of being seen with me?"

"No, of course not. Do you really think that?"

"It's hard not to." Florence shrugged. "Your reaction was extreme. You ran like your life depended on it."

"I'm sorry," Meghan said again, frustrated with herself and still shaken by almost being caught. "I told her I was with Tiger."

"Right. I forgot about that." Florence clenched her jaw. "And where does she think you are?"

"At a restaurant. I kept it vague." Meghan took her hand. "Do you mind if we go to your place?"

"You want to be in my stuffy room rather than outside on a beautiful night?" Florence stared at her, and Meghan was desperate to know what went on in her head. "You kissed me on the beach that night. You didn't care what anyone thought. And we've been out for dinner together. We went on a date. What's changed?"

"I wasn't thinking when we first kissed. I acted on impulse, and I'd just started processing things when we went on the date. But I'm aware now, over aware perhaps. Because it's real, you know? You and me, it's happening." Meghan paused. "I don't care about strangers, it's just Kim."

Florence nodded, but Meghan wasn't sure if she understood. The fear of someone she knew finding out she was sleeping with a woman haunted her like it could ruin her life, even though rationally, she knew that was nonsense. "I have no idea why it frightens me so much."

"Okay, let's go to my place, if that's what you want." Florence leaned close and cupped her cheek. "Manuel might still be home getting riled up for a night out. He can be a bit repetitive after a few drinks, but we can always stay in my room."

"Thank you. And I'm sorry, I—"

"Shh...it's okay." Florence rested her forehead against Meghan's. "I don't want you to be afraid or on edge, ever."

## 42

## FLORENCE

*F*lorence remembered the idyllic scene from her childhood, and not much had changed in the small coastal town called Villajoyosa, which was only a short drive or, in her and Meghan's case, a forty-minute bus ride from Benidorm. It was still as laid-back as ever, especially now that the high season was over, and as they followed the long promenade that stretched all the way from the harbour to the city centre, they passed dogwalkers, local families, fishermen returning from the harbour and countless old ladies with trolleys on their way to the market.

"What a pretty town." Meghan stopped to take a few pictures. Villajoyosa's iconic colourful three-, four-, and five-storey houses lined the promenade and the streets of the old town behind the beach. Painted in every colour under the sun from azure blue to bright pink and soft yellow, it was truly a happy sight. "I've never seen so many colourful buildings."

"Yes, I love 'La Villa', as the locals call it," Florence said, taking in Meghan as she zoomed in on a yellow house behind a group of palm trees. It looked picture-perfect against the bright blue sky, and Meghan was equally alluring and colourful in a yellow sundress. "My parents used to bring me here on daytrips when they were still together. We had a boat, so we'd sail here and spend the day at the beach, playing games and eating ice cream. They're good memories."

"That sounds dreamy." Meghan took her hand as they continued their stroll towards the old town. "Was it hard for you when they split up?"

"It was, especially in the beginning, as my father moved back to the UK and I missed him, but eventually, I saw how much happier they both were after the divorce, so that made it easier. My mother started her own business and became more social, and my father was delighted to move into a modern apartment without crystals and incense. For me, flying back and forth two weekends a month was exciting too. It made me feel grown up."

"You flew by yourself?"

"Yes. I was eight when my mother dropped me off at the airport for the first time. I was looked after by nice flight attendants, who gave me chocolate on the flights, and my father picked me up at the other end."

"I bet that was fun. I'm trying to imagine you as a kid," Meghan said. "You must have been super cute with that full head of curly hair."

"I was." Florence shot her a cheeky wink. "I still am."

"Yes, you are." Meghan bit her lip and grinned as she turned to her. "You're the cutest." She pulled Florence behind a tree, gently pushed her against it and kissed her. "And so, so sexy," she continued, brushing her lips against Florence's. "I crave you all the time. It's constant."

Florence closed her eyes and moaned softly. Flashes of arousal shot through her as she parted her lips and sank into the heavenly kiss. "I wish we had more privacy," she whispered. "I'd love to take your dress off and fuck you right here, right now."

Meghan gasped when Florence turned them around, so she was backed up against the tree. A small smile played around her lips, and Florence could tell by that look in her eyes she had fantasies running through her mind. She pushed herself into Meghan, pressing their hips together, then inched away when Meghan tried to kiss her again.

"Tease."

"Hey, you started it." Florence licked her lips and smiled. "But I'll make it up to you tonight."

"Promise?" Meghan took her hand again, and they turned onto a side street off the promenade.

"I promise I'll make love to you until you're too tired to move." Florence felt Meghan's grip tightening at her words, and although she wouldn't mind heading back to her room right now, they were here to have lunch. "Are you hungry? For anything other than sex?" she added with a smirk.

Meghan laughed. "I could eat." The street ran into a square with equally colourful buildings, most of them housing coffee shops, bars and restaurants. The tables and chairs outside were shaded by red parasols and surrounded by blue planters with pink bougainvillea. She glanced over the cheery terraces and smiled. "How adorable. Want to sit here somewhere?"

"How about the paella restaurant?" Florence suggested. "It's been here since I was little. It used to be really good." She greeted the owner and pulled out a chair for Meghan. "Have you been to any of the other villages around here?"

"Yes, I've been to a few. When we came here on holiday when I was younger, we used to book excursions, but the villages we visited were whitewashed, with white houses and churches. This is so different."

"I know, it's unusual for the area," Florence said. "Some claim La Villa is colourful because the fishermen painted their boats in unique colours so they could easily recognise each other, then used the rest of the paint for the façade of their houses. That's the story my father told me anyway."

"It's a nice story. Are you looking forward to seeing your father soon?"

"Sure. But it's not like we spend a lot of time together when I'm in London. We have dinner or lunch together once or twice a month, and I see him over Christmas. My grandparents and my aunt and uncle from his side live in London too, so we spend the holidays with them. That is, if I'm not working." Florence tried to imagine Meghan's family, but with such young parents, it was hard to picture them. "What about you?" she asked. "Are your grandparents still around?"

"My grandmother from my father's side is still alive, and both my grandparents from my mother's side too. Other than that, we're a pretty small family." Meghan smiled. "We're close, though. I see my parents at least once a week."

"And Kim? How do you know her?" Florence hesitated. "Sorry, am I bombarding you?" She wanted to know everything there was to know about Meghan apart from the thing they'd agreed not to talk about: their future. Ten days into Meghan's holiday and they'd become quite skilled at avoiding the subject, but there was one question she kept asking herself: what was the point in getting to know each other if it might not lead to something lasting?

"No, I like talking to you," Meghan said. "And I have so many questions too. I feel like there's not enough time to cover them all."

*There it is. Not enough time.* It was only more evidence that Meghan was counting down the days until she left and wasn't thinking any further ahead than that. *Don't think about it. Just enjoy the moment.*

"Okay, your turn, then," Florence said, taking the menu from the waiter.

Meghan waved a hand, declining the menu, and pointed to the paella sign by the door. "My friend says you do the best paella, so I'll have that, please." She turned back to Florence. "Want to share?"

"Always."

"Excellent." Meghan brushed her foot under the table, her eyes fixed on Florence. "So, my turn... I guess what I would like to know is, what are your favourite childhood memories?"

## 43

## MEGHAN

"My favourite childhood memory..." Meghan thought about that as they strolled along the beach, back in the direction of Benidorm. It was such a nice day that they'd decided to walk until they got tired and then take a taxi home. "I don't know. Yours are all so idyllic, I can't compete with that." Florence had told her about the boat trips to Vilajoyosa, her first time in London, the first time she went camping with friends as a teenager and a visit to Barcelona with her mother when she was ten.

"It's not a competition," Florence said. "Just tell me whatever comes to mind."

"That would have to be our holidays, then." Meghan bent down to pick up a pretty shell, brushed it off and put it in her handbag. "The anticipation was half of the fun. Weeks before, I'd get all excited and start packing my most precious clothes, and my mother would always take me shopping for a new swimsuit and teen magazines before-hand." She stopped to check out a pile of shells, brushing her bare feet through them. "And then, finally, the best two weeks of my year arrived. The flight, being somewhere sunny and warm, and making new friends to play with in the pool brought me just as much joy as seeing my parents so happy." She laughed. "Looking back, it was probably the alcohol that made them laugh so much, but who cares, right?"

Florence grinned. "That's sweet. I'd love to see some old pictures of you."

"I don't have any on my phone, but I can ask Mum to send some. If you show me yours, I'll show you mine." Meghan put an arm around Florence's waist and pulled her in. Sometimes, when she wasn't overthinking, it felt so natural to be with her, and right now, she could happily have walked for miles, holding her hand and stopping for a kiss each time they reached a quiet spot. She'd been giddy all day and not for another double date with Kim, Andres and Tiger tonight. It was just something she'd have to put up with because doing that allowed her to be here without worrying too much.

"I'll see what I can do." Florence bent down to pick up a tiny piece of something shiny and pink and held it up against the sun."

"I wonder what it is," Meghan said. "Is it glass? Such a pretty colour."

Florence studied it from all angles and gave it to Meghan. "Don't quote me on it, but I think it's tourmaline."

"As in the crystal? How would that end up here?"

"It's not uncommon to find small pieces of quartz or other precious stone on the beach. The sea carries many treasures. My mother used to look for them during our beach outings and quiz me about them. I pretended to have forgotten over the years but I actually remember quite a lot. Keep it."

"Thank you." Meghan opened her wallet and carefully placed it in a side compartment. "Is it worth anything?"

"No. I can get you a bigger piece if you want. My mum has all sorts of crystals in her practice."

"That's sweet, but it's extra special when it's found." Meghan searched the sand for more but didn't find any. "So how does it work? The crystal healing?"

"I think the correct question would be, 'does it work?'" Florence arched a brow. "If you ask me, it doesn't, but the principle is that the crystals give off energy that can balance your chakras. Have you heard of chakras?"

"Yes. They're like energy points in the body, right?"

"Something like that. There are seven chakras in our body, starting with the root chakra at the base of our spine. That's the one that grounds us. It's connected to the earth and regulates our basic need to survive. The last one is on top of our head. That's the crown chakra, and it's connected with the divine and our higher selves. In between, there are five others, each related to certain organs and energy wheels in our bodies. My mother places crystals related to a certain chakra on those energy centres and claims to heal people that way."

"You're talking about her job like she's a charlatan," Meghan joked.

"She used to have her practice at home before she opened her shop, and I've never seen anyone miraculously heal, let me just leave it with that," Florence said. "But it gave her a purpose in life, and that's what's important, I suppose."

"Everyone needs a purpose." Meghan shook her head. "I have no idea what mine is, though. There are lots of things that make me happy, but I don't have anything specific that I'm passionate about."

"I believe love is a good purpose to have in life," Florence said. "That's one piece of advice from my mother I haven't discarded. "Love and you'll receive love in return."

"Karma?"

"Yes. I try really hard not to be an arsehole."

Meghan laughed. "You couldn't be an arsehole if you tried. You're a good person, Florence." She kissed her cheek. There was so much she wanted to say, but all those things still felt too deep to discuss. Anything that came from her heart might be a betrayal; she wasn't even sure if she trusted her heart. Was she getting carried away or was this real? Was Florence an escape? Or was it possible that their dreamy relationship could last in real life?

They'd passed the part of the strip where most of the restaurants and bars were situated, and glancing around, she only spotted a few people on the beach. "Want to stay here for a bit?"

"Are you tired?" Florence asked.

"No." Meghan met her eyes with a look of mischief. "I want to lie down with you and kiss you."

## 44

## FLORENCE

Okay, this was painful. After a beautiful day together, Meghan was with her pretend boyfriend, and it was getting late. Florence had expected a message from her by now, saying she was on her way back, but she was clearly having fun. With Manuel at work, Florence didn't even have him to distract her, so she'd called her ex, who was still one of her closest friends, and they'd met up in a bar in town.

"Stop torturing yourself and let her go," Juan said. "This is so unlike you. I don't see you for two weeks, and suddenly you're besotted with a tourist and acting like the world is going to end when she goes back to where she came from. It's always a bad idea to date tourists. Always. They leave you with promises and then you never hear from them again. And don't even get me started on bi-curious women."

"Because I used to be one?" Florence asked. Juan was long over her, and he didn't hold a grudge, but the reminder that she hurt him badly still stung.

"Exactly. I thought we were going to get married once upon a time, and then you left me because you had to explore your sexuality." Juan held up a hand. "Don't get me wrong. I understand you needed to do that, and it's also exactly what Meghan needs to do. You think that she'll stick with the first woman she crushes on? Nuh-uh. Never going to happen." He looked at her pensively. "And she pretends to have a boyfriend. I mean, that's just stupid."

"I don't think she planned it this way," Florence said in Meghan's defence. "She's just not ready to come out."

"She might never be. This might be a phase. Surely, you can see that. And how do you know she's not in bed with her fake boyfriend right now?"

"Meghan would never do that. I know her and—"

"You don't know her," he interrupted. "You can't possibly know someone after ten days."

"You didn't know Elle either," Florence protested, referring to Juan's fiancée, who was French. "And she was a tourist, so don't be a hypocrite."

"Elle is different," Juan said matter-of-factly. "We just work together."

"Meghan and I work too."

"When it's convenient for her, maybe." He took a sip of his beer, and Florence couldn't help but smirk. Juan still drank beer like some women did; taking tiny sips and wincing like he didn't enjoy the taste of it. He'd always done that, but she thought he might grow out of it one day. "Trust me, I've been there—with you—and it's not going to end well, so take a step back and protect yourself from the pain."

"I can't." Florence shrugged. "I'm already too deep in."

"There's always a way out." Juan took her hand. "Look, you're a good friend, and I truly care about you. That's why I want you to be happy with someone who is open and available, whether that's a man or a woman."

Florence gave him a smile and nodded. "Thank you, I appreciate it. But it's not that simple." She beckoned the waiter for another round and watched Juan light up a cigarette. She felt so fidgety that she was close to asking him for one, even though she hated smoking. "I thought you gave up."

"I did." Juan laughed. "For three months, and then I had a cheeky one after my set one night and I've had a couple since. I only have one sporadically. It's not like I'm back to being a smoker."

"You're smoking. That means you're a smoker." Florence arched a brow at him. "Does Elle know about your sporadic cigarettes?"

"No, she doesn't, and she doesn't need to know. My smoking is innocent."

"Sure. Just a little white lie…"

Juan took a long drag from his cigarette, then stubbed it out in the ashtray on their table. "Thanks, Flo. You've just ruined my cigarette and now I feel bad." He took another tiny sip from his beer. "I'm a DJ. I'm always surrounded by people who smoke. It's hard not to."

Florence studied him in bemusement. "I don't smoke, so it shouldn't be that hard right now. Although I get the sentiment," she admitted. "It must be nice to have something to focus on when you're on edge."

"I'm not on edge."

"Yes, you are." She pointed a finger at him. "If anyone knows you, it's me. You always get nervous this time of year because the season is over, and you're worried you haven't made enough money to get you through the winter." She shot him a teasing smile. "And in your current situation, you're also worried you won't be good enough for your fancy lawyer fiancée if you have to scrape the barrel to take her out for a nice dinner from time to time."

"Bullshit." Juan looked her in the eyes, but Florence

knew she was right. That was the great thing about being friends with her ex; she knew him so, so well. "Elle doesn't care about money," he said.

"You're right. She doesn't. I've met Elle a few times, and she's a lovely lady, but your deep-rooted insecurities and traditional Spanish upbringing still whisper to you that the man should be the breadwinner. That's why you're always so down in winter." Florence tapped the table. "Just tell her that. She's probably wondering why you're so gloomy this time of year, and it's best to be honest. Be honest about the smoking too. It will only improve your relationship, I promise."

"Says the woman who's dating a woman pretending to have a boyfriend." Juan let out a sarcastic chuckle. "Who's lying to who now? Because I think you're lying to yourself, Flo."

"I'm not lying to my—" Florence took in a quick breath and stopped herself when her phone lit up. It was her mother, asking why she hadn't been over in so long. "Sorry, that was my mum."

Juan laughed. "You thought it was Meghan, right? You're suffering from a typical sad case of tourist infatuation." He glanced down at his cigarettes and added, "But to be honest, I'm glad it was your mum. I wouldn't mind having another one. How is your mother?"

"She's good. Still 'healing'." Florence made quote marks in the air, which lingered when another message came in, this time from Meghan.

*I'm sorry it's so late. Kim wanted to play a game and it's going on forever. I'll make my way to your place soon, promise! Can't wait to see you. Meghan xxx*

"I know that look on your face," Juan teased. "Tell her to

come here so I can meet the woman who's got you so twisted."

"Not a chance." Florence took a couple of notes out of her wallet and slipped them under the ashtray. "'Hey, Meghan, come and meet my ex when you're done with your pretend date'?" She chuckled. "I prefer a bit of normality after tonight. No offence to you," she added and gave him a hug. "Thank you, my friend. Drinks on me and enjoy that cigarette."

## 45

---

## MEGHAN

"What have you two lovebirds been up to?" Kim asked as she set the table on the balcony of Andres' apartment. "Any romantic trips? Dinners?"

"We've had a nice time," Meghan said shiftily, leaning into Tiger when he put an arm around her.

"I took her to Benidorm Island," Tiger chipped in. "I borrowed a boat from a friend, and Meghan got a little seasick on the way, didn't you, Meg?"

"Yeah…" Meghan turned to him and forced a smile. "How did all of this roll off his tongue so easily? He called her 'Meg' like they were super close, and he clearly had no problem lying.

"Aww, bless. I didn't know you got seasick," Kim said.

*Neither did I.*

"We went on a cruise together a few years back and you were fine," Kim continued.

Meghan shrugged as her mind was churning. "The sea was rough, and the boat was much smaller obviously, so I guess that made a big difference. But we still had fun."

"I can't tell you how delighted I am that it's working out between you two. I just knew it, didn't I, Andres?" Kim's eyes widened in excitement as she put down place mats and glasses from the tray she'd brought over. "I told him I was convinced you'd fancy Tiger, and I was right."

"She was right," Andres said. "Kim is always right. That's what she keeps telling me."

Meghan let out a dry chuckle. The more elated Kim got, the worse Meghan felt. She was such a terrible friend and eager to talk about something else. She pointed to the apron Kim was wearing. "Since when are you a domestic goddess? I don't think you ever cooked for me, but it actually smells really nice."

"What do you mean?" Kim shot her an innocent look. "I'm a great cook. I entertain all the time in London."

*No, you don't.* As far as Meghan was aware, Kim could barely boil an egg, and she wondered how on earth she'd produced dinner for four people. The delicious waft coming from the oven was suspicious to say the least, but she didn't voice her thoughts. "Of course," she said instead. "I was only joking. Do you want some help?"

"You can help me plate." Kim beckoned Meghan to follow her into the kitchen and lowered her voice. "And?" she asked in a whisper. "How is the sex?"

"It's..." Meghan hesitated. "It's great," she said. "Really great." Kim stared at her, and she shook her head. "I don't want to talk about it."

"Come on. Why so secretive? 'I don't want to talk about it.' That's all I've heard you say this holiday. Give me something, at least."

Meghan let out a sigh of exasperation. "It's mind-blowing," she said, thinking of Florence. "It's unlike anything I've ever experienced. I'm completely sexually free when I'm with he—" She stopped herself. "When I'm with him."

"Wow." Kim giggled, and Meghan was grateful when she finally opened the fridge to take out the salad she'd prepared earlier. "Look, I understand you're uncomfortable telling me all about it while he's outside, but when we get back, we're going to catch up and you're going to give me details. Deal?"

"Deal." Meghan inspected the salad that consisted of tomato, cucumber and onions chopped so precisely into neat squares that there was no way it hadn't been sliced by a machine. "You didn't make this," she whispered. "It's a deli salad."

"Shh." Kim placed her index finger against her lips. "Andres loves my cooking, so don't spoil it." She took out the oven dish that contained four perfectly even squares of lasagne.

"*Your* cooking?" Meghan laughed. At least she wasn't the only one lying. "If your goal is to convince anyone those are homemade, you need to rough them up a bit. Because no one will fall for that." She took a knife out of one of the drawers and sliced a bit off the sides, so the portions were less even. "That's better."

"Shame. They looked so pretty." Kim jutted out her bottom lip as she plated them. "There's a great little deli in town. I go there when he's at work, and they do amazing stuff. Yesterday, I made him a beautiful Spanish stew. He said it tasted just like his mother's." She looked at Meghan and burst into laughter. "I guess I'll have to come clean at some point, but I might wait until after we're married."

"You're so bad." Meghan added salad to the plates and carried two of them outside.

It was a beautiful, mild night, and Kim had lit candles on

the table. If only Florence could be here with them, her night would be perfect. In an ideal world, Kim would know, and they could all hang out and have fun together because every moment without Florence felt like a moment wasted. In an ideal world, she wouldn't have to pretend that she was in love with Tiger, and she wouldn't have the constant weight of guilt on her shoulders—guilt from lying and guilt for leaving Florence on her own.

"Kim really outdid herself today," she said, placing the plates in front of Andres and Tiger. "I forgot how much I love her lasagne."

"It's nothing." Kim batted her lashes as she joined them on the balcony. "Just something I whipped up after I came back from my shopping trip." She sat down and looked so happy that Meghan came close to confessing. With Tiger's arm draped around her shoulder, she felt like she was disrespecting Florence too, and that made it even worse.

"I hope we'll get many more nights like this," Kim said, pouring them wine. "You're all my favourite people in the world."

"Kim talks about you like she's got you on a pedestal," Andres said, moaning as he tasted the pre-made deli dish.

"I do. Meghan's my best friend." Kim turned to her and looked at her earnestly. "I love you, Megs."

Meghan swallowed hard and forced a smile as she took Kim's hand. "I love you too, Kimbo."

## 46

## FLORENCE

*U*ncle Edgar's restaurant had become their go-to place at night whenever Manuel was home. It was the only place Florence could think of where Kim and Andres couldn't possibly go, as they only went there after it had closed for the evening. Meghan was at ease there, and she was happy and flirty, rather than shifty. She'd bought Florence's uncle presents to thank him for having them, and she'd already charmed the hell out of him.

"Will you close up, Flo?" he asked, handing her the keys. The staff had left, the lights were out in the restaurant, and the darkness that surrounded them made the stars look even brighter tonight. "Just drop the keys through my letterbox on your way home."

"Thank you. I promise I won't trash the place again," she joked.

"Again?" Meghan raised a brow at her.

"She did, you know." Edgar turned to Meghan and shot her a grin. "On her sixteenth birthday, I let her have the restaurant after hours so she could celebrate with her friends." He shook his head dramatically. "Boy, did I regret that."

"Hey, it wasn't me! The boys I invited were the ones who drank all the alcohol and got into a fight." Florence laughed. "My friend Marita had an older boyfriend, and he brought some friends along. Before I knew it, there were thirty of us instead of twelve, and most of them I'd never even met."

"She was lucky I came by to check on them so I could chuck them out," her uncle said. "One of the boys had thrown up all over himself and my furniture. I dragged him to the shore and gave him a good wash. Never saw him again."

Meghan laughed. "I bet you paid the price," she said to Florence.

"I did. Uncle Edgar sent me to the restaurant kitchen and made me do the dishes every Friday, Saturday and Sunday night for a month."

"Nothing wrong with a bit of tough love." Edgar crossed his heart. "But I kept my promise. I never told her mother."

"Is your mum strict?" Meghan asked.

"Stricter than Uncle Edgar, that's for sure."

"Her mother never let her get away with anything when she was younger," Edgar said. "But she's a sweet woman. Very spiritual."

"So I've heard. Florence told me she's a crystal healer."

"That's right. You should introduce Meghan to her, Flo," Edgar suggested. He shrugged when Florence hesitated. "Or not. That's up to you two to decide. Anyway, I'd better be going. Have a good night, ladies."

"That was awkward." Florence winced. "Sorry about the meeting-my-mother comment. I'm aware it's way too early for that."

"It's okay. He's a lovely man." Meghan regarded her.

"Would you feel uncomfortable if I met your mum? I'm so curious about her, and I was actually planning on going to her practice before you and I happened."

"Wouldn't *you* feel uncomfortable?" Florence frowned. She really didn't get Meghan sometimes. One moment, she was running away from her, the next, she was asking questions like this. "You're the one who doesn't want to be seen with me. Wouldn't meeting my mother freak you out even more?"

"Never mind. I shouldn't have brought it up," Meghan said.

"No, I'd like you to answer," Florence insisted. "You're sending me mixed messages, and I'm falling for you, Meghan, so please don't mess with me. If I'm just a holiday fling to you, I'll get over that, but if that's the case, don't say you want to meet mother."

Meghan stared at her, clearly taken aback by her outburst. Finally, she took a deep breath and nodded. "Yes, I probably would freak out. I'm freaking out about everything at the moment."

"Would it be easier for you if we didn't see each other?" Florence immediately regretted the question when she saw Meghan's eyes well up. She hated herself for making her cry; it was the opposite of what she'd intended.

"No. I care about you, and I want to see you, but I'm struggling. Can't you see that?" Meghan sniffed. "You're right. I shouldn't have said that about your mother. It was reckless, but I'm trying, okay? I'm trying so fucking hard to come to terms with what's happening to me, and I'm sorry I can't give you answers or make you any promises. I feel stupid for acting this way because I come from a liberal background. There's literally no one in my life who would have a problem with it, and I feel ashamed of myself for being so scared." Bursting into tears, she covered her face with her hands.

"Fuck." Florence got up and pulled her into a hug. They only had a few days left together, and she didn't want to ruin that precious time by putting Meghan under pressure. What she was doing was purely selfish; it was ridiculous of her to think Meghan would come to terms with her sexuality over the span of a holiday. She'd needed much more time herself when she realised she was bisexual, so who was she to judge, now that she was on the other side of the fence?

"I'm so, so sorry," she said, holding her as tightly as she could. "I won't bring it up again." Deciding to be entirely honest, she continued with a tremble in her voice. "That was my insecurity talking. I'm just afraid of losing you, even though I know that will happen eventually. You're too good to be true." There. She'd said it. Meghan was too good to be true, and even if she came to terms with her sexuality, that didn't mean they'd be together forever. She might prefer a woman who was more career-driven, someone who had her life in order, or someone older and more mature.

Meghan looked up to meet her eyes and shook her head. "No," she said. "*You're* too good to be true. No one's ever made me feel his way, and I'm pretty sure no one ever will. I just wish you weren't my first because then this would be so much easier."

Florence let Meghan's words sink in. Yes, she was Meghan's first woman, and everyone knew firsts never lasted. Her first certainly hadn't. It wasn't looking good, so she may as well resign to her fate, however depressing that thought was. After all, it was better having Meghan for now than not having her at all.

"Okay, how about this," she said. "No strings, no commitment, no promises, no nothing. Just this." She brushed her lips over Meghan's cheek, tasting her salty tears before she kissed her. Despite her distress, Meghan met her mouth, and they fell into a kiss that felt like far, far more than no strings. "Just the physical," she whispered. "Let's keep it simple."

# 47

# MEGHAN

"My first kiss was on that bar." Florence pointed to the end of the bar closest to the terrace. "Right there on my sixteenth birthday."

"The disaster birthday?"

"Yes. I was a late bloomer," Florence said humorously. "I can't say I enjoyed it, but I'd had a little alcohol and was feeling brave, so I thought I might as well get it over with. All my friends had already kissed or done more, and I didn't want to be the odd one out. I don't even remember his name, but I do remember wondering if he knew what he was doing."

Meghan walked over to the bar and ran her hand over its smooth surface, imagining a younger version of Florence there. She was feeling much better after their talk and two cups of tea. Then they'd watched the stars and chatted casually about anything but their future. For now, purely physical was what she could handle, and so she tried to set her feelings aside so she wouldn't ruin their time by panicking about the bigger picture.

"Were you sitting on it?" she asked. "And how bad was it?"

"Yes, I was sitting, and he was sort of wedged between my legs with his gropey hands all over me while he kissed me like a tumble dryer." Florence laughed as she raised herself onto the surface to demonstrate, and a flirty twinkle flashed in her eyes when Meghan pushed her legs apart and stood between them, looking up at her.

"Maybe we should erase that awful memory and make a better one," she said in a sultry tone. "So you'll stop associating this bar with the worst kiss ever."

"Oh? You think you can do a better job?" Florence's gaze lowered to her lips, and a flash of arousal shot between Meghan's thighs. When Florence looked at her like that, all else faded, and she felt a yearning so strong she ached for her with every fibre in her being.

"I can't promise you that, but I'm happy to give it a go if you'll let me." Meghan smiled as she ran her hands up Florence's thighs and curled them around her waist.

"If I'll let you?" She leaned forward to meet Meghan's lips, and they lingered close, their breaths quickening.

Meghan's heart was racing, and she cherished the long moment of anticipation. Chemistry oozed between them, and adrenaline coursed through her veins before she claimed Florence's delicious mouth. She kissed her sensually and slowly while she pulled her to the edge of the bar to feel her closer, nipping at her lips and running her tongue over them before diving in and taking the kiss to a searing level that set her on fire.

Florence shifted against her as she wrapped her legs around her waist. "A thousand times better," she whispered against her lips and moaned as Meghan's hands slipped under her shirt to caress her back.

"Excellent. I would say my work is done then, but you're older now, and there's no harm in taking it a little further, right? To help you heal from the memory of that awful kiss," Meghan continued jokingly, fumbling to open the buttons on Florence's jeans. She yearned to taste her, to make her explode against her mouth.

Florence grinned as she kicked off her shoes and lifted her hips to help Meghan pull off her jeans and panties. "No harm," she said, her eyes darkening when Meghan moved her legs apart once again and pushed up her shirt.

Meghan loved it when Florence surrendered to her, and she felt in charge rather than lost and confused in her thoughts and emotions. "I love how you smell," she murmured, running her tongue over Florence's stomach while she inched her hands under her sports bra to caress her breasts. After the nights they'd spent together, Florence's body felt familiar yet thrillingly new at the same time. The feeling of her nipples hardening under her fingertips still baffled Meghan, and the soft touch of her skin was one she thought she'd never stop marvelling about.

Florence's chest heaved fast as she watched Meghan kiss her way down to her belly button and lower. Meghan stopped to look up and shot her a teasing glance as she reached the thin strip of hair, then continued kissing the inside of her thighs.

"You're killing me," Florence murmured.

"Just trying to make your new memory as good as I possibly can, that's all." Meghan met her eyes again and bit her lip. "And I have a feeling this will top your experience with the tumble dryer." She kissed her way up the smooth skin until her mouth was against Florence's sex and inhaled deeply. "Mmm... I love this."

"You are so not straight," Florence said through ragged

breaths. "If anything, you're—" Her words became a moan when Meghan ran her tongue over her most sensitive spot. "Fuck, Meghan." Weaving her fingers through Meghan's hair, she pulled her closer and fell back, knocking a few glasses off the bar in the process.

Meghan's lips pulled into a smile as she dragged her tongue up and down, salivating at the taste of her. Florence was wet and swollen, and she pushed hard against Meghan's mouth, begging her for more. Moving her hands to Florence's thighs, Meghan tightened her grip and closed her eyes as she devoured her, drawing circles with her tongue and drinking her in. It didn't take long until she felt Florence's limbs tremble and heard her moans grow louder in sync with her own.

Pulling her hands away from Meghan's hair to cover her mouth, Florence accidentally smacked another glass to the floor before she stifled a long and intense cry. Meghan didn't stop until Florence became limp, then kissed her way back up to her stomach while she stroked her legs, her thighs and waist, taking in all her gorgeous, feminine glory. Florence was the most beautiful woman she'd ever known, and she felt privileged to have her.

"How about those memories?" she asked playfully, taking Florence's hand to help her back upright. "Do you think you'll have better ones next time you come here?"

Florence opened her mouth to speak, then closed it again. Shaking her head, she let out a chuckle and kissed her. "Undoubtedly," she said. "I'll never look at this bar the same way." She slid off it, took hold of Meghan's waist and turned them around, wedging Meghan between herself and the bar. "But there's one more thing..."

"Oh, what's that?" Meghan asked, her voice hitching

when Florence ran her hands underneath her dress and squeezed her behind.

Florence shot her a mischievous smile before she kissed her again. "The good thing about great memories is we can always make more."

## 48

## FLORENCE

*F*lorence reached for Meghan's hand and kissed it. She'd tried not to let her mood get in the way of having one last, blissful night, but it was getting harder and harder to keep that smile on her face. She didn't want it to end, and although they'd decided to leave their ending open for now, it still felt like this may be the last time she'd ever see Meghan.

"Not to be dramatic, but I'm really, really sad that you're leaving," she said, vaguely aware that she should probably turn off the oven. Meghan had made a stew, and although the smell wafting from the kitchen was delicious, she didn't feel like eating.

"Me too." Meghan turned to her and draped her legs over her lap. Manuel was at work, and they were sitting on Florence's balcony. In between kisses and sweet caresses, there had been mostly silence since they came back from the grocery store. "It's going to be strange being back in the real world." She hesitated. "Because I won't have you."

*But you could have me*, Florence thought. *You can have anything you want, Meghan.*

"I'm also very sorry that I can't take this any further right now," Meghan continued as if reading her mind. "I need to take a step back, clear my head and have some space to think."

"Will you be okay?" Florence asked, noting Meghan's mood was possibly even lower than hers. She'd had a hollow look in her eyes all day, and she'd been far from her usual, cheerful self.

"Yes. I will, eventually. I just have a lot of processing to do. I'm not the same person I was before I came here."

"You are, though. You just happen to like women as well as men. Or perhaps only women, but that doesn't make you a different person."

"You don't understand. It changes my future," Meghan said. "It changes my long-term plans." She dug her fingernail into a mosquito bite on her leg, then scratched it until her thigh was red. "I really want a family one day."

"You can still have children."

"With whom?" Meghan stared at her. "With you? You're way younger than me, and we're in different life stages. It's not the same." She paused as she stared down at the street below. "I don't want to be with a man anymore. I simply don't think I can, and now that I've met you, I wouldn't even be open to..."

"To another woman?" Florence clenched her jaw. "Someone who's more mature? Someone with a better job?"

"No! I didn't mean that."

"You make it sound like I've ruined your future, but who says I don't want children? Don't speak for me when you haven't even asked what *I* want. Besides, you're the one with teenage parents. Out of all people, you should know that age doesn't matter when it comes to parenthood." Her resolve to remain calm crumbled, and she shot Meghan a fierce look.

"I asked you if dating someone like me would be a problem to you, and you waved it off."

"It's not just children. It's..." Meghan's eyes were glazed as she let out a huff of frustration and shook her head. "I don't know."

"Exactly. You don't." Florence got up. "You don't know anything." Parting was difficult enough, but hearing Meghan make up excuses when all she craved was a promise was more than Florence could handle, even though it didn't come as a surprise. "I'll get the food," she mumbled, avoiding Meghan's gaze as she headed for the kitchen.

Taking the pan from the stove, she stared down at the stew and let out a deep sigh. Why was she picking a fight, tonight of all nights? Why couldn't she just be with Meghan without expectations? And why was she acting so bloody clingy when she'd never been clingy before? She turned as she felt a presence behind her.

"Do you want me to leave?" Meghan asked, meeting her eyes.

"No." Florence took her by the waist and tugged her closer. "I'm sorry. I don't want you to leave at all, you know that." This push-and-pull was driving her mad, and she wished she could put her emotions on hold. "Shall we eat?"

"Not for me. I'm not hungry," Meghan said. "I just made it for you."

Florence gave her a sad smile. "I'm not hungry either. If I don't, Manuel will eat it. It looks great, but..."

Meghan nodded. "I feel sick too." She wrapped her arms around Florence's waist. "Look, I have to meet Kim at the hotel in a few hours to pack our stuff and head for the airport, as we have an early flight. Why don't we go to your bedroom? I don't want to fight. I just want to hold you while

I can, but if this is too difficult for you, then maybe it's best if I go."

"No. Please stay." Florence felt a lump form in her throat. She'd miss those big, dark eyes, Meghan's touch, her smell, her kisses, her laugh and her smile. "What time is your bus leaving?"

"Five a.m."

Florence nodded, forcing her focus away from that bloody internal clock that was counting down the minutes. "Then come on." Leading the way to her room, she lay down and spread her arms; Meghan scooted close and held her in return. Their foreheads resting against each other, they lay still, in silence. Knowing this may be the last time, Florence closed her eyes and focused on Meghan's breathing, on her warm body aligned with hers. If these were their final hours together, she wanted to remember it all, no matter how painful it would be.

# 49

## MEGHAN

"Will you walk me to Paradise?" Meghan asked, then let out a sarcastic huff. Right now, the name seemed ridiculous, and 'hell' would be more fitting. She didn't want to go back, but work was waiting, and life was waiting. She wasn't comfortable facing Kim either, after avoiding her for the past three days while claiming she was with Tiger.

"What if Kim sees us?"

"You could pretend to be working?" Meghan suggested. "Put on your work shirt. Then it will make sense that you're there."

"Even if it's the middle of the night?"

Meghan shrugged. "Kim doesn't pick up on details. She's not that observant." She watched Florence get up and take off her tank top. She wasn't wearing a bra, and one last time, she took in her small breasts and lean frame. Her eyes darted over the feminine curves she'd caressed and her strong shoulders and back. "You're beautiful," she whispered, sighing when Florence put on her Paradise polo shirt.

"You're beautiful, Meghan." Florence crawled back on

the bed and straddled her. "You're beautiful and special in every way, and I will never forget this time with you for as long as I live."

"That sounds so definite. It doesn't have to be the end." Meghan felt sick, and she fought back her tears. She wasn't going to cry; she'd cried more than she had in years this holiday, which was strange, as it had also been the happiest time of her life.

"I'm not going to go around in circles with you again." Florence cupped her face and kissed her. The touch of her lips was sweet and soft yet electric, and it awoke all Meghan's senses. "You're not ready. Maybe you'll never be ready, and I don't want to be left hanging. I can't handle it."

"You're right. It's not fair to you." Meghan pulled her back to kiss her again, then turned to the nightstand when her phone rang. "It's Tiger," she said with a frown.

"Why would he be calling you in the middle of the night?"

"I have no idea. Maybe something happened to Kim." Panicking a little at the thought, Meghan picked up and put him on loudspeaker while she got up and searched for her sandals. "Hey. What's going on? Is Kim okay?"

"Yes, Kim is fine." Tiger cleared his throat. "It's just that, she called me earlier, and she sounded like she'd had a few drinks. She wanted to speak to you, but you weren't picking up your phone, so I said you were taking a bath. I think she's expecting me to come and say goodbye."

"Right." Meghan hardly dared look at Florence. "I'm so sorry you're caught in the middle of this."

"It's okay. I can come and pick you up if you want? But you owe me one. Your friend woke me up from my blissful sleep."

"Of course. Thank you. I'll send you the address."

"I guess I can take this off again." Florence removed her polo shirt, sat on the bed with a huff and turned her back to Meghan. Meghan reached out to touch her shoulder, but she shook her off. "Don't. I know you have to do what you have to do, but I just want to be alone."

"Please, Florence. Don't be like this. Not now."

"Not now?" Florence's expression was cold as she turned to her. "What does it matter? You're going back, and I'll never hear from you again. That's the truth."

"But I—"

"No," she continued, her voice unsteady. "I'm going to sleep. You can wait on the balcony until your boyfriend arrives."

Meghan cried as she put on her dress and her sandals and gathered her things. She stuffed them into her big handbag and looked over her shoulder before she left the room, but Florence had buried herself under the covers and was shaking as if she was crying. She felt awful for causing her pain with her insecurity and indecisiveness. She'd been selfish; she should have anticipated how bad this moment would be, for both of them, and she wasn't surprised that Tiger interrupting their goodbye was the final straw for Florence.

"Bye," she said, her voice catching. When she got no reply, she left and closed the door behind her. Descending the stairs on shaking legs, she met a very drunk Manuel on his way up.

"Hey, are you okay?" His voice was slurred, but he frowned when he saw she was in tears.

"I don't want to talk about it." Meghan sniffed as she pushed past him and rushed down. "Take care of Florence, will you?"

"Why? What's going on?"

Desperate to get outside, she didn't answer, and finally reaching street level, she gasped for air and sank down on the pavement with her back against the door. A stripper from the club opposite, who was smoking outside, was watching her, and so was the bouncer. They probably assumed she was drunk, just like Kim would assume she was crying because she didn't want to leave Tiger.

It was all so messed up. Her life had turned into a complete and utter lie. Her best friend knew nothing about her, and she didn't understand that much more about herself other than the pain she felt. The pain of leaving Florence, and the pain of hurting Florence was very, very real.

Tiger's arrival brought her some relief at least. He was the only one who knew the truth apart from Florence, and he'd shown her such kindness. He didn't ask questions. He took her bag, helped her up and hooked his arm through hers.

"Let's do this," he said. "Everything will be okay."

## 50

## FLORENCE

"She's gone," Florence said to Manuel when he came into her bedroom. "Go away. I can smell the beer on your breath from here, and I want to be alone." He'd knocked a few times and clearly decided it was okay to let himself in, even though she'd put the damaged 'do not disturb' sign she'd taken from the hotel on her door.

"Meghan was crying," he said.

"I know." Florence pulled the covers further over her head. "And I don't care."

"Of course you care. You're in love with her, and you're a mess yourself. Look at you."

"Cut the crap, Manuel. You can't even see me. Please just go away."

Manuel didn't take no for an answer and pulled the covers away from her face. Leaning over her and almost making her gag with his alcohol breath, he studied her red cheeks with his bloodshot eyes. "I'm going to make myself a strong coffee and sober up," he said, "and then we're going to talk."

"I don't want to talk. And who do you suddenly think you are? Oprah or something?"

"Joke all you want about Oprah. She's right most of the time, and yes, I'll admit it. I watch daytime TV when you're not here. Talking will help, I promise. I'll get you a beer, and I'll have coffee, and in twenty minutes we'll be able to level. How's that?"

~

Twenty minutes later, Florence was sitting on 'Oprah's couch', crying her eyes out. "And then Tiger called, and he picked her up instead," she said, finishing her story with a sniff.

"So, Tiger took her back to Paradise." Manuel nodded and dropped a pause.

It was incredible how he had indeed managed to sober up after a large protein shake, a coffee and two bottles of water, Florence thought as she sipped her beer. Perhaps it wasn't all selfless on his behalf—she suspected he regretted ruining his training routine and macros because he'd planned a weightlifting session tomorrow morning—but it was still sweet and endearing of him to take the time to calm her down.

"And that's it?" he asked. "You're not going to see each other after this?"

"No. That's it. She can't commit." Florence shrugged. "Anyway, it's probably for the best. I wouldn't want to get my hopes up for someone who will never really be mine."

"She needs time."

"She does, but she was also terrified of being seen with me. We've practically been hiding all week. And then she brought up stuff about kids and how we're in different life stages, and…" Florence groaned in frustration. "Never mind. That's about all there is to tell."

"Kids can be a major factor in decision-making." Manuel said, handing her a second beer as soon as she'd finished the first.

Florence rolled her eyes. "Did daytime TV teach you that too?"

Manuel hesitated for a moment as if his mind was elsewhere. "Yes," he finally said before taking a long drink from his third bottle of water. "A relationship is a long-term decision, and how children fit into that relationship matters. If she's already struggling with her sexuality, it's just confusion upon confusion. I'm not surprised she's all over the place."

Florence was annoyed, as it felt like Manuel was picking Meghan's side, but she didn't defend herself. "You really have been watching a lot of shows," she said dryly. Perhaps she was being immature; sometimes she wasn't sure what caused her to act the way she did. "Do you think I should have been more understanding?"

Manuel tilted his head from side to side. "I can't say. I don't know the two of you together." He regarded her through narrowed eyes. "Do you want kids?"

Florence hadn't expected that question, and she was taken aback. "Yes," she said. "I can't imagine not ever having a family, that's for sure. I'd like to have kids."

"But they're not in your five-year plan?"

Florence punched his arm. "Seriously, Manuel. You're scaring me with your super-serious talk. You're not like this normally."

"Just answer my question." He shrugged as if it was no big deal. "Are they in your five-year plan or not? Because even if you can't imagine it now, soon you'll be open to seeing other people again, and you need to keep stuff like that in mind when you get to a certain age."

"You're one to talk. It's not like you have any experience in mindful dating." Florence propped her feet up on the coffee table and shot him a glare. "You shag your way around town like there's no tomorrow." She contemplated cracking another sarcastic joke, then changed her mind and let out a long sigh. "But okay, since you asked... If it was with the right woman—the one—and I felt like the relationship was stable and long-lasting, then yes, I'd be open to children. I'm not *that* young." She leaned back and stared up at the ceiling. "I mean, I may be relatively young and live a life that seems whimsical to some, but that doesn't mean I'm not focused or that I don't have a sense of responsibility. I want to grow in my career, and I'd like a stable life eventually, but I've been single, so I haven't contemplated making plans. This is easy for the moment."

"But if things would have gone differently with Meghan and you two were in a serious relationship, is it something you'd consider with her?"

"Yes," Florence said without hesitation. "And you know what? For a few blissfully ignorant days, I really thought she was the one."

# 51

## MEGHAN

"When are you seeing Tiger again?" Kim pushed her seat back and flicked through a magazine. She wasn't distraught on their return to London. She had a ring on her finger, after all, and Andres had already booked a flight to come and see her in two weeks. "You were so upset. Just know that you can talk to me. I know what it feels like. This time last year, I was a mess on my flight back, but if it's meant to be, it will all work out. You'll see."

"I'm not seeing Tiger again," Meghan mumbled, pretending she was going to sleep.

"What?" Kim poked her. "What do you mean by that?"

"I mean it's over." Meghan kept her eyes closed so she wouldn't have to look Kim in the eye. "I don't want to talk about it."

"Have you told him it's over?" Kim asked, cupping Meghan's chin and forcing her to face her.

"Yes." Meghan jerked out of Kim's grasp and closed her eyes again.

"But why?"

"Does it matter?" Meghan was getting irritated by her friend's questions. She was falling apart and just wanted to be left alone.

"Yes, it matters," Kim said. "It matters to *me*. You're supposed to be my best friend, but you never tell me anything. You've been so goddamn secretive lately."

"I'm not secretive. I just don't see a future with him, that's all."

"You were upset. You were crying, so you clearly care about him." Kim wasn't letting her off the hook. She nudged her again, and Meghan had no choice but to engage in the conversation. "Tell me."

"I don't want to talk about it. He's not the one for me, it's as simple as that. Tiger is a lovely guy, and I'm sure we'll remain great friends, but going forward, it's not going to be more than that." Meghan thought of Florence, and she wondered if she was sleeping. It broke her heart leaving her like she had, and already she regretted handling things in such a black-and-white way. *You had no choice*, she told herself. It wouldn't have been fair to Florence to leave things open; there was no other solution but to distance herself from the woman who consumed her mind. Hopefully by doing so, she'd gain some clarity because it couldn't be that simple, could it? Go on holiday a straight woman and return gay?

"Has it got something to do with that bartender?" Kim asked. "Florence?" She sighed when Meghan didn't answer. "You were practically swooning over her for days. She even brought you flowers, and then, suddenly, not a word. After meeting Tiger, you spent every waking moment with him, and you were totally besotted—as you put it yourself." She paused. "And now you're done with him, and you won't even give me a reason why, so I'm taking an educated guess."

"It's got nothing to do with...her." Worried she might burst into tears, Meghan couldn't even say Florence's name out loud.

Her short answer wasn't taken lightly, and Kim totally lost it. "Listen, Megs. You've been avoiding me all week, and I let it slide because I was distracted with Andres. I'll admit it. Maybe I should have been around more. I feel guilty about that in particular, but you haven't really talked to me once." She slammed a hand on the folding table in front of her. "Not once. Come to think of it, I feel like you stopped talking to me years ago. Suddenly you were like a closed book. I share everything about my life, but you never give me anything in return. It's like you don't trust me anymore."

"I'm sorry. I do trust you, but there's nothing to tell. I changed my mind. I don't want to be with him." Unable to explain, Meghan knew a simple apology wouldn't suffice, but she had no idea how to answer.

"Yeah, yeah. You're sorry. Whatever." Kim turned away from her and curled up against the window. "I don't even know why we're friends anymore," she mumbled before closing her eyes.

Meghan watched her friend zone out, mentally expanding the space between them. Kim was right, but that didn't change anything, and she felt even worse now, if that was possible. She'd hurt the two people closest to her. Her best friend *and* Florence, her new lover, who somehow knew and understood her better than she understood herself. She'd pushed them both away, and she had no one but herself to blame.

Was Kim right? Had she been closed off for years? She supposed she'd been more withdrawn after the robbery in Paris, afraid to dig into her feelings in case she hit a nerve and everything resurfaced. And yes, she'd had her guard up and steered away from emotional topics in conversations, even with Kim and her mother, but that guard had crumbled to dust with Florence. Over the holiday, her tears had flowed like never before, and she was starting to suspect it might not only be her sexuality she'd been struggling with but also the suppressed trauma she hadn't dealt with properly. Her parents knew what had happened, and she'd seen a therapist, but she'd stopped going to the sessions because she'd dreaded them days in advance. Now, here she was, unable to talk about anything with anyone—apart from with Florence.

"I will tell you," she said to Kim. "I promise I'll talk to you, but I can't just yet."

Either sleeping or pretending to be sleeping, Kim didn't acknowledge her comment. Meghan shifted in her uncomfortable seat and inched away from the woman to her other side, who was leaning against her. Something had to change, and it was time to face her demons.

## 52

---

# FLORENCE

"*F*lorence, can I talk to you?" Stella beckoned her over the moment she arrived back at work after her week off.

"Sure." Florence's first reaction was to assume she'd done something wrong, as Stella rarely called her into one-on-one meetings, but the friendly smile on her boss's face told her she had nothing to worry about. "Do you want me to set the poolside up first?"

"No, we won't be that long, and I've got someone on it already." Stella handed her a coffee, and Florence gladly accepted it after a long, sleepless night. "You look tired. Are you okay? Meghan left this morning, right?"

"Yeah, she left. And no, I'm not great," Florence admitted as they headed for the second bar behind the pool. It didn't open until midday and was generally used for morning meetings. "It didn't work out."

"I'm very sorry to hear that." From the way Stella said it, Florence believed her, and she tried not to choke up as she met her kind eyes.

"Shit happens," she said with a shrug, and took a seat on one of the stools. "What's this about?"

"It's about next season. I'd love to have you back on the team, and not only that, but I was also wondering if you'd be interested in a permanent contract."

"Really?" Florence had never considered working somewhere full-time. When she was younger, she'd started spending time between the UK and Spain because of her parents, but it didn't really matter anymore. Her father didn't need her around, and they could always visit each other.

"Yes. We won't be giving them out until next season, so you'll have lots of time to think about it. Now that we're finally more stable after the pandemic, the board is pushing us to take people on full-time again, so I have the pleasure to handpick my best employees." Stella smiled. "And you're one of them. You've been a bundle of positive energy all summer, and the guests adore you. Besides, you're agile in your role, as you can switch between the bar team and the animation team, and you have your first-aid certificates and lifeguard diploma. I'd be silly not to ask you."

"Thank you, I feel honoured." Florence hesitated. Her mind was a fog, and she was in no state to make decisions of any kind today or even in the near future. "I'd have to think about it, though. It would be a big lifestyle change."

"Of course. I don't need to know until February." Stella handed her a file. "Take this home with you and read it through. It has your proposed new role, perks, pension, salary and hours, and if you have any questions, you know where to find me."

"Are you in the position to tell me who else you've selected?" Florence asked.

"No. Not until someone confirms, and I'd appreciate it if

you could keep this between us, as I don't want any friction in the team." Stella gave her a knowing look. "That includes Manuel. I know you two are close, but even if you don't talk to other team members, he might."

"Sure." Florence flicked through the file but didn't take much in, and even though this was a flattering conversation, she had no idea how she'd get through the day. Glancing at the sun loungers where Meghan and Kim used to sit, she felt a stitch and averted her gaze.

"If you don't feel like talking to people today, I can put you on cleaning and stocking duty," Stella said. "But the distraction of new arrivals might be good for you. It's up to you."

"I'll be okay." Florence put on a brave smile. She would have to get on with things, especially since she'd just had a week off. "Manuel asked me if I wanted to help with his ridiculous dive-bombing competition, so I think I might do that."

"No better distraction than that." Stella laughed. "And someone needs to keep him in check. I'm not sure if the health and safety procedures are being followed." As if on cue, Manuel arrived. With a beaming smile and heaps of energy, he greeted their other colleagues with great enthu- siasm and waved at Stella and Florence from across the pool. "Morning, guys!" He looked at Stella specifically and yelled, "Is there a funeral going on here?"

"Not that I know of. Why?" Stella asked.

"Because it's so quiet, I can hear myself fart. Can I turn on the music?"

Stella chuckled. "Sure, go ahead."

"I don't understand how he keeps going," Florence said, lowering her voice. "He was so drunk last night, he could barely stand when he came in."

"He'll start feeling it when he hits thirty." Stella flinched when the music came on, louder than usual. Manuel's old-school house tunes were close to unbearable in the morning, but it got the guests going, so Stella let him play them. Then there was a lot of back noise from the microphone until his voice blasted over the speakers. "Test, test, test! One, two three, test."

Simultaneously, two of Florence's colleagues opened the pool gates and guests flooded in. Some went straight to the sun loungers for a nap after breakfast, while others headed for the bar. It was easy to pick out the new arrivals; they were still pale in comparison to the rest, a few almost translucent looking. The staff regularly had bets on about who would get the worst sunburn, and Florence often worried about them. She was startled when Manual turned to the microphone again.

"Welcome, guests! It's another sunny day in Paradise. For those birds of Paradise who have just arrived, get ready for a fun-filled week, starting with the Paradise dive-bombing competition! Yes, you heard that right. We're going to make some serious splashes. My name is Manuel, and in an hour, my little assistant Flo and I will host the competition to beat all competitions, in which you will have the chance to be crowned the Dive-bomb Master of Benidorm! Are you ready? You'd better be ready because it's about to get very, very wet."

Laughter filled the poolside and Florence rolled her eyes. "*Little assistant*? Really?" She dropped the file into her bag. "Thank you so much for this, Stella. I'd better go take him away from that microphone. I think the power is going to his head."

# 53

## MEGHAN

*I*t felt surreal to be back at work. Even though Meghan had only been away for two weeks, the significant changes that holiday had caused within her made it feel like much longer. Her shared office that always brought her comfort now seemed like a relic from a former life. Two weeks was nothing, but she was a different person.

"Welcome back," Frank, the account manager, said, getting up from his seat to greet her. "How was the hols?"

"Yeah, how was it?" Louise, the head of HR asked as she glanced up from her screen. "Nice weather? You caught the sun—you look good."

"Thank you, it was lovely." Meghan hung her trench coat on a hanger and turned on the kettle to make herself a cup of tea. "And yes, it was sunny and warm," she added, forcing a smile. She felt heavy and sad. It wasn't just the English weather, of course, although rain had been pouring non-stop since she got back. She missed Florence so much it hurt, and the way things ended didn't sit well with her. Saying goodbye and leaving it as a holiday romance seemed like the right decision at the time, purely because she was unable to offer an alternative, but now, all she wanted was to talk to her.

"Any love on the horizon?" Louise grinned and raised a brow. "A hunky Spanish hombre, perhaps? I'm telling you, if I wasn't married, I'd jump at an opportunity to have some fun with someone a bit more exotic than Bert."

Meghan pretended to root through the wooden box that held a selection of teabags. "No romance. Sorry to disappoint you, Louise." Eventually, she picked the same Earl Grey she always drank, poured water into her mug and added a dash of almond milk. "What did I miss here?"

"Nothing at all," Frank said. "Same old, same old, so you might as well indulge us with your adventures. You went with a friend, right? I bet you had some good nights out."

"I had a good rest, that's what happened," Meghan lied, slowly stirring her tea. She didn't feel like opening her emails and starting her day. As soon as she did, life would go back to the way it was, and she was worried the memories of the past two weeks would fade, blurred by small, everyday challenges that held little significance in the grand scheme of things. She would get back into her routine of working eight hours a day, visit the gym, go home, cook dinner, watch a movie and get her sleep before it started all over again and again and again. Sometimes she'd meet up with friends, and sometimes she'd go for a drink with colleagues after work, but all in all, her life in London wasn't that exciting. Her nights out with Kim were always fun, but Kim hadn't messaged her back after they'd returned home, and she'd been cold and distant when they'd parted at the airport. It was unlike Kim to hold a grudge, and Meghan had a horrible feeling something was broken between them.

Taking in the office, she imagined Florence would be hugely disappointed if she saw it. It wasn't some obscure space in a basement, and there was no safe, let alone a cock-tail bar. Instead, it was rather modern with white walls, lots of plants and three cluttered desks. With big windows, it was the only space with sunlight in the building. Normally, Meghan liked that, but today she felt like hiding.

"I'm going to do a round on the floor while my tea cools off. There are a couple of people I'd like to speak to, so I'll fill you in on the holiday later," she said, placing her mug on her desk.

"Sure. Don't forget we have a meeting at ten," Frank called after her.

"I know. I won't be long." Meghan squared her shoulders and painted on a smile as she headed down the corridor and through the staff door onto the casino floor.

The casino itself was atmospheric with dim lighting, night and day. Blackened windows ensured players lost track of time, and the blinking lights and jingles of the slot machines encouraged risky decision-making. Psychology played a big role in how they used synthetic stimuli. Certain undefinable scents subconsciously linked to luxury and money lured players to the higher-stake tables, while the slot machines were placed near the kitchen and the bar so the smaller players would spend money on food and drinks. The fast-paced music made people increase their play speed at the poker tables, and in the VIP room they used classical music to calm the big gamblers. It was a business that could potentially ruin lives, but it also brought excitement and a fun day or night out to many, so Meghan had always been in two minds about it. In the end, the house always won. Well, not always, but long-term, no one made a profit from spending much time here. Some part of her felt guilty when she saw players get carried away but helping them wasn't her responsibility. If she banned them, they would simply go elsewhere or gamble online.

Meghan counted herself lucky that she wasn't prone to addiction, and she had no interest in gambling herself. Again, her thoughts drifted to Florence, and she realised she'd never asked her if *she* liked gambling. Meghan didn't like her partners to gamble; she was aware she was a hypocrite in that sense as she managed a casino, but it really was a dealbreaker for her. Florence wasn't her partner, though; she'd left like a coward, and she imagined Florence would soon be over her and move on to someone who wasn't afraid to own up to their sexuality. That thought made her stomach churn. She should have been braver, but she wasn't brave, and now she'd lost the only person who had ever made her feel truly alive and desired and safe. Her breath quickening, she leaned against the wall as she pulled at her turtleneck that suddenly felt too tight around her neck.

"Hey, Meghan. Welcome back." Alycia, the restaurant manager, put a hand on her shoulder. "Are you okay?"

"Yes." Meghan closed her eyes and took a couple of deep breaths. "Yes, I'm fine. Just a bit dizzy, that's all."

"Can I get you anything? A glass of water? I think you should sit down."

Meghan shook her head and held up a hand. "I'm fine, I promise." She straightened herself and met Alycia's eyes. "I was actually looking for you. We need to talk about the budget regarding the upcoming Christmas events. Do you have half an hour now, or shall I set up a meeting?"

"Now is fine." Alycia narrowed her eyes at her, but she didn't press the matter. "In your office or in the restaurant?"

"In the restaurant is fine. Let me go get my tea and I'll join you there in five." As Meghan walked off, she noted her legs were unsteady. She'd never felt panic when it involved people, but losing Florence made her feel like her soul had been sucked out of her, and unless she found the courage to tell the world, there was nothing she could do to get her back.

## 54

# FLORENCE

"What's wrong with you, honey? You haven't touched your food."

Florence picked up her fork and took a bite of the rice dish her mother had made. "It's really good, Mum. I'm just not very hungry."

Her mother nodded but pushed the salad bowl towards her anyway, encouraging her to pile even more food onto her plate. "Have you booked your flight to London yet?"

"Yes. I'm leaving in a month." Florence scooped as little salad as she could get away with onto her plate. "I've found a room in a house share too, but I'll be staying with Dad for the first couple of nights before I get the keys."

"That's good. Is your father okay?"

"Yes, he's fine. You know Dad—always working." The subject of her father as well as her leaving for the winter was always touchy, so Florence decided not to elaborate. If it was up to her mother, she'd be living here all year round, and being closer to her mother than her father, the end of the season was never easy for Florence either. Although she and her mother often met up for a coffee in town, she preferred coming to her mother's apartment for dinner once a week. Located between Benidorm and Altea, they had moved there after the divorce, and it had felt a little small when Florence still lived at home, but it was perfect now her mother was alone. The living room was always cool in the summer, and in the winter, the little wood burner kept the intimate space warm. Decorated with typical Spanish sturdy, rustic, wooden furniture, carved wooden doors, an archway that led into the kitchen and local terracotta tiles on the floor, it was the opposite to her father's modern apartment in London, but it felt so much more like home.

"And you?" her mother asked. "How are you? I've seen less of you lately, but I find it hard to believe you're doing overtime since the season's practically over." She paused, clearly gauging if Florence was open to talking today. "I've also noticed your aura is off. You're sad. Is it love related?" She looked Florence up and down. "Don't lie to me, I can tell by the green around your heart. It's diluted."

"No. I'm just dealing with some stuff." Florence focused on her food and braced herself to eat at least half of it. "It's no big deal," she lied, still missing Meghan every minute of the day.

"Well, I'm your mother, and I'd like to know if something's bothering you. Is it a boy or a girl?"

Florence hated it when her mother used the terms 'boy' and 'girl'. It made her feel like a teenager. "A woman," she finally said. "It's over. It was only short-lived, and I'll be fine. I just need some time."

"Who is she?"

"Someone who was staying at Paradise. An English tourist." She sat back and sighed, meeting her mother's eyes. "I'd rather not talk about it. It's not going to change anything."

"A little motherly advice might make you feel better."

*I doubt that*, Florence thought, but she didn't have the heart to say so. "Her name is Meghan, and she's from London. We were seeing each other while she was staying at Paradise, and I got my hopes up. I really liked her, but it's over."

"Why? What went wrong?"

"She was straight before she came here."

"Before she met you?" The expression on her mother's face would have been funny in any other situation, and for a moment, Florence thought she was going to laugh, but instead, she gave her a warm smile. "I'm not surprised. You're special. You've always had a wonderful aura of love and energy surrounding you. You glow, you know that?"

Florence suppressed a groan. Her mother's life revolved around auras, crystal healing and alternative medicine, while Florence was sceptical and tended to brush off her mother's observations. "My wonderful aura wasn't enough, I'm afraid."

Her mother regarded her with interest. "I haven't seen you like this since you broke up with that boy. What was his name again?"

"Juan. I saw him a few weeks ago. He's getting married."

"Yes, Juan. Good for him. He's a lovely soul." Her mother paused. "Are you not going to see Meghan when you're in London?"

"No. As I said, there's no point. Meghan's not ready, and even if she was, I doubt I'd be enough for her. She's ten years older, and she's got a real job and a real life."

"Nonsense. Every job is real and valid, and so is every life. You know it, I know it, and she knows it." Her mother stood up. "Wait here. I have something for you." She headed through the kitchen and into what Florence suspected was her bedroom before returning with a black velvet pouch. "This is for you. I tried to give it to you after you broke up with...what was he called?"

"I literally just told you, Mum."

Her mother narrowed her eyes, digging through her recent memory. She'd never been good with names. "Juan," she said after a moment's hesitation. "See? I remember. You didn't want it back then. Perhaps you weren't spiritually mature enough, but you are now, and I won't take no for an answer."

Florence opened the pouch and pulled out a chunky, light-pink crystal. "What's this?" she asked, even though she knew exactly what it was. She'd picked up on more than she liked to admit over the years and could easily identify over a hundred different crystals.

"It's rose quartz," her mother said, confirming her suspicion. "Rose quartz is a master healer, associated with the heart chakra." She folded her hand over Florence's, who was holding it. "The heart chakra is—"

"I know, Mum."

"I know you do, honey, but let me finish and refresh your memory anyway. The heart charka is off when we're traumatised, wounded or broken. And when we're in recovery, we need to heal the heart chakra. Take my word for it." She took the crystal from Florence and held it up against the lamp over the dining table. "See the colour? That's the colour of love in its purest form. It radiates healing, self-care and self-love, as well as love for others. Do you know what happens when you squeeze quartz?"

Florence shrugged. "Nothing?"

"Keep your scepticism to yourself for now, okay?" Her mother shot her a warning look before she continued. "When we squeeze quartz, it gives off a tiny electric current, almost like it's acknowledging the contact. You can look it up. It's been scientifically proven. Quartz reacts to us and our emotions, and in return, we can charge this amazing creation of nature and use it as support to heal our wounds. Connected with the feminine divine, I would say that in your situation, this is the perfect crystal for you, right here and right now."

Florence managed a smile and took the crystal back. It felt warm in her hands, like it had immediately adapted to her body temperature. "Thanks, Mum," she said. "I know you mean well and that this is your lifestyle. I hate to disappoint you, but I'm not the kind of person to heal myself with a crystal. I feel like shit, and only time and distraction will change that."

Her mother looked at her and sighed. "You're so much like your father, but one day you'll understand there's far more to this world than meets the eye. Just try it for a few days, will you promise me that?" She pressed on when Florence didn't answer. "As you're not into meditation, simply hold it and focus on it. The best way to use it is to wear it on your heart, like a talisman, but you can also carry it around in your pocket. As long as you feel it's there with you. Rose quartz is a powerful reminder that we are all worthy of love, and you, my sweet pea, are so, so worthy of love."

Florence glanced at the piece of rose quartz and squeezed it, then met her mother's eyes. "Okay," she said, for the first time deciding it wouldn't harm her to make her mother happy by fully accepting one of her quirky gifts instead of just shoving them in a box. She loved her mother, and it was time she started embracing her support, even if that support was a little 'out there'. "Thanks, Mum. I'll try."

"Please, Florence. Negative experiences can be destructive and make us close off, so it's important not to get sucked into a downward spiral. What we want is to be lifted because in the end, all that matters is the pureness and openness in here." She crossed her hands over her heart. "In our fourth chakra—the heart chakra."

# 55

## MEGHAN

"How was your holiday, love?" Meghan's mother put the roast chicken on the table and her father brought out the side dishes while Meghan set the table in their small living room.

"It was good, Mum. Spain was fun, as always." She tried to sound as upbeat as she could because her mother always knew when something was wrong. She'd dodged their past two Sunday lunches, using the excuse of work, but she couldn't avoid them any longer.

Her father was still wearing his work gear: an old pair of paint-stained jeans and a hoody that was torn at the left sleeve. He loved being a carpenter and sometimes worked Sunday mornings if there was a deadline on a building project. Her mother was wearing a tight black dress that would have been more suitable for a nightclub, and her hair was styled into a seventies beehive and curled at the tips.

"Are you guys thinking of going again next year?" Meghan asked.

"Of course, Megs!" her mother said. "We've already booked it because we wanted the same room. You know, the one that looks out over the pool bar? Why did you go to a different hotel?"

"Because I'm not hung up on tradition like you two, and Kim picked it." Meghan realised then that it was because of Kim that she'd met Florence. If they hadn't stayed at Paradise, she wouldn't have struck up a conversation with Florence on that first night. She'd have still panicked wherever they were staying because she'd have had to sleep in her room alone, which meant she probably would have told Kim about her trauma out of desperation.

Everything would be different now if she hadn't ended up in Paradise. She and Kim would still be besties and speaking every day like they used to, and she wouldn't be so confused and upset. Most of all, her heart wouldn't be broken because what she felt was the worst pain she'd experienced in her life. Looking back, though, she wouldn't change it for the world, no matter how hard it was. Part of her knew she'd get through this, and when she was out at the other end and able to think straight again and be open about her feelings, Florence might want to talk to her. It was a tiny spark of hope, but it was enough to keep her going.

"Kim should have left the booking to you," her mother said, unaware of Meghan's inner turmoil. "You're the Benidorm expert, after all. How was the bar there? Free flow? And the music?" Her mother wiggled her shoulders. "Did you get your jiggle on?"

Meghan chuckled. "Yes. All free and great music." Her parents were the epitome of British working class, and even though their life hadn't always been easy, they certainly knew how to have fun and make the most of their lot. "There was an event on," she continued. "The hotel was closed when we arrived, as they were busy with the preparations and they'd failed to inform us about it."

"So you had it all to yourselves? How fun!" her father said.

"*I* had it to myself," Meghan corrected him. "Kim went to see her boyfriend, who is now her fiancé."

"Really?" Her father chuckled. "I didn't see that one coming. Knowing Kim, I honestly thought she was making more out of the relationship than was there."

"No, they're very happy and they're getting married next year."

"Good for them." Her mother regarded her as they sat down around the dining table. "But she left you alone? Were you uncomfortable because of..." She stopped herself, and her smile dropped. She had just a much trouble talking about it as Meghan.

"It was fine, Mum. I spent the night with the bartender," Meghan assured her. "She was really cool, and we became good friends." For some reason, she felt compelled to talk about Florence.

"Oh, good. So, you had company while Kim was being all loved up?" her father asked, equally eager to steer away from the subject of his daughter's assault.

"Yes, I hung out with Florence a lot." Meghan tried to keep a straight face as she said it because Florence's name made her want to cry and smile at the same time.

"Great, love. I'm glad you made a new friend. And what about the event? Any nice men?"

"Actually, it was a women-only weekend." Meghan helped herself to food. "A Pride event."

At that, both her parents burst into laughter, and her mother nearly choked on the piece of chicken she was chewing. "Oh, God. I'm imagining you and Kim surrounded by lesbians." She giggled. "You must have been so popular, being such pretty girls."

"It was fun," Meghan said, laughing along but only half-heartedly. "Everyone was super nice, and no, it wasn't like they were hitting on us."

"But there was a little flirtation?" Her mother winked, then laughed even harder as she pointed to Meghan's cheeks. "Are you blushing? Ross, look at that, our daughter is blushing." She reached over the table to rub Meghan's shoulder. "Don't worry, love. I was curious at one point. Being with your father my whole life got me a little bored in the bedroom department, and I figured trying it with a woman wouldn't be the same as cheating."

"Gross, Mum." Meghan cringed. "I don't want to know, and besides, it's *exactly* the same as cheating."

"I disagree. I told you father about my desires—I've always been a little curious—so he knew about it and was happy to get involved. Right, Ross?" Her mother shrugged as if talking to her daughter about a threesome was nothing out of the ordinary, then continued without waiting for a reply. "Anyway, we found a woman online and invited her over one night, but it wasn't for me, after all. It was clumsy and a little awkward because—"

"Stop!" Meghan covered her ears with her hands. "I don't want to know, and I don't understand why you're even telling me this. I'm not gay."

"We never said you were." Her father frowned. "We were simply reflecting on our experience, and guess what?" He paused for dramatic effect. "It brought us even closer together because we realised we only wanted to be with each other. Your mother and I are what they call kindred souls."

"It's true," her mother agreed. "I had this woman in my salon the other day, and she was into weird stuff—energies and auras and other things I'd never heard about. And guess what she said?"

Meghan glanced at her blankly. "I don't know."

"She said I had an abundance of love in my life and that I'd hit the jackpot with my partner. She also said that was rare, and that I was very lucky." Her mother slammed a hand on the table. "And of course I know that, but we'd never met before and she could see it in the colours surrounding me. Isn't that amazing?"

"You are lucky, darling." Meghan's father kissed his wife on her cheek. "And so am I. Very lucky."

"You are," Meghan said. She reflected on that and thought it was peculiar that the topic of auras had been brought up twice in a month, as it wasn't something she normally talked or even thought about. "How on earth are you two still so happy together? Most of my friends' parents are either divorced or in the process of getting divorced, and the few who are still together can't stand each other from what I've seen. And how did you know that Dad was the one for you? I mean, you were so young. How could you possibly make the decision to marry him? Or vice versa," she added, turning to her father.

"When it's real, you just know," her mother answered. "You're consumed with the other person, and you can't imagine a life without them." She smiled. "Yes, we were young. Too young, perhaps, but it all worked out fine, and I wouldn't change it for the world."

Despite her low mood, Meghan felt a warm buzz course through her. Her parents were sweet together, she'd always thought that, but they'd never had a conversation like this with her. Florence consumed her mind as well as her body. Meghan felt it everywhere each time she thought of her— the longing, the missing, the pull, even if they were twelve hundred miles apart. What if Florence was the one and Meghan let her get away?

If there was a time to tell her parents the truth about her holiday, it was now. She wanted to. Meghan took a deep breath, summoning the courage to speak, but her mother beat her to it.

"I'm sorry to change the subject, but we need to talk about your birthday, as it's coming up soon. Any ideas on what you'd like to do?"

Meghan shook her head, regretful the moment had passed. "No. I haven't thought about it yet." There would be other opportunities, she thought. Maybe some other time.

## 56

## FLORENCE

*R*ainy days were the worst at Paradise, and Florence struggled to keep up with the orders. When it rained, their guests were grumpy and looked at her as if *she* were responsible for the bad weather. With the lack of other distractions, they hung around the bar all day and drank too much, boring her with their negativity. It was understandable, of course. Some saved up the whole year to spend a week here, and if that week happened to be a rainy one, they felt like their holiday was ruined. No pool, no beach, no sightseeing. And all that was left was the free bar.

"We need another keg of lager," she mumbled to Manuel. "Would you mind?"

Manuel pulled her to the back of the bar and lowered his voice. "How about this," he said. "You try to smile for a while, and I'll get the keg. You've been miserable for weeks and it's getting old."

"Sorry." Florence shrugged. "I'll do my best."

"Please. I know Meghan fucked you up, but it was only a holiday fling, so get over it." He cupped her face and used his thumbs to pull the corners of her mouth upwards. "There you go. Much better."

Despite her state, Florence couldn't help but laugh. "Okay, go." She slapped his behind before he walked off.

"You two seem intimate. Is that your boyfriend?" a woman at the bar asked her.

"Manuel?" Florence chuckled wholeheartedly this time. "Gross. No."

"I wouldn't exactly call him gross. I've rarely seen such a beautiful specimen." The woman grinned. "Is he single?"

"Always," Florence joked. "But we're not allowed to get involved with guests, so don't get your hopes up."

"Too bad." The woman downed the rest of her white wine and pointed to her glass for a refill. "And you? Are you single?"

"It looks like it." Florence grabbed a bottle from the fridge and topped up her glass. She felt sick every time she thought of Meghan. Not because she hated her but because she missed her.

"That's a vague answer. Are you in the doghouse or something? I am, that's why I'm here alone. My husband had enough of me because he thinks I was flirting with my colleague. I wasn't," she added. "He's just got a paranoid personality."

Considering the woman's interest in Manuel, Florence was more inclined to give her husband the benefit of the doubt, but she smiled and said, "I'm sure it will all work out. Sometimes people just need some time apart." She wasn't convinced of that. So far, she hadn't heard from Meghan, and she hadn't contacted her either. She'd been sad and down and it hurt, but if Meghan decided it was only a holiday romance, or if she wasn't ready to admit she was gay, there was nothing Florence could do about it, and she'd have to move on. Moving on wasn't easy, though, and she'd been far from her bubbly and chatty self at work. She tried her hardest to engage with the guests, but at the end of her workday, she was so exhausted from pretending she was fine that she just wanted to sleep.

"I disagree about the time apart." The woman gulped down her wine like it was water. "I thought so too, at first, but since I've been here, all I want is to have wild sex with a stranger who I'll never see again."

"I'm always up for a jiggy." A bald British man who had overheard their conversation held up his hand. "I'll give you one, babe. Free of charge." He stroked his hairy, bare chest, then patted his chubby belly with a roaring laugh, causing everyone else to laugh along.

Florence sighed and rolled her eyes as more people joined in, both men and women joking about how they wouldn't mind straying from their partner for once. The standard of conversation was basic at best, but at least she could close up in two hours and go back to bed, where she'd sleep through her heartache for as long as she could.

"Here you go. Flo." Manuel came back and attached the full keg. He ran the tap until the cheap lager flowed without foam, then yelled, "Beer is back! Who wants a beer?"

The enthusiastic cheers that followed drowned out the already loud music. The word 'beer' clearly brought out the beast in the guests.

"Thank you, I'll take it from here." Florence forced her lips into an awkward grin that made Manuel laugh as she shoved him aside and took over the tap. "See? I'm smiling. Now go take your break. You've been pulling the weight today." She didn't mind being busy, as distraction was the best remedy. Before Meghan, distraction in the form of someone else had been the best remedy, but she didn't feel like going out and meeting other men or women.

What had changed? And why was it even harder to move on than it had been after she'd broken up with Juan? Was it because deep down, she'd seen real potential with Meghan? Was it because she'd truly believed it could work out long-term? Some part of her had held that hope, sure, but that was the naïve girl in her who still had a lot to learn.

*Grow up. Life isn't about getting what you want all the time. Like Manuel said, it was a holiday fling, nothing more. Meghan will move on, you will move on, so suck it up.*

"Any chance of getting that beer?" a man asked, pointing to the glass that was overflowing and running down Florence's hand and wrist. "It hurts my heart to watch liquid gold go to waste." He spread his arms in a dramatic gesture.

"Oh, sorry. I was in my own world." Florence looked down at her soaked hand, shook off the beer and handed him the pint before she placed another glass under the tap. "Here you go. Who's next?"

## 57

# MEGHAN

"Shoot. You have ten minutes." Kim's demeanour was cold and all business as she sat down opposite Meghan, and it was hurtful to realise how they'd gone from best friends to two women who were just meeting up because Meghan had begged her to. She'd messed up, and it would be hard to come back from it, but at least Kim was here now. "Because I'm done with your apologetic messages," she continued. "They mean nothing to me unless you're finally honest with me. I know you weren't with Tiger. Someone spotted him in a bar chatting up women while you claimed to be with him. Andres told me after I came back."

*So she knows.* It explained why Kim had been so unforgiving. Meghan wished she could have invited her to talk sooner, but she hadn't been ready; she still wasn't sure she was ready.

She took a deep breath, bracing herself before she finally met Kim's eyes. "I'm so sorry, I've been a bad friend," she said. "You're right. I haven't been honest." She already regretted her choice of pub, as it was busy and noisy.

"No, you haven't." Kim's eyes welled up. "You used to tell me everything, in detail. And then I get engaged and all of a sudden you shut down. What's that all about? Are you jealous or something? Because you should be happy for me."

"I'm not jealous," Meghan said. "I'm truly happy for you, but I had a really strange stay at Paradise, and it changed everything."

"Everything?" Kim's eyes widened. "What the fuck, Meghan? That's still way too vague, so please enlighten me."

Meghan was silent as she picked at her fingernails. "I've fallen for Florence," she finally said. With those simple words, her most private feelings were out in the open. As expected, Kim gasped. "We're not together anymore. I think I've ruined it, but what it comes down to...is that I'm pretty sure I'm gay."

Now it was Kim's turn to be quiet. She stared at her, open-mouthed. "You're in love with the bartender?" She frowned. "I know I teased you about her, but I didn't think you'd actually go there or even be into it if you did."

"Well, I did go there." Meghan bit her lip as she looked down at her hands. "I spent most of the holiday with her." It felt surreal to say it, and she was terrified, but it was out, and the world hadn't ended. "Every night."

"Every night?"

Meghan nodded, still picking at her fingernails. "It was just friendship at first." She hesitated. "I was scared to sleep on my own, so she stayed with me."

"But you're not scared of any—"

"You're right, I wasn't," Meghan interrupted her. "Not until a few years back." She hated talking about it again, but it also felt easier now that she'd already told Florence. "Do you remember that time I went to Paris for work?"

~

Kim took Meghan's hand after she'd finished. Her eyes were glazed, and her bottom lip was trembling as if she was about to burst into tears. "Why didn't you tell me?"

"I couldn't talk about it," Meghan said. "And I didn't know I had a problem until I got to the hotel. I'm seeing a therapist again, and I'm dealing with it."

"I wish I'd known. I wouldn't have left you on your own if I had."

"I'm sorry, I couldn't talk about it," Meghan said again. "And besides, you were there to see the love of your life. You were so happy."

"And you were afraid." Kim's eyes welled up. "Traumatised."

"I wasn't afraid. Florence was with me. She didn't mind sleeping in our room, and we became very close very fast because we spent so much time together." Meghan gave her a small smile. "And I had a crush on her, you were right about that. I've never felt that way—so infatuated with someone." She sighed. "But again, I couldn't tell you."

"I want you to feel like you can tell me anything. We're best friends." Kim squeezed her hand. "Why can't you open up to me?"

"I am now, aren't I?" Meghan took a sip of her wine. "I realised I wasn't the person I thought I was, and that wasn't easy. I had to figure out who I was first."

"And? Have you?"

Meghan shrugged. "All I know is that I can't imagine dating men again. And that I miss Florence and want her in my life. I don't think anything else matters."

"Then why are you so sad when you talk about her?"

"Because I left her hanging. I couldn't make any

promises or commit in any way, and that hurt her. She also thought I felt ashamed to be seen with her." Meghan paused. "She was right. I wasn't ready to be open. Not then."

"What about Tiger?"

"He was my excuse whenever I went to see Florence—his idea. He's a lovely guy. We're still in contact."

Kim let go of her and sat back. "Thank you for telling me everything," she said. "I'm not going to lie. I didn't expect any of this. Obviously, I couldn't have known about the Paris incident, but I should have sensed you were seriously into Florence. I should have tried to talk to you instead of making fun of the situation. You were acting differently, and I didn't pick up on that because I was too busy with my own stuff."

"You got engaged. That's not just stuff." Meghan met her eyes. "Are you still angry with me?"

"No." Kim shook her head. "Of course not." She frowned. "So, are you and Florence speaking?"

"I haven't spoken to her since I left Spain. She's probably moved on."

"Or she might feel the same. Why don't you call her? Tell her you miss her. Or get on a flight to Spain."

"She's coming to London next week," Meghan said, her heart racing at the idea of Florence being close again. "She works here in the winter."

"Even better." Kim slapped a hand on her thigh. "Make a statement and invite her to your birthday."

"My birthday? With all my friends and family here? My colleagues?" Meghan stared at her. "I can't do that."

"Why not? Are you ashamed?"

"No... I'm not ashamed, but if I invite her, everyone will know."

"So?"

Meghan thought about that. If this was her life now, if she really was gay, she couldn't keep it to herself forever. The idea of telling everyone close to her had seemed absurd this morning, but she felt so much lighter after telling Kim, and it wasn't unthinkable anymore.

"Are you shocked?" she asked. "To hear that I'm gay?"

"Honestly, yes. I never saw you that way, but I'm also glad you figured this out, and I really hope it works out for you," Kim said earnestly. "And this is London. It's not a big deal to be gay." She pointed to Meghan's phone. "Look, I don't want to pressure you. This is your process, and I understand you need to do it your own way, in your own time. But I need you to know that you're making this bigger than it is in your head. No one is going to judge you, and nothing needs to change apart from one thing. You'll be so much happier."

# 58

## FLORENCE

*F*lorence stopped what she was doing and stared at her phone when she saw Meghan's name pop up. She stood there, glued to the floor, and couldn't seem to move her hand to pick it up. Five weeks had passed, and although getting up in the mornings had become easier, she still felt down and couldn't understand how a holiday romance had messed her up so badly. If she checked the message, she might fall back into that black hole she'd found herself in when Meghan first left. All she wanted was to forget about her, and if they were in contact, that would only make it harder. *Don't look.* That was a ridiculous thought. Of course she would look. The only way to avoid that was if someone snatched her phone away and threw it under a bus.

Finally dropping the T-shirt she was folding into her suitcase, she sat down and opened the message.

*Hey, Florence. I'm sorry. I know it might be unfair of me to contact you. Maybe this is as difficult for you as it is for me, or maybe you've moved on. But I want you to know that I miss you even more than I feared I would. I'm celebrating my birthday in*

*London next week. I'd love it if you came, even if it's just as a friend. I told Kim about you. Hope you're okay. Meghan x*

"I'm not okay," Florence mumbled with a frown, mildly irritated at the warm glow that spread through her body. It felt wonderful, but that could only mean one thing: trouble. She resisted the urge to jump at Meghan's invitation because if she'd learned one thing from this experience, it was to stop throwing herself in at the deep end. She had a good idea of what was going on here; Meghan felt guilty, and she wanted to wash away that guilt by going back to being friends. It was the easy and lazy way out; Florence had done it herself a few times.

*Thank you for your message. I'm okay. I'm glad you told Kim. That can't have been easy, and I'm proud of you. But I can't come to your birthday. Maybe one day we can be friends.*

She waited and waited, then cursed herself for staring at her phone and flung it across her bed. What was she expecting? For Meghan to beg her after she'd turned down her invitation? And why the hell had she done that? Even though Florence knew it was a terrible idea, she desperately wanted to see her again.

*Damn it.*

She took all her remaining clothes out of the drawers and stuffed them on top of her neatly folded piles in her suitcase. What did it matter if she arrived back home with creased clothes? What did anything matter? She zipped closed her suitcase and piled it on top of the other two in the corner of her room. The luggage allowance would cost her an arm and a leg this year. She always arrived with the minimum amount but left with so much more, and she had no idea how that happened.

Staring across the room, the shelves were as empty as she felt inside. The blackboard Manuel used to write on to warn her about his lady visits was wiped clean of his naughty messages, and she'd removed her family photos from the walls. Saying goodbye to Spain was always a sad time, but this year, it felt so much harder.

"Almost done?" Manuel appeared in the doorway with two beers, and Florence gladly took one.

"Yes, I think I'm done."

"I don't like that you're leaving," he said. "I'll do my best to make so much noise the new tenant will leave before you come back next year, but I can't promise anything."

"I know." Florence chuckled. "You're a good guy, Manuel. I enjoyed living with you, believe it or not. There's a room free in the house I'm moving into in London."

"Nah. I'm fine here. London is too busy and rainy for me, and besides, I asked Paradise for a permanent contract and they gave it to me, so I'll be able to work my way up now."

"That's great! Congratulations." Florence took a drink of her beer and patted his cheek. "You're not supposed to tell me that, though, are you?"

"No, but it's not like you'll be back there gossiping tomorrow, and—" Manuel stopped himself. "Wait. How do you know I wasn't allowed to talk about it?"

"Because Stella offered me a permanent contract too."

"That's fantastic!" He ruffled a hand through her hair. "So, we'll be working together full-time?"

"I haven't made up my mind yet, but it's a nice offer." Florence looked up at him. "Anyway, since when are you ambitious? You said you'd rather lose your six-pack than take on a managerial role, and now you suddenly want to work your way up?"

Manuel shrugged. "Since I found out I'm going to be a father."

"What?" Florence laughed, then slammed a hand over

her mouth when he didn't laugh along. "Are you..." She pointed her beer bottle at him. "Are you joking?"

"No. It's your mother's fault," he said matter-of-factly.

Florence regarded him as she tried to make sense of the nonsense he was telling her. "Okay, I know you tend to lower your standards when you're drunk, but please don't tell me you're about to become my stepfather. You've only met my mum a few times when she was here, she's too old to have a baby, and anyway, I like to think you'd never do that to me."

"I didn't sleep with your mum!" Manuel shook his head and shot her an incredulous look. "Jesus, Flo. Of course I didn't." He tapped the triangular, ochre-coloured precious stone attached to a leather string around his neck. "She gave me this one time she came here for dinner, remember?"

Florence frowned as she studied the necklace. "Yes, I forgot she was the one who gave it to you. You've worn it a lot." She'd been given a few pieces of jewellery herself, but she'd stored them in a box and only wore them occasionally when she saw her mother.

"I wear it night and day," Manuel said. "I like it, and women love it too. I tell them it's a magic talisman gifted to me by a witch, which isn't that far from the truth." He dropped a pause. "However, what your mother failed to tell me is that it's a fertility crystal. I didn't know that until a woman I hooked up with looked it up the other night. It's moonstone. It all makes sense now. Your mother put a spell on me."

"Wait. You think that necklace is the reason you're going to be a father? I'm sure you're aware of how babies are made. And you know those things don't hold any power, right? They're just pieces of pretty crystal." Florence chuckled, but Manuel remained serious. Half grateful for something to take her mind off Meghan and half in shock as she was actually inclined to believe him, Florence stared at him. "How?" She shook her head. "I mean, in a way, I'm not surprised the way you live your life, but I thought you were careful."

"I've always been careful, but I got really drunk one night and had unprotected sex. Just one time, that was all it took." Manuel paused. "I was upset at first, even in denial. Luckily, the mother is Spanish, and she lives here. After she told me she was pregnant and that she was keeping the baby, I needed some time to get used to the idea. And now... I don't know." A small smile played around his mouth. "I think I'm looking forward to it."

"You're serious." Florence got on her tiptoes and gave him a long, tight hug. "What about you and the mother? Any chance you'll get together?"

"I don't think so," he said, shaking his head when she stepped back. "But we've talked, and we've come to the agreement that we're going to raise our child together, so I had to start thinking about my future. I only found out three weeks ago. She wasn't sure if she wanted to tell me initially, so she was already five months in when she finally did."

"Oh my God."

"Yeah. I didn't tell you earlier because I needed to let it sink in, you know? It's not easy when you realise your whole life is about to change. And there's no point sharing when you're confused. I had to get things straight in my own head first." Manuel rubbed her arm. "But I wanted to tell you now, before you go. Apart from my mother, you're the only person I've told." He smiled. "I'm going to have a little girl."

"Oh, how sweet." Florence returned his smile and hugged him again. Resting her chin on his shoulder, she fought her tears. Were they tears of joy or tears of sadness? A bit of both, she supposed, and they clearly needed an outlet. "It feels so surreal. You're going to be a father." Her thoughts drifted to Meghan, and with Manuel's words lingering in her mind, she realized she'd put too much pressure on her, expecting too much too soon. Perhaps it was all her fault that she'd lost her. "I'm so happy for you."

"Thank you. I'm excited too, believe it or not." Manuel squeezed her.

"So next time I see you, I'll meet your little girl?"

"Of course."

"And you'll be leading an entirely different life," Florence continued. "You might even be a responsible grown-up."

"To some extent—at least, two days a week when I have custody. But I'll still be living here for a few years. I can't afford to buy a property just yet." He laughed. "It'll work out one way or the other. My mother has assured me of that, she's going to help me out. So, what about you? How are you feeling about going back?"

"In two minds," Florence said. "I'm looking forward to seeing my father and some of my friends in London, but I'll also miss Mum and my friends here. Especially you."

"I'll miss you too, Flo." Manuel held up his bottle and clinked it against hers. "And what about Meghan? She lives in London, right? Any plans of meeting up?"

"I don't think so. I'm done with straight women," Florence said half-heartedly, then turned around at the sound of another message. She searched for her phone, which had landed between her pillows, and held her breath as she read it.

*Hi, it's Kim here, Meghan's friend. I stole your number while she went to the bathroom, hope you don't mind. Can we talk?*

# 59

## MEGHAN

*M*eghan had partied in Soho on numerous occasions, but tonight, she felt as if she were here for the first time. The bars in Dean Street were crowded as always on a Friday night. Most of the patrons drinking outside were men, she noticed, and that confirmed her research before she came here. There were dozens of gay bars for men in London but only a few for women. She'd never realised that before when she strolled through these very streets full of confidence, looking for a fun place to have a final drink with friends before heading home. It wasn't a big deal back then, but it was now.

She felt like an outsider, some curious weirdo who was eager to find out what the gay community got up to on the weekend. Everyone seemed to know each other, as hugs and kisses were exchanged, and Meghan made sure not to look anyone in the eyes. They would immediately recognise her insecurity and maybe even feel sorry for her since she was wandering around on her own looking lost and out of touch with herself and the world at large. Tightening the tie on her trench coat and re-wrapping her scarf around her neck, she walked two blocks, then turned a corner. The bar looked the same as it did on her Google search, only less busy. A few women were waiting by the door, but the queue wasn't as long as the ones in front of the men's bars.

"Want to come in?" a young girl waiting in the front of the queue asked Meghan when she noticed her looking. "Make up your mind. We're going in any minute, and you can pretend you're with us."

"Ehm...yes, sure," she said, joining them as the security guard opened the door. "Thank you."

"No worries. I'm Ashton."

"Meghan." She shook Ashton's hand.

They headed down to a basement, a modern, white space filled with women. It felt like a secret meeting place, even though she doubted any of them made a secret of coming here.

"Can I buy you a drink, Meghan?" Ashton shot her a flirtatious smile.

Meghan had a suspicion the girl was no older than twenty, but she was nervous being here by herself and any company was better than none. "How about I buy you a drink instead?" she suggested. "But I don't want anything from you. Let's just be clear on that. I came here because... well, because I've never been here before."

Ashton laughed. "Okay, your loss, lady. But I'll have that drink. A lager, please."

Meghan nodded and made her way to the bar while Ashton talked to her friends. She was way too young for her, and Meghan had no interest whatsoever, but she did admire the girl for her confidence, and her carefree attitude reminded her of Florence.

"Here you go," she said, handing Ashton the pint after waiting forever for her turn to order. She'd bought a double vodka and soda for herself, as she needed something strong. "Cheers."

"Cheers." Ashton regarded her. "So, what are you doing here? Forgive me for saying this, but you look like you're totally out of your comfort zone."

"I'm not surprised you noticed." Meghan gave her a smile. "I've never been to a women's bar."

"I thought so. I could tell from the way you were standing there, staring at the door." Ashton chuckled. "That's why I gave you a nudge."

"I appreciate that. I'll admit, I'm uncomfortable and I'm not sure why I'm here."

"I was wondering about that too," Ashton said, narrowing her eyes at her. "I was just trying my luck, but you don't give off an 'I'm available' vibe, and I'm sorry to disappoint you, but requests to join women and their husbands in bed is not welcomed with open arms around here." Ashton pointed to a woman who was trying to climb on the bar only to be pulled off by the bouncer. "Apart from Shanita over there. She's up for anything, anytime."

Meghan sipped her drink and laughed. She finally managed to relax a little now that she was absorbed in the crowd and didn't feel so visible anymore. "There's no husband," she said, then decided to be honest. "I'm gay, I think."

"You think?"

"No," Meghan said, changing her mind. "I'm gay, period."

"Oh." Ashton gave her a lob-sided smile. "And you only realised now?"

"Hey, I'm not *that* old," Meghan protested. "But yes, I'm a late bloomer. I honestly had no idea I liked women."

"How are you so sure you like women now? Have you gone there? Because I can help you with that."

"Don't push it, junior," Meghan joked. "Yes, I have gone there. I kissed a girl and I liked it," she added, trying to relate to Ashton's generation. "And I've done a lot more than just kissing."

Ashton laughed too. "And you want more?"

"Not with just anyone. Not right now, anyway. As I said, I don't really know why I'm here. I guess I'm trying to find myself or something."

"That's admirable." Ashton set her beer aside and clapped her hands together. "And where is 'the girl' in question now?"

"Far away and she wants nothing to do with me." Meghan shrugged.

"Ouch. That must hurt."

"It does," Meghan admitted. "But I wasn't ready."

"Hey, it's not your fault. Take as much time as you need," Ashton said. "You're here and that's a start. Welcome to the wonderful world of women, baby dyke."

Meghan chuckled. "What does that make you? A foetus dyke? Because I'm pretty sure I'm old enough to be your mother."

"It's just an expression. You're finding your purpose in life." A blonde woman walked in, and Ashton followed her with her eyes. "And I think I've just found mine. Excuse me for a moment, will you?"

## 60

### FLORENCE

*I*t was on days like these that Florence wished she had a car. Her mother, who was taking her to the airport, had clients today, so she'd asked Florence to meet her at her practice in Altea. Dragging her three cases onto the bus while balancing two weekend bags on one shoulder, Florence groaned as she searched for her bus pass in her pocket. As she pulled it out, her crystal fell out too, and for a second, she worried it was broken. A queue was gathering behind her, and as she bent down to pick it up, one of her suitcases fell over, blocking the aisle.

"Sorry about this. I'm moving," she said in Spanish so the driver wouldn't mistake her for a tourist and curse at her. She tapped her pass and pulled her luggage to the standing area in the middle of the bus, then let out a long sigh as she studied her crystal. Was she worried about it now? That was ridiculous, but the truth was, she *had* been carrying it around with her, and just knowing it was there gave her a sense of comfort. It wasn't chipped, and it didn't look 'injured' in any way, so she gave it a stroke as a weird form of apology, then put it back in her pocket. She'd never admit to her mother it was growing on her; that would defy all the rebelling she'd done over the years. It would also mean she'd get bombarded by information she wasn't particularly interested in, and there would be no end to it. No. Against all odds, this crystal would be her dirty little secret.

The bus drove past Paradise Hotel and bars she'd spent many nights in. She'd be back again, but saying goodbye to Spain was always painful. During the journey, she seriously considered Stella's proposal to become part of the full-time staff at Paradise. If she did, she'd never have to start over, and she'd never have to go through this difficult and chaotic time of year again. She could find a flat, have a real home, settle down and build a life. There was only one thing pulling her back to London, and that was Meghan. Kim had called her and told her Meghan was still completely hung up on her, and she'd begged Florence to come to her birthday dinner tomorrow. Florence wanted to see her again, but she wasn't convinced it was a good idea. Meghan would probably freak out the moment she saw her and fall back into her old habits of hiding. In fact, she was worried Meghan might freak out last-minute and avoid her own birthday party if she knew Florence would be there.

"Altea station," the bus driver shouted as the bus came to a halt on the main square.

Florence dragged her suitcases out of the bus and pulled them in the direction of the small crystal practice located in a narrow street off the square. Apart from the occasional staff pizza night at Stella's house, she hardly ever came to Altea, as she had no reason to, but she liked the small town that was riddled with antique stores and art galleries. Maybe she would move here if she accepted her contract. She'd be closer to her mother, and it seemed like a friendly community.

The crystal practice, called *Pure Therapy*, was wedged between a florist and an odd little gallery that sold portraits of dogs. Big chunks of amethyst and quartz were displayed in the window, along with a terribly dated photograph of her mother wearing a purple cape and holding a clear crystal in front of her chest like she was some kind of psychic. Nevertheless, she had a lot of repeat customers, and even some of Florence's colleagues came in for a session from time to time.

"Hi, Mum," she said, keeping her voice down as she let herself in and stowed her cases behind the till.

"Hi, honey. I'll be right there," her mother whispered from behind the curtain at the back of the store. Besides offering crystal therapy, she also sold crystals and crystal jewellery, and the small space was packed with display cabinets and tree branches that held bracelets and necklaces—or talismans, as her mother called them.

Florence picked up one of the silver chains with a single, green crystal attached to the end. It was simple and pretty, and she wondered if Meghan would like it.

"Thank you. I feel so much better already." A woman appeared from behind the curtain, followed by her mother. "I'll be back soon."

"Anytime, Abby. Just give me a call." Her mother took the woman's payment, then waved her out. "And be mindful of your throat chakra. Try to hold a few days of silence. It will do you good after the session."

"Silence? Are you telling her not to speak?" Florence stared after the English woman now conquering the cobbled street on her high heels.

"Abby gossips a lot, so there's no harm in a few days of

reflection. She might come to insights I can't give her directly, as it would be rude to comment on her tittle-tattle." Her mother smiled and gave her a hug. "I can't believe you're leaving already. This season has flown by." When she stepped back, she noticed Florence was holding the necklace. "Do you like that one?"

Florence glanced at it and hesitated. "It's beautiful, but it's too much for me. I don't wear jewellery apart from the small bracelets you gave me." She held up her wrist to show the leather band with a green crystal she'd put on to please her mother.

"Still, you were drawn to it," her mother said. "I could tell you all about which ones would be suited to you, but in the end, sometimes crystals choose us, not the other way around. It was calling to you, honey."

"I'm not so sure about that," Florence said. "I'd never wear it."

"Then maybe you're supposed to give it to someone." Her mother took it from her, found a velvet pouch under her counter and dropped it in. "Take it. Do you know what it is?"

"Jade?"

"No, but close. It's malachite, a stone of transformation," her mother said. "It will give the wearer a sense of stability if they're feeling overwhelmed and help them move on to the next chapter in their life, as it encourages risk-taking and change. Interestingly, it's linked to the heart chakra, just like that piece of rose quartz I gave you." She smiled. "Please take it, it's a perfect gift."

"Thank you." Florence carefully placed it in the side pocket of her weekend bag.

"You're welcome, honey." Her mother seemed beside herself that Florence was finally showing some interest in her life's work. "Have you said goodbye to your friends? Manuel must be sad that you're leaving. He's such a nice boy."

"Yes." Florence hesitated as she regarded her mother. "Mum, why did you give him a fertility crystal?"

An amused expression settled over her mother's face. "Because it felt right," she said. "Sometimes my intuition guides me when I choose presents for people, and my intuition with him was very strong when I met him for the first time, so I made him something he could wear. Has he worn it?"

"Yes. And he's going to be a father."

"Oh?" Her mother's eyebrows shot up, but she didn't look all that surprised. "Well, then, I suppose destiny has run its course. How nice for him."

"But you can't just give someone a fertility crystal and not tell them what it is," Florence said, then realised the implication. "I mean, not that I believe it would actually work..."

"If you don't believe it, what's the problem?"

Florence shook her head. "Never mind." She was grateful her alarm went off, reminding her it was time to leave. "We have to go."

"Yes. Let's." Her mother searched in her overfull handbag for her car keys. "Wait here. I'll drive the car up."

# 61

## MEGHAN

*nother year older.* It wasn't so much the number that bothered Meghan, but more the fact that she felt like she was starting from scratch. She'd thought she knew herself, and she had a plan. Grow in her career, find a man, buy a house together and have children at some point. And now she'd have to rethink all of that, at least the man part. Well, children would be a different matter too, she supposed, as they wouldn't just magically materialise. So yes, there was that.

Starting over and making a new plan was daunting, but at the same time, she also felt immensely grateful for the two weeks that had opened her eyes to something incredible. Even though it wasn't going to work out with Florence, maybe she could have that again one day with another woman. Meghan found it hard to believe that anyone could make her feel the way Florence did, but no matter how much she missed her, tonight, she would smile and try her hardest to enjoy herself with all the people she loved.

She'd done a lot of reflecting in the past six weeks, and she'd been so close to telling her parents on numerous occasions, but every time she'd chickened out. She agreed with Kim that tonight was a good night to come out because then she'd only have to have the conversation once, but without Florence here, it seemed pointless, so she told herself she was off the hook once again.

A group of friends from university, a handful of colleagues from the casino, her parents and some other relatives were already here, and she greeted a few more friends who arrived, then pointed to the two long tables in the back of the pub.

"Thank you so much for coming, guys. Find a seat, I'll be there in a minute."

Seconds later, Kim arrived. "Am I late?" she asked, panting as she steadied her hands on her knees. "I took a taxi because I was running late, but the traffic was horrendous."

"Don't worry, babe. This is London. No one is ever on time." Meghan kissed Kim's cheek and gave her a squeeze. "Besides, since when are you worried about being late?"

Kim straightened herself and scanned the pub, taking in Meghan's guests. "Right. Of course. I just didn't want to miss the best part."

"Thank you. But what do you mean by the best part?"

"The start, of course!" Kim chuckled. "Never mind. Just take this so I can get rid of my coat," she said, pressing a small giftbag from a lingerie brand against Meghan's chest.

Meghan opened the bag and spotted delicate black lace. "You bought me lingerie? Kim, this is really expensive!"

"It's beautiful, you'll look stunning in it, and you never know when you might need it," Kim said, glancing at the tables again. "Now, where am I sitting? Oh my God, your mum looks younger than me nowadays."

"I know. It's not fair." Meghan smiled at her mother, who

was waving Kim over. She'd had some rejuvenating injections lately, and she'd had her eyebrows done for tonight. Her mother dressed very young for her age, even promiscuous at times in Meghan's opinion, but tonight she looked great in a low-cut top, jeans and a black leather jacket. Her father was going through a phase, she supposed, as he'd rocked up wearing his usual work cap paired with a T-shirt by some obscure heavy metal band she'd never heard of.

"You should see my parents." Kim chuckled. "Twenty years older and retired. My mum dresses like she's going to church and collects fridge magnets." Her eyes darted to the pub entrance, and her lips pulled into a wide grin. "Oh my... look who's here."

"What?" Meghan followed her gaze and almost fell over when she saw Florence coming through the door. "Fuck... Is that... Did you...?"

"Yes, I did, and you can thank me later." Kim rubbed her shoulder. "I'll go order a drink and join the party." She lowered her voice. "Don't worry. I'll distract them so you won't have all eyes on you while you snog her face off."

Florence's breath visibly hitched when she saw Meghan, and she seemed unsure of herself as she walked up to her.

"You came." Meghan met her eyes and lost track of everything around her. She'd missed those eyes so much, and she'd missed that smile. The lips she'd kissed more times than she could count, the wild curls she used to run her fingers through, the hands she used to hold. The doubt that had lingered in the back of her mind all along—the doubt that had nothing to do with Florence and everything to do with herself—was gone, and she'd never been so sure of anything in her life. "You came," she said again, her eyes welling up as she fell around Florence's neck. She held her until Florence let go and inched back; she looked emotional too.

"Is this okay?" Florence asked. "Do you mind if I'm here?"

"Mind? I'm so happy you're here." Meghan smiled, lowering her eyes to her lips. "Do you mind if I kiss you?" Shaking on her legs, she was vaguely aware that people might be looking their way, but her desire to kiss Florence was stronger than any trace of insecurity still lingering.

Florence looked shocked, but she didn't shy away and, inching closer, she cupped Meghan's face. "Please," she whispered.

Meghan let out a soft breath as their lips brushed, and when she pressed firmer against her, it felt perfect. The noisy pub was suddenly a lot quieter; no doubt her friends and family had spotted what was going on, but she blocked that thought out. This was their moment, and she desperately wanted Florence to understand she was ready. The kiss was explosive. It sent euphoric waves throughout her entire body; warm and lovely and so, so right. Hot tears mixed as they trickled down their faces, and she could taste the salt on Florence's lips. Meghan had her back, and she wasn't going to let her go this time.

It was Florence who pulled them out of the moment, and she broke away with a startled expression. "I think we should probably save this for later," she said as her eyes darted to the two long tables in the back from which two dozen people were staring at them. "Are you sure you're comfortable with this?"

"It's too late for that question now." Meghan smiled as she ran her hand over Florence's cheek. She was buzzing; part of her wanted to jump up and down and scream with excitement, and another part of her was fighting the nervous flutters that re-surfaced. "I can't believe you're here."

"Kim called me."

"I figured as much." Meghan hesitated but only for a moment before she took Florence's hand. "Will you join us?"

"If that's okay with you."

Meghan didn't really know what to say, as all eyes were fixed on her. The only one who didn't look shocked was Kim, who gave her a thumbs up and mouthed, 'You can do this.'

"Everyone, this is Florence," she finally said. "Florence is...she's..." She glanced at Florence, who gave her a warm, encouraging look. "I'm... I'm in love with her."

## 62

## FLORENCE

*F*lorence's first twenty-four hours in London had been a whirlwind. Seeing her father again last night was emotional, and then there were a ton of things to organise before heading to the West End today. Until an hour ago, she hadn't been sure if she'd even make an appearance. Nervous and insecure beyond belief, she'd thought of messaging Kim to call it off, but as she sat in the pub opposite—drinking a double gin and tonic for liquid courage—and saw Meghan arrive, her physical reaction was off the charts. Her breath caught as Meghan turned around before she entered the pub, almost as if she knew someone was watching her. Florence froze in her seat; her palms felt clammy, and her heart started beating wildly. That was the moment she knew she'd never be at peace if she didn't try again. Because how could she let Meghan go if she made her feel like this? Still shaken and at the risk of having her heart crushed again, she'd crossed the road to meet the woman who made her feel insane in the best and worst ways.

Meghan was wearing a tight, black turtleneck dress and

a long, black trench coat, and her hair fell down her back in waves so shiny and bouncy Florence fought the urge to run after her and touch it. And then, when they were face-to-face, Meghan kissed her, and she'd melted all over again as if nothing had changed. Things had changed, though. It was a kiss that felt real to the very essence of her core, but it was also a statement in front of everyone, and Florence still found it hard to believe Meghan had done that. She'd never expected her to come out to her friends and family. All she wanted initially was for them to be able to go outside without feeling like Meghan was ashamed of being seen with her. She'd come as a friend, but there was nothing friend-like about the way Meghan had greeted her, and she was still trembling in the aftermath.

Now, sitting between Meghan and Kim at the end of one of the tables, she tried her best to remember everyone's names. Meghan's colleagues stared at her in an awkward yet friendly manner, and to everyone's amusement, a few of Meghan's friends took the 'I knew it' approach. Florence doubted anyone had seen it coming, but she smiled and played along. The sentence, 'I really had no idea' had been thrown around a few times too, and Meghan's mother especially seemed puzzled.

"Why didn't you tell me before? You know your father and I wouldn't have a problem with it," she said, reaching out to pat Meghan's shoulder. "We've already discussed my phase of—"

"I know. I needed time, Mum," Meghan said, swiftly cutting her mother off before she gave her a smile. "But thank you for saying that. I'll fill you in tomorrow, but tonight, I just want to celebrate my birthday. You'll get to know Florence soon enough," she added, squeezing Florence's hand under the table.

"Okay, no more questions. I'm just so glad to see you're happy." Meghan's mother leaned around Kim and smiled at Florence. "You should come for dinner soon, so we can get to know each other better. I make a great Sunday roast, and Meghan claims my gravy is better than anyone's."

"I'd love that. Thank you." Florence looked her and her husband over and took in Meghan's mother's 'Duffy hair', her attractive features and her toned body. Meghan's father's heavy metal T-shirt stretched taut over his muscles, and he wore a cap with the logo of a building company that she imagined he only took off in bed. Meghan had talked about her parents, but it was still a little shocking to see them in comparison to her own mother. "You both look so young. How long have you been married?" she asked, purely to start a conversation, as she already knew the answer.

"Thirty-five years and a bit, and we're still very happy," Meghan's mother said with a hint of pride. "We got married when I found out I was pregnant with this little mysterious munchkin. A bundle of surprises, she is." She winked at Meghan. "So, how long have you and Meghan been together?"

Meghan shot her mother a warning look. "Mum, I said we'd discuss it later." She turned to Florence and lowered her voice as she leaned closer. "I'm sorry. I should have anticipated questions like this. I don't even know where we're at and how you feel about this and—"

"Hey, don't worry," Florence assured her. "Just tell her the truth. Your truth."

"*My* truth?" Meghan shook her head. "I didn't even know what my truth was until I missed you so much that I had no idea what to do with myself."

"Then what *is* your truth?" Florence asked, fixing her eyes on Meghan's.

"That I'm madly in love with you and want to be with you for as long as you'll have me." She gave Florence a shy smile. "But I'm not sure you want that too, and I'm sitting here counting down the minutes until I have you to myself so we can talk about it."

"Then how about this?" Florence whispered in her ear. The moment felt right, and she wanted clarity as much as Meghan did. "Will you please be my girlfriend?"

Meghan's lips pulled into a huge grin, and she let out a quiet chuckle. "It's the first time anyone's asked me that so blatantly."

"It's a simple question."

"The answer is simple too," Meghan said in a hushed tone as her expression turned more serious. "Yes." She inched back to look at Florence, and her rosy cheeks were so sweet Florence couldn't resist kissing one of them. "So, am I your girlfriend now?"

"It looks like it." Florence laughed at their conversation. It was secretive and clumsy, like the exchange with her first ever boyfriend. Meghan's face said it all, so she smiled. "Okay, girlfriend. Do you want to tell your mother we've officially been together for thirty seconds, or shall I?"

## 63

## MEGHAN

"This is home." Meghan closed the door behind Florence, then steadied herself against it. She was just as nervous as that first night they'd slept together, perhaps because she'd had so long to reminisce about it, hoping it would happen again. Tonight had been the most surreal night of her life and she was mentally drained, but her body was giving off very different vibes; she was starving for Florence.

Finally pulling herself away from the door and following her, Meghan imagined seeing her apartment through Florence's eyes. It was dull in her opinion. She hadn't put much effort into making it cosy; when she was home, she was usually cooking or chilling out in her bedroom. The furniture was basic, and her dining table was small. She rarely entertained, as there were so many better places to meet with friends in her neighbourhood. A white corner sofa, a wooden coffee table, a couple of bookshelves and a few artworks and plants were as far as she'd gotten with her decorating, and she'd given none of it much thought because this apartment had always felt like a temporary space, even though there was no reason for her to believe she'd move on anytime soon.

"It's cool." Florence walked into her small living room and then into her kitchen. "Okay, it might not be casino-boss-worthy," she joked, turning to her, "but it's lovely and it suits you." She ran her hand over the back of the sofa. "It's nice to see where you live."

"I didn't bring you here to admire my IKEA furniture," Meghan shot back at her. "But feel free to indulge."

Florence closed the distance between them and gave her a flirtatious smile. "I'm good. I've seen it all." She paused as her gaze darted down to Meghan's lips. "What about your bedroom?"

"You want to see my bedroom?" Meghan grinned as she took Florence by her waist. It was thrilling being alone with her, and the energy between them was just as electric as before, if not more so. Having her so close again felt like coming home, and looking back, she couldn't understand how she'd ever doubted something that was clearly so right.

"Yes." Florence's wild curls tickled Meghan's cheek as she brushed her lips against her neck and inhaled. "Mmm... I just want to drink you in." She inched back to look at her. "Or...do you want to talk first? It's been a big day for you."

"No," Meghan whispered. She shivered when Florence lowered her hands to her behind and pulled their hips together. "Tomorrow. For now, I just want to be with you." Leading the way into her bedroom, Meghan held her breath as her body went into overdrive. Closing the door behind her, she glanced from Florence to her bed and back, already anticipating how it would feel to have that beautiful, warm body against hers again.

Florence sat on her bed and bounced a few times, then kicked off her shoes and scooted back against the pillows.

"It's so messy, babe," she said playfully. "I didn't expect that of you."

Meghan laughed when she realised she still had clothes strewn over the floor, as she couldn't decide what to wear before she left earlier. There were also a handful of empty Coke cans on the bedside table, and the wax of the candles she'd been burning had dripped down her console. "Sorry about that. I wasn't expecting company tonight. It's only ever me in here."

"Oh?" Florence arched a brow. "That must be lonely. We should do something about that." She patted the mattress. "Come here."

Meghan's lips parted in a smile at her command. "What did you have in mind?" She contemplated turning on her bedside lamp, then decided against it. The flashing street-lights left a glow in the room that lit up Florence's face in various colours, and she liked the effect.

"How about you start by stripping off?" Florence kept a straight face; she didn't even blink or smile as she looked Meghan up and down, and there was something very arousing about that.

"Like this?" Meghan took off her coat and dropped it to the floor.

"Hmm... I think you can do better than that," Florence said with a cheeky smile, taking off her own coat. "A bit more, maybe?"

"Oh..." Meghan fanned her face dramatically. "You want more?" She pulled her dress over her head, leaving her in a black bra and matching panties. At least she'd bothered to put on her nicest lingerie tonight; she only wore the black lace set for special occasions, even if no one saw it. "Better?"

"Much better." Florence's eyes were fixated on her, and although she was clearly trying her hardest to play it cool, she finally lost it and spread her arms. "Fuck, you're gorgeous. Just come here, will you? You're driving me crazy."

Meghan laughed as she joined Florence on her bed and straddled her. Florence raised her hands to Meghan's waist, encapsulating it like a lava corset, steadying her and heating her. She closed her eyes for a beat, savouring the sensation of Florence's touch. "I love your hands. They're so right for me."

Florence looked up at her and ran a single finger along her cheek, down to her breasts, where she lingered for a moment before she continued down. "Yeah?" Moving down Meghan's waist until her finger was resting on the edge of her panties, Florence suddenly wedged her hand between Meghan's spread thighs and cupped her centre hard. "You don't mind me groping you, do you?"

Meghan gasped as her eyes fluttered closed. "No..." Florence's fingers pushed against her clit, making her buckle. "I don't mind at all."

Florence moved back up to her breasts and cupped them, gently caressing them with her thumbs until Meghan's nipples were so hard and sensitive that she shuddered under her touch. Florence reached around her back to unclip her bra and smiled. "Can I take this off?"

Meghan shimmied her arms, letting the straps fall down her arms, and stalled for a beat at the sight of Florence's expression. "You're looking at me like you're seeing me for the first time," she said.

"It feels like that." The look in Florence's eyes spoke of sincerity and lust and so much more that she couldn't phantom, that it flustered Meghan.

"Every time we kiss feels like the first time," she whispered. "It shocks me and strikes me like lightning right here." She touched her stomach.

"Is it too much?" Florence asked, sitting up to touch her face.

"Too much, yes, but in the best ways." Meghan kissed her softly and smiled. "Take your clothes off. I want to feel you."

Florence nipped at her lips, then kissed her so deeply and passionately that Meghan drowned in her embrace. Florence's lips, her tongue, her need seeping out of her and pouring into Meghan felt like she was giving her life, and, in a way, she was. She gave her energy, power, passion and a sense of self that made her whole. Meghan ground into Florence and kissed her back until their lips were sore.

Florence turned them around so she was on top, stripped off her jeans, shirt and bra, then lowered herself onto Meghan with a sigh. "I almost forgot how good you felt," she whispered.

Already close to climaxing by the overwhelming arousal of Florence's actions, Meghan was unable to reply, and falling into another kiss, she rode the waves that took her higher and higher. "Please stop," she finally muttered. "I'm about to—"

"I know," Florence whispered back and lowered a hand in between them, into her panties. Meghan gasped as Florence's fingertips skimmed her swollen lips. "I want to feel you come, Meghan. Come for me." She entered her with two fingers, slowly, as their bodies rolled together and, in that moment, Meghan felt insane. She reached into Florence's briefs and found her so wet and sensitive that Florence cried out at her light touch. Moving into her faster, Florence's lips parted as she stared down at her.

"Yes..." Meghan muttered, holding her gaze. "Yes!" She clung to her while her body convulsed, overflowing with ecstasy, and Florence followed with a loud moan. They held each other, never losing eye contact. When their breathing became normal again and she felt Florence relax into her, an unplanned announcement slipped out of her as she smiled shyly. "I love you," she whispered.

Caught by surprise, Florence flinched, and Meghan felt her heart pounding hard. "You...?"

"Yes," Meghan said softly. She was sure of it; that yearning she felt even when Florence was with her, was love of the deepest kind.

"Babe..." Florence returned her smile and cupped her cheek. Her eyes became shiny as she swallowed hard. "I love you too."

# 64

## FLORENCE

"Good morning, gorgeous." Meghan rubbed the sleep out of her eyes, pulled the covers further over her and Florence, and scooted closer. "Did you manage to get some sleep?"

"A little." Florence smiled as she wrapped her arms around Meghan. They'd been up most of the night, making love until the early hours. "How are you feeling today?"

"Ehm..." Meghan narrowed her eyes and grinned. "Great, I suppose." She sighed as she sank into Florence's embrace. "This is a nice start to the day, that's for sure. And it doesn't even feel strange to have you here."

"No regrets?" Florence looked at her pensively. She wasn't just referring to Meghan's coming out but also to their exchange in bed last night.

"No regrets whatsoever. I feel light and hopeful, and I can't understand what I was so afraid of." Meghan picked up her phone and scrolled through dozens of messages. "Look. These are all from my friends and family, telling me they're happy for me."

"I'm glad." Florence felt hopeful too, and for the first

time since she'd met Meghan, she could relax and stop doom-thinking. This was a beginning, not an end, and the clock that was ticking wasn't counting down. It was ticking towards their future. "Do you have somewhere you need to be today?"

"I'm working tonight," Meghan said. "I work late shifts two days a week so I can keep track of the night staff and the occasional event, but I'm free until seven."

"I bet they'll be talking about you today."

"No doubt." Meghan kissed her way down Florence's forehead and cheek until she met her mouth. "I can't believe I'm saying this, but I genuinely don't care. Waking up with you and knowing I won't have to worry about a thing anymore is so, so liberating." She ran her tongue over Florence's upper lip and lingered there, breathing against her mouth. "Are you free?"

"Yes. I'm starting my first shift tomorrow at a cocktail bar in Belgravia." Florence let out a quiet moan; Meghan's seductive moves were turning her on. "It's a fancy place, so I'm hopeful the tips will be generous."

"Nice. Will you be making Unicorns?"

Florence laughed. "No. No Unicorns. But I have my own Unicorn now," she said in a playful tone as she ran her hands through Meghan's hair. "You're so gorgeous." Remembering the gift she'd brought, she picked up her jeans from the floor next to the bed and took the small velvet pouch out of her back pocket. "I forgot to give you your birthday gift."

"Aww, is that for me?" Meghan sat up in bed and pulled out the necklace with the green pendant. "This is beautiful."

"You don't have to wear it if you don't like it."

"I love it. Will you help me with it?"

Florence took the necklace and fastened it around

Meghan's neck. It looked stunning against her naked skin. "It's malachite," she said. "It symbolises starting over."

"How appropriate. Did you get it from your mother?"

"Yes." Florence felt her cheeks burn, as she was about to confess something she still hadn't told anyone. "Mum gave me a piece of rose quartz, and I've been carrying it around with me. It seemed ridiculous at first, but as crazy as it may sound, it gave me comfort in the past weeks."

"I don't think it sounds crazy." Meghan stroked the pendant that was hanging at the perfect height, against her heart. "I'm so sorry I hurt you."

"Don't be," Florence said. "I'm sorry if I pressured you."

"You didn't. The way you acted was totally reasonable." Meghan leaned in to kiss her cheek. "Confession?"

"What?"

"That tiny piece of tourmaline you found on the beach..." Meghan opened her bedside drawer, took it out and held it between her thumb and index finger. "I've been looking at it every night. It reminded me of you, and that gave me comfort too." She smiled. "I looked it up. It's supposed to calm negative emotions."

"So it's not just me who's losing it." Florence watched her put it back in her drawer with as much care as if she were handling a diamond.

Meghan shook her head and chuckled. "We're not losing it. We're just gaining some spirituality, and there's nothing wrong with that. And you know what else? I've been thinking a lot about what you said that day on the beach. That you think love is the purpose of life."

"You have?"

"Yes, and I agree wholeheartedly." Meghan pulled Florence on top of her and kissed her. "Because how could this not be the greatest purpose of all? You make me whole, and isn't that what everyone searches for? Their other half?" She paused. "I meant what I said last night. I love you."

"I love you too." Florence met her gaze, and she believed her. She saw so much emotion and sincerity reflected in those beautiful, dark eyes, and it made her feel safe and secure. "What about those things you mentioned about our age difference and kids?" Florence asked.

"I think I was overcomplicating our situation. Maybe I was looking for excuses, like you said. But I know we can make it work."

"Of course. We can talk about these things," Florence said, wondering if she'd ever been so happy as she was now. "There's nothing you can't talk to me about."

"I know. But there's no rush. Let's just enjoy this glorious time in bed together." Meghan kissed her and ran a hand down her back to her behind. "I've finally got you back and I want to make it a morning to remember."

Florence's breath hitched at Meghan's touch, and she shot her a mischievous smile. "Oh, don't you worry. I'll make it so memorable that you'll still shiver in forty years' time when you think back to it."

"I know you can do that." Meghan giggled as she imagined them both as older women. "Do you think we'll still be together in forty years?"

"I hope so." Florence ran a hand up her thigh, and it made Meghan twitch in anticipation. "And you know what? We'll have a cool story to tell."

"Oh, yeah? What's that?"

"When people ask how we met," Florence said, pausing as she brushed her fingers between Meghan's legs, "we can tell them we met in Paradise."

# EPILOGUE – MEGHAN

"I do," Kim said through sniffs. She wiped away a tear as Andres put the ring on her finger, and their kiss resulted in happy cheering and clapping from their friends and family, who had gathered in Spain to witness their wedding ceremony. Standing under an archway of greenery and little white daisies that Meghan, Florence and Tiger had helped set up, Kim looked striking in her white lace veil and mermaid dress that showed off a little baby bump of just over three months.

Clapping along, Meghan shed happy tears from the front row of chairs set up on the beach, and smiling widely, she turned to Florence. "That was beautiful, wasn't it?"

"It was. I'm so happy for them." Florence took Meghan's hand and kissed it. The sun was setting, and Kim and Andres were standing in front of the glowing horizon, their silhouettes framed by the last light of the day. Wedding guests got up to get a glass of Champagne, and Florence pointed to the bar. "Want one?"

"Yes, please." Meghan straightened her peach-coloured

bridesmaid's dress and followed her, then waited for Kim to join her. She was in charge today, and although she was a little nervous about that, the venue seemed to be on top of things and she hadn't come across any hurdles so far.

"That was perfect," Kim said, hugging her tightly. "Thank you. You guys have made it so beautiful for us."

"I'm so glad you're happy and yes, that was a touching ceremony. Congratulations." Meghan put her hands on Kim's shoulders. "But the night is only just starting, so let me know if there's anything you're not happy with. Anything, and I'll fix it, okay?"

"Thank you, but it's already exceeded my expectations." Kim beamed. "I love all the little touches in the decorations and those tiny cupcakes they're serving with the Champagne. It's such a nice surprise."

"I actually have another surprise for you," Meghan said, squeezing her as she dropped a dramatic pause. "I'm moving here."

"What?" Kim screamed with joy and flung her arms around Meghan. "I thought you and Florence were going to live in London together. She was practically living with you already."

"That was the initial plan, but I've been job hunting in the past few months, and I've found something in Benidorm. I'll be managing a hotel—I'm starting in July." Meghan smiled. "Florence just signed her permanent contract at Paradise. She's moving here in a few weeks, and I'll follow later, as I still have to work my notice at the casino."

"Oh, my God. That means you'll be here when our son is born!"

"I'd be here for that, no matter what," Meghan said. "But

yes, it will be so much easier to see my godson grow up when I live nearby." She stepped to the side when Andres' parents joined them. "Anyway, we can talk about that later. Go greet your guests."

It was wonderful to be back in Spain again, especially for such a special occasion. March was pleasant with a dry, warm wind that made the linen canopies dance over the tables where they would have dinner later. The small beach bar just outside Altea had pulled out all the stops for the wedding and placed long rows of immaculately laid tables on its concrete terrace. With the big, white centrepieces made of fresh flowers and plenty of candles, the night would no doubt be very romantic.

"You told her?" Florence asked, handing her a glass of Champagne.

"Yes." Meghan kissed her. "Sorry, I couldn't resist."

"That's okay, babe. I think we should tell my mother too while we're here."

"Of course. It'll be great to finally meet her in person, although I won't deny I'm a little nervous."

"There's no need for that." Florence put an arm around Meghan and nuzzled her neck. "She loves you already after all the video calls."

They'd talked about their future a lot until they finally settled on the decision to move to Spain. Meghan didn't want to be away from Florence seven months of the year, and although Florence could have easily found a full-time job in London, they both realised their quality of life would be much better here. So far, Meghan hadn't told anyone apart from Kim, but she suspected her parents would take it well; she and Florence had found a sweet rental with a big, spare bedroom on the outskirts of town, so they could visit whenever they wanted. It was close to the beach and walking distance from shops and restaurants, and Meghan could already picture herself living there.

"I can't wait to move here with you." Her eyes rested on Florence's beautiful, confident smile. She looked striking in her white suit and peach-coloured shirt that matched Meghan's dress, and she wore a white rose in her hair. Florence still had the same effect on her as when they first met, and she smiled each time she saw her and was immensely grateful for every day they had together.

"It will be fun, I promise," Florence said. "I'll do everything in my power to make you happy, and if you change your mind, we can always move back to London."

"You don't have to try. You already make me happy." Meghan glanced at Kim and Andres, who were surrounded by friends and family. Kim was glowing as she held onto her bump. "She's going to be such a great mum, and I'm excited to be a godmother."

"It's a huge honour and you'll be the best godmother." Florence took Meghan's hand as she followed her gaze. "Expect to be roped in for regular babysitting, though. Manuel already asked if we could look after little Gabi while we're here so they can have a date night. He sounded desperate."

Meghan laughed. "Of course, I'd love that." They'd been to Spain for the baptism of Manuel's daughter, who was now Florence's goddaughter. Against all odds, Manuel and the mother rekindled their relationship after Gabi was born, and they were living together.

So much had changed over the past months, and soon, their new life would start. It seemed like only yesterday Meghan arrived here with Kim, completely oblivious to what lay ahead of them. Neither of them had any idea they'd return for good. For love.

The sun sank into the sea, and as shadows fell over the venue, hundreds of tiny lights over the canopies sparkled to life, bathing the tables in a dreamy glow.

"Do we have time to go down to the beach before dinner?" Florence asked. "It's a beautiful night and I've missed the sea."

Meghan took in the party and noted the guests were topped up with Champagne and happily mingling, so she took off her heels and hiked up her satin dress. "Yes, let's go now before they'll miss us. I've been wanting to dip my toes in there too. The water is so calm tonight."

As they descended the wooden steps to the beach, the rough sand glistened in the dim light from the restaurant behind them. Meghan took in a deep breath, relishing the salty air that was about to become the smell of home.

"The sand's still warm," Florence said, brushing her feet through it. She rolled up the hems of her trouser legs and waded in to her ankles.

Meghan followed, holding up her dress with one hand and taking Florence's hand in the other. "This feels good." She closed her eyes as the current pulled the sand from beneath her feet. Shells tickled her skin, and she looked down to watch them shimmer.

Florence lowered her hand into the sea to pick one up. "This is pretty," she said, shaking it to dry it before holding it in front of them.

"What's that?" Meghan narrowed her eyes at the sparkly object, suspecting the darkness was playing tricks on her mind. "Wait...is that a ring?"

"It's *your* ring." Florence took her hand and put it on her finger. "Don't panic, I'm not asking you to marry me." She winked. "Not yet, anyway."

Meghan's eyes welled up when she saw it was a silver ring that encased the piece of tourmaline they'd found on the beach last year. "Babe, it's beautiful..." She always carried the crystal with her when she travelled, and she'd panicked when she couldn't find it before they'd left London. "I thought I'd lost it."

"I'm sorry about that, but it was a surprise..." Florence put it on her ring finger, then inched closer and cupped her cheek. "I know this crystal means a lot to you, and since we won't see each other until you move here permanently, I wanted you to have something you can wear and think of me."

"Thank you. I'll cherish it forever." Meghan wrapped her arms around her neck and rested her forehead against Florence's. She'd let go of her dress and could feel the tide pulling at the hem, swirling it around her legs. "I love you." She felt it everywhere; in her heart, in her mind, in her bones... Florence was a part of her.

"I love you too. So, so much." Florence lifted her chin to kiss her softly. "But this ring is also a promise," she continued. "I promise I'll give you a real ring one day."

"Not if I beat you to it," Meghan whispered against her lips. "But just so you know, this ring is more special to me than any engagement ring could ever be." She rubbed her thumb against the silver. It fitted her perfectly, and it felt natural around her finger, as if she'd always worn it. From the near distance came the sound of the musicians at Kim and Andres' wedding, playing a Spanish song with a slow rhythm, and Meghan smiled as their eyes locked. "Want to dance?"

"With you, always." Florence pulled her closer by her

waist, and together, they swayed to the music as gentle waves brushed past them.

Meghan rested her head on Florence's shoulder and sighed in deep contentment. She was calm, she was happy, but most of all, she was whole.

# AFTERWORD

I hope you've loved reading *Paradise Pride* as much as I've loved writing it. If you've enjoyed this book, would you consider rating it and leaving a review? Reviews are very important to authors and I'd be really grateful!

# ABOUT THE AUTHOR

Lise Gold is an author of lesbian romance. Her romantic attitude, enthusiasm for travel and love for feel good stories form the heartland of her writing. Born in London to a Norwegian mother and English father, and growing up between the UK, Norway, Zambia and the Netherlands, she feels at home pretty much everywhere and has an unending curiosity for new destinations. She goes by 'write what you know' and is often found in exotic locations doing research or getting inspired for her next novel.

Working as a designer for fifteen years and singing semi-professionally, Lise has always been a creative at heart. Her novels are the result of a quest for a new passion after resigning from her design job in 2018.

When not writing from her kitchen table, Lise can be found cooking, at the gym or singing her heart out some-where, preferably country or blues. She lives in London with her dogs El Comandante and Bubba.

Sign up to her newsletter: www.lisegold.com

# ALSO BY LISE GOLD